Also by Alan Gratz

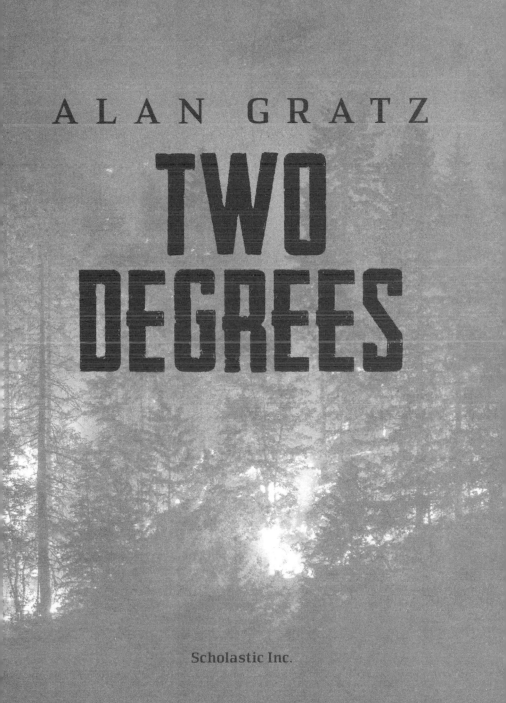

ALAN GRATZ

TWO DEGREES

Scholastic Inc.

ISBN 978-1-338-86512-7

10 9 8 7 6 5 4 3 2 1   22 23 24 25 26
Printed in Italy   183
First printing 2022
Book design by Christopher Stengel

For Claire and Maddie Gratz.
The future is yours.

PART I

RED FLAG WARNING

"Dad, look. A wildfire!" Akira Kristiansen cried. She pointed down the mountain trail, where a thin gray wisp of smoke rose from the trees in the valley.

Akira's father rode just ahead of her on a black Friesian horse named Elwood. Akira was riding Dodger, her chestnut gelding quarter horse. Dodger had been the first one to sense the fire below, stopping and turning his ears toward the smoke to let Akira know there was trouble.

Akira's father pulled to a stop and glanced over his shoulder. A first-generation Norwegian American, Lars Kristiansen looked like a real-life Paul Bunyan, complete with blue jeans, a red plaid shirt, and a bushy brown beard.

"Don't worry about it," he told Akira. "I'm sure it's nothing."

Akira frowned. She'd checked the fire conditions before setting out on their ride that morning. The National Weather

Service had issued a red flag warning for the Sierra Nevada range today, as they did almost every other day in the fall. A red flag warning meant warm temperatures, dry conditions, and strong winds—which all added up to the possibility of a forest fire. How could smoke in the foothills *not* be a problem?

Akira looked at the ground, where brittle leaves and pine needles were ready and waiting to burn. "Shouldn't we at least let Cal Fire know?" she asked.

"A little fire is good for a forest," her dad told her. "It gets rid of all the dry stuff before too much of it builds up and burns out of control."

Yeah, but it seems like there aren't any "little fires" anymore, Akira thought. Not since the temperature of the earth had risen nearly two degrees, and the hotter air and longer droughts had sucked the moisture out of everything, making California a tinderbox. Now almost every fire was a megafire that burned up half the state. And it was all thanks to human-caused climate change. Akira had learned about it in school last year, and it had scared her. But when she'd come home and told her family what she'd learned, her dad said the same thing then that he said now:

"Nature can take care of itself."

He clicked his tongue for Elwood to walk on, clearly done with the subject.

Akira shook her head. Her dad had seen all the same changes in the Sierra Nevada that she had in the past few years: bigger, more frequent, more destructive wildfires. Smoke warnings that caused her to stay home and miss school. Drought conditions that had made their well run dry.

But she knew better than to say the words *climate change* around her dad. All he would do was challenge her on it, and Akira didn't have the energy for that. Her father *got* energy from engaging with other people. It recharged him to be social. Akira was the opposite. She liked people, but being "on" all the time drained her. After a week of the normal chaos of school and family, she needed these peaceful, restorative Saturday morning rides with Dodger.

And arguing about climate change was definitely *not* peaceful.

Akira looked over her shoulder at the smoke and sighed. Then she gave Dodger a pat on his withers to let him know she'd gotten his message.

"Thanks, Dodger. Everything's okay," she told him.

I hope, she added silently.

KING SEQUOIA

It was October, and the hillsides were awash in oranges and yellows and reds and greens. Akira loved this time of year, when the air was crisp and cool and smelled like cedar and Douglas fir. There were a few dark clouds in the sky, but Akira knew it wasn't going to rain.

It never rained anymore.

Akira closed her eyes and took a deep breath, letting Dodger have the reins. He and Elwood carried Akira and her father up into a tall canopy of Ponderosa pines, where bearclover and white alder grew among granite boulders. The horses climbed higher, to the top of the mountain, and at last Akira and her dad came to the place they'd been headed all along.

A hush fell over Akira like she'd entered a church, and her skin tingled.

"'Do behold the King in his glory, King Sequoia,'" Akira's father whispered, quoting a line from the naturalist John Muir.

All around Akira and her dad were dozens of giant sequoias, some of the biggest trees on the planet. The largest sequoia here was twelve feet wide, and it stretched so high up into the sky Akira had to crane her neck back to see the top of it. Full-grown giant sequoias like these were called monarchs, because they were the kings and queens of trees. Some of them were over two thousand years old.

Akira and her dad shared a smile. They both loved this place.

Up here, Akira felt like she was outside of time. Like the rest of the world didn't exist. This grove was Akira's escape. Her sanctuary.

Akira hopped off Dodger and walked deeper into the grove while her horse grazed. *This is what it must feel like to be an ant among elephants*, Akira thought. The giant sequoias made her feel small and insignificant, but in a good way. They reminded her that she wasn't the center of the universe. That there were things that were far older and bigger than she was.

Her father got down from Elwood. "Oh no," he whispered theatrically. "What will happen if your wildfire makes it all the way up here?"

Akira scowled. She knew as well as her dad did that giant sequoias were adapted to withstand wildfires. Their bark was two feet thick, and their shaggy evergreen leaves were high up, where forest fires couldn't reach them. These trees even *needed* wildfires to reproduce—their seed cones only opened up when exposed to extreme heat. A wildfire was never going to burn these trees down, and her father knew it. He was baiting her, trying to get her to argue with him about climate change.

Akira huffed and turned away. Why did her dad have to ruin this? These rides into the mountains were when Akira felt *closest* to her father. He was the one who'd taught her the names of all the plants and animals in the forest, and all the facts about giant sequoias. Who'd taught her how to recharge her batteries in nature.

How could her father be wrong about climate change, but right about everything else?

Akira shook her head. She wasn't going to bite. She wasn't going to argue. This was *her* day. Her time away from everything, in her favorite place in the whole world. And she wasn't going to let anybody spoil it.

"Whoa! Cool!" a girl's voice shouted behind her, and Akira jumped.

TRESPASSERS

Akira turned around. The girl who'd intruded on her sanctuary looked to be about thirteen, like Akira. She had short raven-black hair and light-brown skin, just like the man who was walking beside her. *Father and daughter*, Akira guessed.

"And there are horses too!" the girl added, running for Dodger and Elwood. Halfway there she saw Akira and stopped. "Oh, hi. Sorry."

"Hey there," Akira's dad said to the newcomers. "I'm Lars, and this is Akira."

"Daniel and Sue," the other dad said. He and his daughter had a bit of an accent, but Akira couldn't place it.

"Where you from?" Akira's dad asked.

Akira groaned inwardly. Her dad loved chatting with random people. He talked to everybody from drive-through attendants to parents in the pickup line after school. That was embarrassing enough, but now his friendliness was going to encourage these strangers to stick around.

"We drove up from Fresno," the man said. "Parked in the lot on the other side of the mountain and hiked up. How about you?"

"We live close. Rode up from the other side," Akira's dad said. "My wife and younger daughter are back home."

"Can I pet your horse?" Sue asked Akira as their dads made small talk.

"Sure, I guess," Akira said, swallowing her frustration. Why did this girl and her dad have to be here now? They were trespassing on her refuge.

At least Sue knew enough to rub Dodger's neck, not pet his head like a dog. And Dodger seemed to like her, giving Sue a nudge with his nose that made her giggle. Dodger was a good judge of character, and that made Akira relax a little.

"These giant trees are incredible," Sue said, her voice quieting. Maybe she was starting to feel some of the grove's magic too.

"Yeah. Is . . . this your first time seeing them?" Akira asked, making an effort to be sociable. It wasn't easy for her. If she was honest, Dodger was her best friend. At least since Patience had moved back to Florida.

Sue nodded. "We just moved here last year."

"I grew up here," Akira told her. "My dad's been bringing me to see the sequoias since I was little."

"He's your dad?" Sue asked, then immediately blushed. "I'm sorry. It's just—"

Akira waved it away. She got that all the time. She didn't look entirely like either of her parents, sharing her dad's broad shoulders and high cheekbones, and her Japanese American mother's straight black hair and brown eyes.

"We were a little worried to move to California, what with all the wildfires you've been having," Akira heard Sue's dad say, and alarm bells went off in her head. She took a step toward the two dads, trying to think of something she could say to change the subject, but it was too late.

"You know, because of climate change," Daniel added.

Akira froze. *Oh no. Oh no oh no oh no*, she thought. *He said the words.*

Akira's dad laughed. "There's no such thing as 'climate change,'" he told Sue's dad. "I mean, the earth goes through hot and cold cycles, but humans don't have anything to do with that."

Daniel looked taken aback. "You're kidding, right? You don't think the huge amounts of greenhouse gases we're releasing into the air by burning fossil fuels has anything to do with the fact that the earth keeps getting hotter?"

Akira and Sue shared a worried glance, anticipating the coming storm. Even Dodger's ears flicked toward the two men.

"The earth is a huge ecosystem," Akira's dad said, like he was explaining it to a dummy. "We're just one tiny part of it."

"Dad—" Akira started, but her father ignored her. Dodger danced nervously, sensing her anxiety. Their beautiful, perfect morning was going up in smoke.

"All those gases trap the heat in our atmosphere," Sue's dad said, "which causes droughts and melts the ice caps and raises the sea level. Climate change is real, and we're causing it. Which means we have a responsibility to do something about it."

"Do you hear yourself?" said Akira's dad. "Look at these trees. How can you stand among these giants and think anything *we* do could change anything? The idea that we caused climate change, or could stop it if we wanted to, is the height of arrogance."

"I'll tell you what's arrogant—" Daniel said, but he never got to finish.

"*Fire!*" Sue screamed, making them all jump. "There's a wildfire down the other side of the mountain!"

Akira looked back the way she and her father had come, and gasped. The little trickle of smoke they'd seen a short while ago had turned into a huge, raging wildfire. The fire was growing fast, eating up the forest with impossible speed.

And it was headed right for them.

"We have to get back to the car now!" Daniel cried.

"You'll never make it on foot. Not with how fast that fire's moving," Akira's dad said, their argument forgotten in their panic. "Get on the horses. We'll take you to the parking lot."

Akira grabbed her father's arm. "But Dad, that's the opposite direction of our house!"

"We'll drop them off, then go around the long way," he told her. "We'll be all right. But we have to get these people to safety. Now hurry! Go!"

A FIRE NAMED MORRIS

The horses moved at a quick canter down the trail. Akira's dad rode on Elwood with Sue, and Akira was on Dodger, with Daniel sitting behind her.

Dodger's ears kept flicking forward and back, and his muscles and gait were stiff. Was he picking up on Akira's fear and the urgency of their run through the woods, or was he sensing something more? How close was the fire behind them?

Akira pulled out her phone and tapped the screen.

"What's that?" Daniel asked, looking over her shoulder.

"Fire tracker app," Akira told him. "Shows you where fires are in real time."

A map of the area loaded, and seconds later Akira watched as a big red blob appeared, covering everything behind them. She zoomed out, but the red blob kept going, and going, and going.

Akira sucked in her breath. "That's impossible," she whispered.

"How bad is it?" Akira's dad called, glancing back at her.

"*Bad,*" Akira said. It had been less than half an hour since she'd first seen that trickle of smoke. Now the fire covered a huge part of the map beyond the main road around the mountain. The road Sue and her dad would have to take to get out of here.

Worse, the big red blob already had a label on it.

"They're calling it the Morris Fire," Akira said.

She and her father shared a worried look. They both knew

what it meant when Cal Fire gave a wildfire a name. That meant it was a big one.

As Akira watched, the app updated and the leading edge of the fire jumped closer to the road.

"It's moving so fast!" Akira cried.

"We're going to be all right," her dad called back. "We're almost to the parking lot."

Akira could feel Daniel trembling behind her on the horse. Akira was frightened too. More frightened than she'd ever been in her whole life. She'd seen fires like this on the news. Breathed in their smoke from miles away. But she'd never been this close to one. When wildfires got big, when the wind whipped them up and they grew quickly out of control, that's when they were really dangerous. That's when they ate up houses and towns and hundreds of thousands of acres of forest.

And people.

Akira tried to tamp down the panic rising inside her. Was that smoke she was smelling in the air, or was it her imagination? And was it getting darker, or was that just a cloud passing by above the trees?

We should have called somebody when we first saw the smoke, Akira thought. *We should have tried to do something about it.*

Now it was too late.

The horses burst from the wooded trail into a small gravel parking lot. There was only one car there, a sleek-looking four-door hybrid. Very different from the heavy-duty gas-guzzling pickup truck Akira's dad drove.

"That's our car!" Sue cried.

Akira pulled Dodger to a stop. Sue's dad slid off the horse and went to help Sue dismount from Elwood.

Dodger whinnied and danced around nervously under Akira, and she put a hand on his withers to calm him. "What is it, boy? What's wrong?"

Akira checked the fire tracker app again and blinked. The blue dot that marked her location was showing her *inside* the fire!

"*What?*" Akira cried, and as she looked up, she saw the first tongues of orange flame licking the trees along the road.

The fire was here.

BURNING QUESTIONS

"Dad!" Akira cried. She pointed to the edge of the parking lot, where trees were igniting like matchsticks.

"No," her dad said, spinning around on Elwood. "No no no no."

Akira could feel Dodger wanting to bolt, and she fought to rein him under control.

Daniel hugged Sue close. "What do we do? Where do we go?" he asked.

The little gravel lot was too small to protect them. Akira could see that. If they stayed where they were, the fire would engulf them.

Akira's dad hopped off Elwood. "Into the car," he told everyone. "Now! Quickly! We have to drive through it."

"*Drive through it?*" Daniel cried.

"Better than staying here as it sweeps over us!" Akira's dad said. "The asphalt will act as a natural firebreak. See? It's the trees and brush that are on fire, not the road."

Her dad was right. The fire was spreading through the forest, but not onto the pavement. Driving was the only way out. For them.

"But what about the horses?" Akira asked. She put a hand on Dodger's neck again.

"Hiyah!" her dad yelled. He slapped Elwood on the rump, and the black Friesian took off into the woods, away from the fire. "The horses are better off on their own," he told Akira.

"What? No!" Akira cried. She jerked away, and Dodger backed away with her.

"Akira, get down off the horse! We have to go!" her dad said.

Daniel and Sue were already in their car. Burning orange embers swept past Akira on the wind, hitting the car, the gravel, the dry grass and pine needles behind her. Little fires were springing up everywhere, even on the gravel. Dodger snorted and capered.

Tears streamed down Akira's face. "He'll burn up in the fire! So will Elwood!"

"The horses are faster than us. They can outrun the fire," her dad told her.

Akira knew her dad was right. Horses spooked easy. Open an umbrella near them and they would gallop halfway across a meadow and stand there giving the umbrella the stink eye. Elwood was already long gone. And he and Dodger could find their way home in a fog, with or without Akira or her dad there to guide them. But to just leave Dodger behind—

"We have to go!" Daniel yelled from inside the car. The fire was spreading around the edges of the parking lot.

Akira's dad grabbed her and lifted her off Dodger, and she sobbed guiltily.

"*No! Dodger!*" she cried, reaching out for him. Pleading silently for him to be all right. To return home to her safe and sound.

"Hiyah!" her father cried. He gave Dodger a slap on the backside, and Akira watched her best friend run away into the woods.

Akira's dad hustled her into the back seat of the car next to Sue, then ran to the passenger side and hopped in next to Daniel.

"Go! Go!" Akira's dad cried.

Daniel hit the accelerator. The hybrid's tires spun on the gravel, and then the car launched forward, throwing Akira back in her seat as they drove straight into the heart of the inferno.

INTO THE FIRE

The top of a burning tree fell onto the road in front of the car, and Akira ducked in fear as Daniel plowed over it. *WHOOMPH. CRUNCH!*

The little car rocked. Akira's dad yelped and threw a hand out to brace himself on the dashboard. Sue screamed. Akira fell on the floor of the car.

"Seat belts!" Daniel roared.

Akira scrambled back up. As she and Sue bent over to latch their seat belts, Akira noticed three shiny pinkish lines on the left side of Sue's forehead. They were all half an inch long, and ran parallel to each other before disappearing into the roots of Sue's dark hair. *Scars*, Akira realized with a start. *But from what?*

The car bumped and thumped over more debris in the road, and Akira's eyes were drawn back to the hellscape outside her window.

Even though it was still morning, the world looked black as night. The only light came from the trees on either side of the road. They glowed yellow-orange, burning like someone had dumped gasoline on them and then lit them up with a flamethrower.

The car passed by a hillside that was a sea of flames, so bright Akira had to look away. Sweat coated her forehead and ran down her back. Her dad tried turning on the AC, but all that did was blast smoke into the car, and he quickly turned it off.

Daniel's phone auto-connected to the car stereo, and a pop song Akira liked started playing. She blinked at the absurdity of it and glanced at Sue, who looked as stunned as she was. They had just met, and here they were riding together through a wildfire as if they were heading off to see a movie.

"Turn on the radio," Akira's dad said. "See if you can get any emergency information."

Daniel mashed buttons on the big screen on the dashboard. "Sue, how do you get the radio on this thing?"

"I don't know!" said Sue.

"Forget it. Just stay focused on the road," Akira's dad said. "I'll call home."

Home! Akira's heart thumped a steady canter in her chest. Were her mom and little sister, Hildi, okay? Akira checked the fire app, but it hadn't updated since the parking lot. The red blob marking the wildfire was a long way off from her house, but what if the winds changed? And the flames were moving so quickly.

Akira thought of Dodger and Elwood. Had the fire caught up to them? A black hole of guilt ate her up from inside, and she bent double against the pain. How could she have let Dodger go? He was her everything. He'd been her horse since they were both ten years old. She fed him and talked to him every morning and night. Took him out on the trails around their house. Mucked out his stall. Brushed and combed his mane and tail. Cleaned and conditioned his leather saddle, his bridle, his halter. *Oh, Dodger!*

If only they'd headed home at the first sign of the wildfire. If only they hadn't taken Sue and her dad back down to the parking lot—

A burning ember hit the windshield and burst into a thousand bright sparks, and Akira jumped. More embers rattled on the roof like hail.

"I can't get through to your mother," Akira's dad said, lowering his phone.

Sue looked at Akira with worried eyes, and Akira felt sick all over again.

"I'm sure she's all right," Sue told her.

Akira hoped so. Sue was lucky, at least. Her own mother was down in Fresno, far away from the fire.

Akira texted her mom:

We're in a stranger's car trying to drive through the fire. Watch for Dodger and Elwood. We sent them ahead. Are you and Hildi okay?

She hit send and waited, watching for the little dots that would show her mother was writing back. The dots didn't come, and Akira wilted.

Daniel leaned forward, his eyes locked on the road ahead. "It's too much. I can't see. The whole canyon's a death trap!" he said, his voice shaking. He sniffed, and Akira realized Daniel was crying. Akira pulled back, more scared of hearing a grown-up cry than the world of fire outside.

"It's okay. We're going to be okay," Akira's dad told him. His own voice was strained and nervous. "Just keep driving slow and steady. You're doing great."

Daniel drove intently, his hands tight on the steering wheel. The main road acted as a natural firebreak, just as Akira's dad had said it would, but the flames were so high they scaled the pine trees and rode the wind across to the other side, creating a kind of fire tunnel for the little car. Oaks and maples lit up like Christmas trees, their burning leaves glowing like strands of orange bulbs. Sometimes an entire tree trunk was on fire, the whole thing outlined in bright orange. Akira had never seen anything like it.

They came around a curve in the mountain road, and Daniel hit the brakes, throwing them all against their seat belts. A dark shadow loomed ahead of them, blocking their way.

Daniel inched closer to the thing in the smoke, and at last Akira was able to make out what it was. It was a car, half-on and half-off the road. Its front end was stuck in a ditch, and its back end hung in the air.

And it was on fire.

A metal car was on fire.

THE CAR IN THE DITCH

"Do you think somebody's in there?" Sue asked, giving voice to what everyone else was thinking. Akira squinted, but she couldn't see inside the burning car.

Daniel honked his horn. "Hey!" he yelled, even though there was no way anybody in the other car could have heard him. "Hey, if you're in there, get out!"

Nobody honked back, and nobody got out of the burning car. Akira shuddered, imagining what it would be like to be trapped in there. Burning alive.

"What do we do?" Daniel asked.

Akira's dad suddenly threw his car door open and jumped out.

"Dad! No!" Akira cried.

Akira watched with her heart in her throat as her father ran through the thick brown smoke toward the burning car. As her father bent to peer inside the windows, Akira felt sweat beading up on her forehead. It was getting hotter in Sue's car. And if the car in the ditch had caught on fire . . .

Akira's dad hurried back to their car and threw himself into the passenger seat, hacking and coughing and covered in sweat.

"Dad! Are you all right?" Akira cried, reaching out for him.

"Was there someone inside?" Sue asked.

Akira's dad shook his head and waved Daniel forward. "Nobody there," he croaked. "I'm okay. Go."

Daniel hit the accelerator, and they swerved around the burning car.

Akira worried about her father as he continued to cough, but there was nothing she could do. She checked her phone, and her heart leapt when she saw she had a text from her mom:

We're okay. Stay with your father, and let us know when you're safe. ❤

"Mom just texted me!" Akira announced. "She and Hildi are okay."

Akira's dad reached his hand back, and Akira squeezed it.

What neither of them said was that *they* weren't okay, and neither was anybody else in the car.

Everybody was quiet as Daniel drove on. Glowing embers drifted through the air, and Morris's flames were almost purple in the smoke. A burning house looked to Akira like a glowing skull, its broken windows hollow like eye sockets, its exterior walls black against the bright orange fire that filled it. It felt like they were driving through a movie about the end of the world.

How big is Morris now? Akira wondered. She tried her fire tracker app again, but it still wasn't updating.

"Please just let us get through the fire," Akira whispered.

And then, as if in answer to her prayer, the little car rounded a turn and the flames were completely gone. There was still smoke all around, but the road had curved out of the path of the fire.

They all let out gasps of relief, and Daniel turned to smile reassuringly at Sue.

"I told you everything was going to be all right," Akira's dad said, and Akira laughed. They were free from the fire! They were going to make it after all.

And then another car came flying out of a driveway next to them and smashed into the side of their car.

CHURCHILL, MANITOBA

PART I

THE TUNDRA BUGGY

A big male polar bear stood up on his hind legs and put his front paws on the tundra buggy with a *thump*, and the tourists sitting inside jumped back and gasped.

Standing behind them in the aisle, thirteen-year-old Owen Mackenzie smiled and rubbed his hands together. He was *definitely* going to get good tips on this trip.

"They don't call Churchill the Polar Bear Capital of the World for nothing, folks!" Owen said.

The tourists shook off their surprise and leaned in to *ooh* and *ahh* and take pictures of the polar bear, and Owen's dad turned around in the driver's seat and gave Owen a quiet fist bump.

Owen's parents were the owners and operators of Tundra Treks, a company that took people to see polar bears in the frozen wilderness outside Churchill, Manitoba. Churchill was a tiny town in northeast Canada, a thousand kilometers south of the Arctic Circle on the western side of Hudson Bay.

Polar bears mostly ate seals, but could only catch them out on the ice that formed when the ocean froze over in the winter. When spring came and the sea ice melted, the polar bears came back on land and spent the whole summer going hungry. Then, every October, a thousand polar bears made their way to the place where the sea ice re-formed first: Churchill, Manitoba. As soon as the bay froze over, the bears headed out to hunt seals again and begin their annual migration north.

But for one glorious month, lots of chilling polar bears meant lots of tourists.

Which meant lots of money for families like Owen's.

The polar bear outside the tundra buggy stretched his nose up to sniff one of the windows, and the tourists laughed with delight.

"Most male polar bears are about two and a half meters long, and weigh around four hundred and fifty kilos," Owen said, reciting facts from his memorized script. "That's nine feet tall and a thousand pounds, for you folks from the US." Owen had learned to explain things in ways that people from lots of different places could understand. Every year, ten thousand tourists visited Churchill from all over the world. Just today, he'd heard American English, British English, German, Spanish, and Korean.

Owen had been working as a tour guide for his parents since he was ten. He was white, with blond hair like his dad and blue eyes like his mom. He'd always been comfortable around adults, and he loved any chance he could get to grab a microphone and be the center of attention. Which made him a natural as the tour guide on his family's tundra buggy.

Tundra buggies looked like huge white buses on black monster truck tires. The big tires helped protect the fragile permafrost below, *and* kept the tourists up high, out of the reach of curious polar bears. Benches inside the tundra buggy could hold up to forty people, but this late in the season, there were only about twenty people on Owen's tour.

"Can we pet the polar bears?" one of the passengers asked. He was a boy around Owen's age, with light-brown skin, black hair, and arching eyebrows that made him look continually skeptical.

"*No,*" Owen said, answering for everyone. "Polar bears are the largest land predators on Earth. Even though they look like big, cute dogs to you, to them you look like a big hot dog with mustard and relish!"

The tourists laughed again. Owen loved a responsive group like this one.

"Thankfully, polar bears prefer to eat seals," he went on. "But they've been known to attack humans. And they're sneaky about it. Everybody in Churchill leaves their houses and cars unlocked this time of year, just in case we meet a polar bear while we're out and have to duck inside someplace to get away."

"Does that often happen?" a lady with a German accent asked, her eyes big at the thought. "Have you ever encountered a polar bear in town?"

"Not me, personally," Owen told her. "But bears come into

Churchill all the time. A few years ago, a girl from my school was attacked on Halloween night."

The crowd gasped.

"It's okay. She survived," Owen said quickly. "Another time, a man in town came out of the shower and was drying off when he looked up and saw a polar bear peeking through the window," he said, and everyone laughed again. "Sometimes polar bears bust right into houses, looking for food," Owen added.

"Back when I was a kid," Owen's dad said from the driver's seat, "the Department of Natural Resources shot any bears that came into town. Now we tranquilize them and send them to Polar Bear Jail, where they stay until the sea ice forms and they're airlifted out by helicopter and released in the wild."

"The scientific name for polar bears is *Ursus maritimus*, which means 'sea bear,'" Owen said, shifting back to his tour guide script. "That's because polar bears are such great swimmers "

"Wait. Can we *swim* with the polar bears?" the dark-haired kid from before interrupted.

Owen took a deep breath. "No," he said. "Again, the polar bear would *eat you*. Besides, the water around here is freezing this time of year. You'd probably die of hypothermia first."

The annoying kid shrugged. "If I was trying to get away from a polar bear, I would just dig a hole in the snow and hide where the bear couldn't see me," he said.

"That is *also* a bad idea," said Owen. He turned to the rest of the group. "Maybe you've heard the old saying about bears: 'If it's brown, lie down. If it's black, fight back. If it's white, say good night.'"

"Because you're going to go to sleep with the bears?" the annoying kid asked.

"No," Owen said, trying to keep his cool. "Because you're going to be *dead*. Polar bears are big, fast, strong, and smart. And you can't hide from them. Polar bears can smell seals miles away through two feet of ice. If you *do* have the misfortune to come face-to-face with a polar bear, don't run, and don't play dead. And never, *ever*, turn your back on a polar bear. Just back away slowly, making as much noise as you can, and *maybe* you'll survive."

The bear outside moved away from the tundra buggy, and Owen's dad started the engine again.

"Looks like it's time to head back in," Owen said, and everyone groaned.

"We were hoping to see a mother and her cubs!" a Canadian woman said as they rolled back to town.

Owen smiled. Cubs were always a major attraction, but it was the end of the season and most of the bears were out on the ice already. "Sorry. Cubs are super cute. We do see them sometimes, but momma bears are very protective of their cubs. You do *not* want to come between a cub and its mother. Momma Bear will wreck you," Owen said, getting a laugh.

"What about climate change?" a man with a Scandinavian accent asked. "I read that the warmer temperatures mean there's less ice for polar bears to live on."

"That's true," Owen told everyone. "The sea ice is melting earlier and coming later every year. But hey, that means we get more time with the polar bears," he added brightly.

The tundra buggy pulled into its big parking lot on the out-skirts of Churchill. Owen went down the steps first and stood by the exit as the tourists came out. He thanked each of them for coming, and graciously accepted their compliments and tips.

When everyone was gone, the kid who'd asked all the annoy-ing questions came down the steps and stood near Owen, staring at him quietly. Owen squinted at him, waiting long moments for him to say or do something.

They both broke down in laughter at the same time.

"Dude! Seriously?" Owen cried. "'Can we pet the polar bears?' 'Can we *swim* with the polar bears?'"

George Gruyére was laughing so hard he had to hold his stomach. George had been Owen's best friend since they shared crayons with each other on the first day of kindergarten. They had been pretending not to know each other on the tour for laughs.

George was Mushkegowuk. The Mushkegowuk were an Indigenous people sometimes referred to as the Swampy Cree and now registered with the Canadian government as the York Factory First Nation. George's ancestors had lived in this part of the world for millennia and had been the ones to greet the first French trappers who ventured north from Montreal in the 1600s.

Owen's father came out of the tundra buggy and chuckled. "George, I almost lost it when you said you'd just dig a hole to hide from a polar bear," he said. He put a hand on Owen's head. "Good job today, kiddo. You guys going out to the cabin now that you have the weekend off?"

Owen nodded. Ordinarily this was the weekend the Weather Lady flew in from the States for her annual Arctic tour, renting out the whole tundra buggy for herself and her crew. She did wild stunts like crawling inside polar bear dens and lighting ponds on fire, which was always exciting. But her flight had been canceled because of bad weather or something. Owen was bummed but glad to have the whole weekend to spend at George's family's ice fishing cabin instead.

"I just gotta get my bag from Mom," Owen said, darting off across the parking lot.

Owen's dad grabbed him by the shoulder and hauled him back, saving Owen from being run over by one of the tourists' rental cars that was driving away.

"*Owen*," his dad scolded him. "I know there aren't tons of cars in Churchill, but you still have to *pay attention*."

"Right!" Owen called, breaking away. "Sorry!"

Owen banged inside the office of Tundra Treks, and his mom looked up at him with a smile from behind the counter.

"The tourists were raving about you," she told him. "They're going to go home and tell all their friends about Tundra Treks."

"Sweet," Owen said, running for his bag.

"I packed you and George some brownies," Owen's mom said.

"Aw, yes," Owen said. "Thanks, Mom!"

"You have everything you need? Phone? Flares? Air horn? Bear spray? Cracker shells?"

"Yeah, yeah," Owen said. His mom always worried, but most of the polar bears were already out on the sea ice, and he and George had been out to the cabin by themselves plenty of times before.

He was ready to run, but his mother curled a finger at him and he slunk over to her.

"Owen, *remember*," she said, tapping his forehead. "You have to pay attention and *think*."

"I know, I know. Dad already told me."

"I mean it," she said. "You're really good at focusing on what you're interested in, but really bad at noticing that you're about to step into an ice hole."

"Heh-heh. 'Ice hole,'" Owen said.

Owen's mom narrowed her eyes. "That is exactly what I'm talking about, young man. Think *big picture*."

"Big ice hole?"

"*Owen*," his mother warned.

"Okay, okay," Owen said, pulling away. "Big picture! I got it."

"Have fun!" his mom called as he ran outside. "And watch out for polar bears!"

ICE HOLES

Owen and George powered through the newly fallen snow on George's snowmobile. George drove, and Owen sat behind him. It was cool that George had a snowmobile they could use, but Owen was trying to save up to buy his own. Then he wouldn't have to ride shotgun anymore.

"Mom told me to look out for ice holes," Owen told George, the wind clipping his words.

"You *are* an ice hole," George said back, and Owen laughed.

George throttled down to steer around a slow SUV that didn't know how to drive in the snow or didn't know where it was going. Or both.

"Ugh," George said. "I hate all the tourists."

"Tourists are good!" Owen told him. "Tourists are *money*."

Owen smiled and waved at the tourists in the SUV as they passed, and they happily waved back. In a few weeks, the last of the tourists would be gone, along with a lot of the tour guides and workers who only came to town for polar bear season.

Owen loved both times of the year. Quiet season was great because then the tiny town would be theirs and theirs alone. But he loved the excitement and influx of new people that came with the tourist season too.

And he loved the polar bears, of course.

A blue pickup truck with flashing yellow lights blocked off the road they were taking out of town, and George slowed the snowmobile again. "Aw, now this?" he moaned.

The truck belonged to the Manitoba Department of Natural Resources—what everybody called the DNR. The DNR were in charge of running off polar bears that came into town. Someone in a second DNR truck was doing that right now—firing cracker shells into the air from a shotgun as they chased a big dirty polar bear back to the tundra.

PAKOW. PAKOW-PAKOW.

Cracker shells weren't real bullets—they just made a lot of noise, which tended to scare off most polar bears. Most, but not all. Every year the DNR ended up killing one or two polar bears that attacked a person or killed someone's dog.

"Gotta be one of the last bears of the season," Owen said. "I'm surprised he's not out on the ice yet."

"I know the feeling," said George. "We're never going to get to the ice fishing cabin!"

Tourists always wanted to see the DNR chase polar bears, but Owen and George had both seen it happen so many times they didn't need to stay and watch. George revved the snowmobile and turned to find another way out of town.

MAC AND CHEESE

George finally found a clear road, and they zoomed past the big inuksuk that stood beside the broad, flat lake right outside Churchill. *Inuksuk* was an Inuit word for a tall stack of stones in the shape of a person. Inuksuks marked things like travel routes, or good places to fish or camp, or special places people believed were close to the spirits.

The city of Churchill had put this inuksuk up for tourists to take pictures with. A family was there now, posing for a selfie, and Owen gave them a friendly wave.

George opened up the throttle on the snowmobile, and Owen closed his eyes and enjoyed the mix of warm sun and cold air. Like George, he wore colorful snow goggles, a knitted ski mask, a dark, heavy parka, and insulated boots and wool mittens. They both wore thick wool socks and thermal underwear too, even though it wasn't the darkest, coldest part of winter yet. That came in January and February, when the temperature dropped to around -56 degrees Celsius and the sun was only up for six hours a day. Now it was only -16 degrees Celsius, and they had plenty of daylight to make it to the fishing cabin before sundown.

"Your mom send you with brownies?" George asked, his voice whipping by on the wind.

"Is Churchill full of ice holes?" Owen called back. George nodded and raised his fist in salute. Owen's mom's brownies were legendary among the kids in town, made with caramel, nuts, and crushed pretzels.

They zoomed east, running parallel to the shore of Hudson Bay. From the back of the snowmobile, Owen could see white chunks of ice floating on the turquoise-blue water. That was enough for the polar bears to head out and start hunting. Soon the chunks would grow and pile up and form one solid mass that would cover the bay for months, making it impassable for ships and shutting down the Port of Churchill for the season. The port was where George's dad worked.

Owen felt a gust of warmer air and frowned. Was it his imagination, or had that come in off the freezing bay?

"I wish we could see the new Marvel movie this weekend," said George.

Owen wanted to see it too, but he was used to waiting. "The Polar Cinema will get it in a month," he said. The Polar Cinema was Churchill's lone movie house, a single-screen theater in the Town Centre Complex that showed new movies about a month after they came out everywhere else.

"I'm just saying it would be nice if we lived someplace where the closest first-run movie theater wasn't seventeen hours away by train," George groused.

Owen frowned behind his friend. It was true—you had to use a train, a plane, or a ship to get anything in or out of Churchill. Even their cars and trucks had to be imported. But Owen *liked* that isolation. He liked that this was their little corner of the world, disconnected from everything else. And he'd thought George did too.

"First it's the tourists, now it's the movie theater. You sound like your brother," Owen said.

George's brother was sixteen, and couldn't *wait* to get out of town.

"Why are you so down on Churchill all of a sudden?" Owen asked.

"How are you *not* down on Churchill?" George asked.

"Are you kidding? It's a kid's dream up here!" Owen argued. "We get to ride wherever we want on snowmobiles, go ice fishing, see polar bears. We can go kayaking with beluga whales in the summer, and see the northern lights all year long. There's a movie theater and a library and a bowling alley and a pool in the Town Centre, and—"

"Maybe I just want to live in a place where I don't have to put on ten layers of clothes to go outside in the winter," said George. "Where the mosquitoes aren't so thick in the summer they can drain a pint of blood from a dog in a day. Where there are more than seven girls our age, and we haven't known them all since we were in kindergarten."

Or boys, for that matter, thought Owen.

Was that what was eating George? The small dating pool? Owen hadn't thought much about it, but with only nine hundred year-rounders in town, everybody *did* know everybody else here. There were only fifteen kids in the eighth grade at Duke of Marlborough School, and two hundred kids total from kindergarten up through grade twelve. Churchill was a town with more polar bears than people.

"I'm just saying that maybe there's more to life than

what you can get in Churchill, Manitoba," George said.

Owen was sad to hear his friend say that. He could sense that George didn't want to talk about it anymore though, so Owen let it go.

Neither of them said a word as they passed Miss Piggy, the graffitied wreckage of the old cargo plane that had crashed trying to fly out of Churchill back in the 1970s. They were still quiet half an hour later, when they passed the SS *Ithaka*, the big rusted and broken-down ship out in the bay that had run aground in a storm in the 1960s and been stuck there ever since.

The *Ithaka* was the landmark for where to turn inland toward the Gruyéres' fishing cabin, and George silently steered them south, away from the bay.

The snowmobile zoomed around shallow frozen lakes, and dodged clusters of smooth gray rocks that stuck up out of the white blanket of snow like icebergs on the ocean. All the while, Owen felt the silence between him and George growing. He didn't know what was up with his best friend, but he didn't want it to ruin the fun weekend they had planned.

"Hey," said Owen. "Hey, George."

"What?" said George.

"I just thought of something," Owen said.

"*What?*" said George.

"I need to pee," Owen said.

George laughed in spite of himself, and he stopped the snowmobile near some rocks where they could both go to the bathroom with a little privacy.

"Hey, George," Owen said, calling over his shoulder as he got unzipped. "I have an idea for what we can call ourselves."

"You mean besides 'George and Owen'?" George asked, trying to write a big yellow *G* in the snow.

"*Mac and Cheese,*" Owen called back. "You know, because my last name is Mackenzie. So I'm Mac."

"I am not the cheese," George told him.

"The cheese is good!" Owen argued. "You could be the *Big* Cheese. You know. Like the boss."

"How am I the cheese at all in this scenario?" George asked. "Because you couldn't think of anything else to go with Mac?"

Owen looked back at George over his shoulder. "Dude. Your last name is Gruyére. That is literally *a kind* of cheese! It's perfect."

"Just hurry up, ice hole," George told him.

Owen turned back to zip up his pants and saw the cutest thing ever a few meters away. It was a tiny polar bear cub, rolling around on its back and looking up at Owen like it wanted to play.

Owen's heart melted. He'd seen plenty of polar bear cubs from inside his parents' tundra buggy, but never one this close-up, and suddenly he was cooing like the sappiest tourist.

As he watched, the cub grabbed its back legs with its front paws and fell sideways in the snow with a tiny *fwump*.

"Awww! George, check it out," Owen said. The cub was So. Freaking. Adorable.

Suddenly Owen's tour guide script came back to him, and he heard his own words: *Cubs are super cute, but you do not want to come between a cub and its mother. Momma Bear will wreck you.*

Momma Bear, he thought. Where was Momma Bear?

Owen spun around. George had turned to look at him and the cub.

Which meant George didn't see the big polar bear standing right behind him.

"George!" Owen cried, but too late. Momma Bear swatted the back of George's head, and Owen's friend went down in a spray of red blood.

MOMMA BEAR

Momma Bear stood up on her back legs, and Owen had never felt so small in his entire life. She was easily two hundred and twenty-five kilos big and two meters tall, and her fur was stained a yellowish white from being off the ice for so long. All except for her right front paw, which was red.

Red with George's blood.

Owen reached around for the shotgun on his shoulder, but it wasn't there. His stomach sank. Because George always drove the snowmobile, Owen got to carry the shotgun. That was the deal. But Owen had been so busy clowning around to get George to lighten up that he'd forgotten to grab the shotgun from the snowmobile.

Which was parked *behind* the polar bear.

Owen stood frozen in terror as Momma Bear thumped back down on all fours in the snow, less than a meter away from George's body. George wasn't moving. He didn't look like he was even breathing. Was George playing dead, or was he *really* dead?

Momma Bear opened her mouth wide and swung her head back and forth, low and mean, showing off her huge, sharp teeth. She reared back to lunge at George again, and Owen finally found his voice.

"Hey," he squeaked. There was no air in his lungs. He took a quick breath. "Hey, bear!" he yelled, getting some volume behind it this time. Owen waved his arms. "Look at me! Let's go!"

Momma Bear stopped mid-attack and locked in on him with a furious glare. It suddenly reminded Owen of how his mother had looked that time he and George started a fire in the microwave trying to slow cook baked potatoes.

How could a bear look so *human*?

Getting Momma Bear's attention had bought George a precious few seconds of not being attacked, but Owen didn't know what to do next. He had no phone or flares or air horn, no bear spray or shotgun and cracker shells. All that was back in the snowmobile.

Because I wasn't thinking, Owen berated himself.

Momma Bear stepped over George's body toward Owen, and Owen instinctively took a step back. His throat was dry as ashes, but he swallowed down a gulp. *Oh crap*, he thought. *Oh crap oh crap oh crap.*

Momma Bear was coming for him next.

The polar bear huffed like a dog. *Hrooof. Hooof.* She opened her mouth wide again to show her teeth and popped her jaw. It sounded like somebody tapping a wooden spoon against a wooden bowl. *Tok-tok-tok-tok-tok.* Owen knew that polar bears huffed and popped their jaws to warn people off, but he'd never heard it up close like this. Never felt that deep-down, icy-cold certainty in his bones that a polar bear was about to charge him.

But he sure felt it now.

The urge to run was like one of those big hooks that came

out in cartoons to yank people offstage. Owen couldn't resist it. Every centimeter of him was screaming at him to *run run run run run*.

And that's exactly what he did.

Owen turned in his tracks and ran away from the big polar bear as hard and fast as he could. *THUMP THUMP THUMP THUMP*. Was that the sound of his boots stomping in the snow, or was it his heart, hammering in his chest? His boots, his big parka, his rasping snow pants, they all dragged at him. Weighed him down. He was too slow. Too slow!

He heard the thumping crunch of Momma Bear's paws in the snow as she loped after him. *Th-thump, th-thump, th-thump*. Owen's breath blew out in great white clouds, fogging his snow goggles. He couldn't see, didn't know where he was running. All he knew was that he *couldn't stop*.

One of Owen's boots slipped in the snow. He stumbled, slid, started to fall forward—

And then something big and strong and sharp *whacked* his arm and sent him spinning into the snow.

MIAMI, FLORIDA

PART I

THE BIG ONE

Natalie Torres sat on the edge of her couch, her eyes glued to the television and her weather journal clutched tight in her hands.

"Hurricane Reuben has gone back and forth between Category Four and Category Five—the highest, most powerful category we have," Maria Martinez said on TV, pointing to the huge swirling mass of white clouds projected behind her.

Everybody in Miami knew Maria Martinez, the chief meteorologist for one of the local news channels. They may not have watched the weather forecast every night like Natalie did, but when there was a hurricane, everybody in South Florida turned to Maria for the latest.

Natalie knew that Hurricane Reuben had already brushed Puerto Rico, where Natalie's mother had been born and Natalie's father still lived, and made a devastating landfall in the Dominican Republic. After that it had picked up strength again and swept along the top of Cuba, and now it was deciding where to go next.

"Our current projection models show Reuben possibly hitting the Florida Keys and heading west, into the Gulf of Mexico, the way Katrina did in 2005 on its way to New Orleans," Maria Martinez said. "Or it could round the Everglades and travel north up the west coast of Florida. And of course there's still a strong possibility that it will make a right turn at the Bahamas and drive straight up I-95, hitting Miami and Fort Lauderdale and West Palm Beach and everything in between."

Natalie shuddered. That was what she and everybody in Miami feared the most.

The Big One.

The giant, mythical hurricane that would destroy the entire southeast coast of Florida.

"For a hundred years," Maria Martinez was saying, "hurricanes have hit all over South Florida *except* for Miami. Andrew, Wilma, Irma—they all came close, and did a great deal of damage. But the last hurricane to hit Miami directly was in 1926, when only a hundred thousand people lived here. The Great Miami Hurricane leveled the city, killing hundreds of people and leaving tens of thousands more homeless." She paused. "Now there are close to three million people in Miami-Dade County alone."

Natalie swallowed. Back when she was in second grade, everybody had thought that Hurricane Irma was going to be the Big One. It wasn't. Irma ended up barely missing Miami. But it had come close.

Close enough to rip Natalie's roof off while she and her mother huddled in the bathroom.

Ever since Irma, Natalie had become obsessed with weather. She'd started keeping a weather journal, where she wrote down the daily high and low temperatures, the cloud formations, the wind speeds, the amount of sunshine and rain. She asked for a barometer and an anemometer and a rain gauge for Christmas, and hung them outside her bedroom window. Every time she had to do a science project or write a paper in school, she did it on a different hurricane.

If the weather was going to shape Natalie's life, she wanted to know everything about it.

"Is it the Big One?" Natalie's mother called, coming in the front door with groceries.

"They don't know yet," Natalie said, hopping up to take two of the bags.

Natalie and her mother had the same brown skin and brown eyes, but Mama's black hair was straight and never frizzed in the Miami humidity the way Natalie's did. Natalie didn't know how her mom could wear jeans and a blouse in this heat either. The most Natalie could bear to wear were shorts and an old tank top. But Mama always looked put together, even when there was a hurricane coming.

"The store was pretty picked over," Mama told her. "I got what I could."

Natalie followed her mother to the kitchen and helped her put away the food. Everything she'd bought was canned or dry and didn't need to be cooked or refrigerated, for when the power went out. She'd bought candles and matches too, and batteries for their flashlights.

Natalie glanced back at the television, where Maria Martinez was now showing a map of Miami. The city sat between the Atlantic Ocean to the east and the vast wetlands of the Everglades to the west, northwest, and south. Whether Reuben hit them directly or not, water was going to come at them from every one of those directions—plus down from the clouds and up through the porous limestone underneath the city. Maria Martinez was predicting storm surges of over ten feet.

During Irma, Natalie's house had flooded up to her knees. And that was *before* the roof had come off.

Natalie felt a surge of panic. "We have to get everything ready!" she cried. She grabbed her weather journal and showed her mom the list she'd made. "We have to fill the bathtub with water so we can flush the toilet once the power goes out, board up the windows, take all the pictures off the walls so they don't fall and break, put all our valuable stuff up high out of flood range, charge our phones—"

"Mija. *Mija*," her mother said, putting a hand on Natalie's head to calm her down. "I know you're overwhelmed. But we'll get through this together."

Natalie took a deep breath and nodded, and they got to work.

She and her mother were filling up water bottles in the kitchen sink so they'd have clean water to drink when Natalie's phone dinged. It was a text from her friend Shannon.

OMG the roads are full of cars.

Are you leaving town? Natalie texted back.

No. Dad says we're safe in our building. It has a generator. He says if the power goes out it will be like a camping trip. 😟

Natalie shook her head. Shannon went to school here in Hialeah, their city within a city in Miami. But Shannon lived in one of the new high-rise luxury apartments in nearby Doral, not in a small single-story house like Natalie and her mom. Natalie and Shannon had met in homeroom last year at the beginning of sixth grade and had immediately bonded over their shared love of boba tea, K-pop, and extreme weather shows.

Shannon texted her a picture of an interstate that skirted Miami, taken from her window. The highway looked like a parking lot. Every lane was packed bumper to bumper with cars headed north, out of the city.

"Look," Natalie said, showing the picture to her mom.

"Hunh," said Mama. "Must be nice to be able to get out of town."

Natalie's mom worked as an administrative assistant at a doctor's office, and Natalie knew her salary wasn't that big. If they went to Tampa or Orlando and stayed in a hotel every time there was a storm, they'd be broke.

When the water bottles were full, Natalie and her mother went outside to cover the windows with plywood. There was one small transom window above the front door that was too high to reach, but it hadn't broken in any previous storms.

It was hot and muggy, and Natalie was panting and sweating by the time they finished hammering. The October sun was bright, and there wasn't a cloud in the sky. It certainly didn't *look* like a hurricane was coming, but something still felt off.

Natalie glanced around and began to understand what was wrong. No cars drove by. No birds twittered on the power lines. There weren't even any airplanes taking off and landing at the airport just south of them. Everything was quiet and still, like Natalie and her mom were the only two people left in Hialeah.

Natalie knew that wasn't true. Most of the people in her neighborhood couldn't afford to leave. They were holed up in their houses already, preparing to ride out the storm.

Into the creepy silence came a loud, frantic sound—*weeoo-weeoo-WEEOO-WEEOO*—and it took Natalie a moment to realize it wasn't an alarm or a siren. It was *frogs*, croaking in the nearby canal.

Natalie's mom pointed. Half a dozen snails were oozing up the cinder-block foundation of their house, getting as high as they could. In the house next door, Natalie heard their neighbor's little Chihuahua growling and barking.

The animals know, Natalie thought.

Something was coming.

Something big.

DIABLITO

"Tía Beatriz!" Mama exclaimed. The sound of Tía's dog barking made her look next door. "Her windows aren't boarded up. Her son must not have come by yet. Where could he be?"

Tía Beatriz wasn't really Natalie's aunt, but Natalie and her mom still considered her family. The elderly woman who'd emmigrated from Nicaragua years ago had been their neighbor for as long as Natalie could remember. When Natalie was younger, Tía Beatriz had babysat her after school until her mother got home from work.

"Maybe her son's stuck in traffic," Natalie said, remembering Shannon's picture of the interstate.

"I'll bring her over to stay with us," Mama said. "You keep working through the list."

Natalie ran back inside and took all the photos off the walls: Natalie winning the sixth-grade science fair. Mama graduating from night school. The time she and Mama had gone to Puerto Rico to see her father. Next, she put their books and electronics high up on shelves and cabinets, where they would be out of any flood.

On the television, Maria Martinez said Hurricane Reuben's wind speeds were being clocked at 165 miles per hour. Natalie grabbed her weather journal and wrote that down. One hundred and sixty-five miles per hour was high! When Irma had made landfall, Natalie remembered, its wind speed had been 130 miles per hour.

Natalie heard a *yip* from the front door and looked up. Her mom was back with Tía Beatriz and Tía's Chihuahua.

"Ay, Elena, I would have been fine," Tía Beatriz told Natalie's mother. "I've been through hurricanes before."

"Not like this one, Tía," Mama said. "I got her son on the phone," she told Natalie. "He was sitting in his car halfway here from Homestead. I told him Tía was with us and to go home to his family."

"Princesa," Tía said, holding out her arms to Natalie. She had seen her only yesterday, but Natalie still gave Tía a big hug.

Tía Beatriz's skin was dark brown, and her face was squished and wrinkly with age. The wrinkles radiated out from her eyes and mouth in a sort of perpetual smile, matching her personality.

At their feet, Tía's tiny dog growled.

"Churro, you hush now," Tía scolded, but Natalie knew that was impossible.

The dog's name was Churro because his fur was cinnamon colored, like a churro, and his black snout made it look like he'd been dipped in chocolate. But Churro was anything but sweet. At least not to Natalie.

Churro bared his teeth and snapped at her, and Natalie narrowed her eyes at him.

"Diablito," Natalie whispered at him. Little devil. The hurricane was going to be stressful enough without having to tiptoe around Churro the whole time.

Tía Beatriz waved dismissively at Maria Martinez on the television as she sat down on the couch.

"Shouldn't hurricane season be over already?" Tía Beatriz asked. "It's almost the end of October."

"Hurricanes are coming earlier and ending later," Natalie told her. "It used to be that most hurricanes hit in August and September, but now we're getting hurricanes almost nonstop from May through November."

"Natalie's become something of an expert," her mother explained.

"Yes, I see," said Tía Beatriz. "Estoy impresionada."

"The storms are getting bigger too," Natalie said. "And it's all because of climate change. Burning fossil fuels puts carbon dioxide in the atmosphere, which traps the earth's heat."

Natalie started to get worked up. Years of studying the weather and diving down the rabbit hole of climate change science online had prepared her for this moment.

"Ninety percent of the heat trapped in the earth's atmosphere goes into the oceans," she went on. "Hurricanes are formed over the ocean, and they feed on warm water as they move. So now the warmer water supercharges them, making hurricanes stay stronger and last longer."

"Okay, mija, okay," Mama said, patting her shoulder. "I wish you wouldn't dwell on these things."

"But Mama, if we don't do something about climate change—"

"I know. But it's too much," her mother told her. "You're just making yourself upset, and there's nothing you or I can do about it."

"There's lots of things we can do about it," Natalie said. She grabbed her phone. "I read an article online: 'Fifteen Things You Can Do to Stop Global Warming'—"

"*Natalie,*" her mother said, trying to get her to slow down.

"We have breaking news on Hurricane Reuben," Maria Martinez said in an urgent tone, and Natalie, Mama, and Tía Beatriz looked back at the TV.

"The Category Five storm has changed course, and is now headed *directly* for the Miami metropolitan area. The National Weather Service has issued a *mandatory evacuation* for all of Miami-Dade, Broward, Palm Beach, Collier, and Monroe counties."

Natalie felt the bottom drop out of her stomach.

"I'm calling it, everybody," Maria Martinez said. She swallowed hard and looked right into the camera. "Our lucky streak is over. The Big One is here."

THE PARTY'S OVER

The rain came down in sheets, and the lights in Natalie's house flickered. She, Mama, and Tía Beatriz sat together on the couch, listening to the oscillating roar of the storm outside— low, then loud, then low again. Natalie had to keep working her jaw and swallowing to pop her ears. She'd never felt anything like it before, and she was scared.

It hadn't been like this the *whole* day. Natalie and her mother had finished their storm prep soon after Maria Martinez had called Reuben the "Big One," but that still left hours before the hurricane actually hit. They couldn't go anywhere with the windows boarded up and the door blocked with a mattress. And since the power was bound to go out, it made sense to finish off anything in the freezer that was going to melt or spoil. So while Reuben bore down on Miami, Natalie, Mama, and Tía Beatriz settled on the couch to eat ice cream and watch telenovelas. It had almost been like a party.

But now the party was definitely over.

Thunder boomed close by, shaking the whole house. Churro had been whimpering and quivering for the last hour, and now he threw up. Natalie was no fan of the mean little dog, but she felt sorry for him. She felt sick too. They had repaired their roof after Irma. Made it more secure. But Reuben was stronger than Irma had been and was going to hit them dead on. What if

Reuben ripped their roof off again, and they were swept away into the storm?

Something crashed into the side of the house and Natalie flinched. Was it a tree branch? A trash can? There was no way to look outside to see. Natalie couldn't check the rain and wind gauges she had mounted outside her boarded-up bedroom window either.

Greenish-yellow lightning flashed around the edges of the plywood boards they'd put up, and—*poom*—the electricity went out for good. Natalie jumped—it always scared her when the lights went out in a storm—but she quickly got over it and helped her mom light a handful of small votive candles.

Natalie's phone lit up with a text, and she unplugged it from the wall charger. No use keeping it plugged in now.

The storm looks so cool from up here! Shannon wrote, and she sent a picture of palm trees below bending over sideways in the wind.

It's pretty bad here, Natalie wrote back. *We just lost power.*

Shannon replied with a sad face emoji.

Rain lashed the house, and thunder boomed again.

Tía Beatriz crossed herself. "Reminds me of Hurricane Joan," she said, her thin voice barely audible over the storm. "Came straight across Nicaragua in 1988. Wiped out all the trees and farms. Washed away all the roads and bridges. Destroyed everybody's houses. Joan came just as the civil war was ending, when we already had next to nothing. There was no government to aid us, so we shared what we had with each other. It helped, but it wasn't enough. So I came here, to el norte. I miss some of the way things were before. But now my children are better off than I ever was."

Natalie went to sit beside Tía Beatriz and put her arm around her.

The walls rattled and shook. Natalie closed her eyes and tried to picture herself somewhere calm and sunny and safe.

Someplace like Mariposa.

Mariposa! She'd forgotten to save Mariposa!

"I'll be right back!" Natalie cried, and she grabbed a flashlight and ran for her bedroom.

MARIPOSA

Natalie opened her bedroom closet door and pushed aside her hanging dresses and jackets. On the floor at the back, her flashlight found a stack of shoeboxes covered in glitter and bright paint.

Mariposa.

Natalie lifted the boxes and carried them carefully to her bed. She felt a pang of guilt for forgetting to rescue them earlier. The truth was, she hadn't thought about Mariposa in a long time.

Mariposa was the fictional country Natalie had invented when she was in third grade. The kingdom of Mariposa had started as drawings and maps and stories from her imagination, but soon she began to see her real-life neighborhood through its lens, transforming the everyday into the fantastic. The dirty canal along Okeechobee Road became the sparkling blue Mariposa River. The old coral-stone water sanitation building with its arched walkways and terra-cotta roof was a royal castle. The small park where people walked their dogs was Mariposa's rural countryside.

Natalie glanced around her bedroom. Before her walls had been covered with posters of lightning storms and Greta Thunberg and K-pop bands, they had been covered with all things Mariposa. Natalie had spent hours turning the crinkly checkerboard wrappers from food trucks into Mariposa money. Cutting and coloring the thin cardboard from cereal boxes to make Mariposa passports for her friends and family. Writing a Mariposa constitution and drawing up maps with provinces and states and territories.

Natalie sat on her bed and ran her hand across the blue construction-paper butterfly glued to one of the shoeboxes. *Mariposa* meant "butterfly" in Spanish, and emblazoned on every piece of money, every official proclamation—on the very flag of Mariposa itself—was a Miami blue butterfly.

Natalie felt bad for forgetting Mariposa. But she wasn't a kid anymore. She was in seventh grade. She couldn't keep believing in fairy tales. Still, Mariposa had meant so much to her once, and she didn't want to lose it forever.

Natalie stood on her desk chair and put the Mariposa boxes up as high as she could on her bookcase, higher up than her laptop, where her memories would be safest from a flood.

The house shuddered, and Natalie quailed. Outside, Reuben raged.

Natalie shone her flashlight along the seam of the roof, looking for cracks. Nothing.

Yet.

Natalie hurried back to the living room to huddle with her mother and Tía Beatriz on the couch.

"I got a message from your father," Mama said, holding up her phone. "He's all right."

Natalie nodded. She was glad her dad was safe, but she didn't know him very well. Her parents had gotten divorced when she was a baby, and Natalie had only met her father twice in her life. She knew how hard it was for everyone in Puerto Rico right now though. They still hadn't completely recovered from Hurricane Maria, which had hit Puerto Rico the same year Irma hit South Florida.

Natalie's phone dinged. It was another text from Shannon.

There goes Halloween, I guess. And after all the work we did on our costumes!

Natalie had totally forgotten about Halloween. She and Shannon were going to go as a pair—Shannon as a hurricane and Natalie as Maria Martinez reporting from the storm, complete with blowing newspapers pinned to her windbreaker and an inside-out umbrella over her shoulder.

Natalie smiled at the thought of their costumes, then frowned. *That* was what Shannon was thinking about now, while Natalie was watching to see if her roof was going to blow off?

Natalie's fingers hovered over her phone as she thought about how to respond. She wanted to say that she had bigger things to worry about, but she didn't want to offend her friend.

Turning off my phone to save the battery, she wrote instead.

CRASH!

Everyone jumped at the sound, and a blast of wind blew the mattress in front of the door down.

The storm had smashed the little window above the door. Natalie and her mother dodged the broken glass on the floor and tried to right the mattress, but a river of brown water started gushing in under the door, flooding the room.

"We have to stop the water!" Natalie yelled, but her mother couldn't hear her. The wind whistled like a freight train's horn outside—*BWAAAAAAAAA. BWAAAAAAAAAAAAAAA.* It was the loudest thing Natalie had ever heard, and she had to cover her ears.

Natalie ran to the bathroom for towels, but when she got back to the front door there were already two inches of water on the floor. She watched in horror as the ceiling wobbled and the walls rippled like waves.

No. Not the roof, Natalie thought. *Not again!*

As she was looking up, as she was praying the roof wouldn't lift off and go flying away again, the back wall of her house came crashing in.

THE OCEAN COMES
TO HIALEAH

A chest-high wall of gray water swept into the house and lifted Natalie off her feet.

She banged into the coffee table, swallowed salty water, and was dragged along the floor until she finally fought her way to the surface, choking and spitting. It was too much. Everything was coming at her at once. The water pulled her under again and hammered her with parts of the wall, the table, all the things they'd put up high to keep dry. Natalie was sinking. Drowning.

Suddenly Reuben pulled back like a fighter dancing away after delivering a punch, and Natalie pushed herself up against the front wall, half in, half out of the water. She spluttered and coughed, her throat raw. Her arms and legs ached. "Mama?" Natalie croaked. "*Mama?*"

Her words were immediately eaten up by the freight train roar of the storm. Natalie had lost her flashlight and her phone in the flood, and the candles had drowned with everything else. It was pitch-black in the house except for the blinding flashes of lightning she could see outside through the missing wall.

The back wall of our house got knocked down by a wave, Natalie thought wildly. That wasn't supposed to happen. It wasn't like they lived by the beach. Hialeah was miles from the coast. But the water was just over her knees now, and it rose and fell with the swell of the storm like when she went to the ocean and waded out into the waves.

Only now the ocean had come to her.

Natalie's mother burst up out of the water beside her, gasping for breath, and Natalie grabbed her. It was hard for Natalie to stand, to keep her feet planted in the shifting water, but she braced her legs and held her mother up as she coughed and spat and retched.

Mama clutched at her arm and pulled her close. *"Tía Beatriz!"* Mama shouted in Natalie's ear.

Tía! Where was she? Natalie looked up in time to see another wave rolling into the house. It lifted the couch and the table and the television console and threw them against Natalie and her mother, slamming them into the wall. Natalie saw stars as pain shot through her, and she fought to stay conscious. The waterlogged mattress knocked her under again, and Natalie's scream was swallowed by another mouthful of warm, salty water.

Natalie fought her way back up again and found Mama beside her, coughing and gagging but all right. And there was Churro too, clinging to the sofa. The little dog was still alive! The sofa was upside down, and Churro stood on top of it, barking his head off as though the couch had personally attacked him.

Natalie still didn't see Tía Beatriz, and she suddenly wondered if Churro was trying to tell them something. She pulled Churro off the sofa and flipped it over, and up floated Tía Beatriz.

"No! Tía!" Natalie cried, but the old woman didn't respond. Tía's eyes were closed, and Natalie couldn't tell if she was breathing.

Natalie put Churro back on the sofa and waved frantically for her mother to come and help. Natalie slipped her arms under

Tía's armpits, but she'd only managed to get her neighbor's head above water before the next wave hit, pushing them all into the front wall again.

Natalie's mother swam over and took Tía Beatriz from her. Natalie didn't want to let Tía go. She couldn't bear the thought of Tía being dead, and she had to look away from the old woman's slack, ashen face.

"Try to open the front door!" Mama yelled over the roar of the storm.

Natalie nodded, ready to do anything that might help. She unlocked the door and tried to pull it open, but the rising water held it shut.

No, no, no! Natalie thought. She tried the windows next, but she and her mother had boarded them all shut from the outside, trying to keep the hurricane *out*. She banged a fist against the plywood. How could they have known Reuben would come in through the back wall instead?

Churro barked angrily—*Rrrrr-rar-rar rar rar-rar! Rar-rar-rar-rar-rar!*—like he could scare the hurricane back out to sea. But Reuben wasn't going away. The water was getting higher. Furniture from their own house crowded them, joined by a lawn chair, a small metal table, and a plastic bag full of trash swept in from outside. A whole bush crashed into Natalie and clawed at her face.

Natalie tried pushing past it all and escaping through the open wall at the back, but the storm surge was too strong.

They were trapped. And if the water kept rising like this, they were all going to drown.

INTO THE STORM

Mama pointed to the little window up above the door, the only one they hadn't boarded up, and Natalie understood at once. It was just big enough for her to wiggle through. If she could reach it.

Natalie climbed the moving stack of furniture and debris under the window. The pile shifted underneath her, but the next wave lifted her high enough to reach the windowsill. She grabbed on and pulled herself up.

Arms burning, stomach scraping over broken glass, Natalie wriggled out headfirst into the storm. She worried about the fall to the steps outside, but the water was just as high outside as in. She splashed down backward, like doing a flip into a pool.

Natalie was an excellent swimmer, but nothing had prepared her for diving into a hurricane. The dark, swirling water pushed and pulled at her. Rain lashed her face. Wind howled in her ears. Lightning blinded her. Little bits of things flew into her—plants? rocks? parts of houses?—she wasn't sure. Couldn't know.

Natalie felt her panic rising. The water was up to her chest now, and she could barely stand. She tried to push her front door open from outside, but it wouldn't budge. She pulled at the plywood on the windows, but they'd done too good a job. The boards were nailed tight.

Natalie grabbed the sill of the high window from the outside and pulled herself up—easier now that the water was higher—and saw her mother's frightened face. Mama's arms were wrapped around Tía, who still wasn't awake.

"Mama! I can't get the boards off!" Natalie cried, but Reuben swallowed her words.

Natalie's mother started to tell her something, but another wave came through the back of the house, and Mama and Tía Beatriz went underwater again.

"No!" Natalie cried. She hung on to the windowsill for a long moment, waiting with growing despair for her mother to resurface. Her mother came up spluttering at last, struggling to keep herself and Tía Beatriz above water. The storm surge was taller than they were now.

"Climb out through the window!" Natalie yelled.

Natalie's mother shook her head. They both knew she wouldn't fit—and neither would Tía Beatriz.

Mama and Tía Beatriz went under in another wave, and Natalie felt herself being pulled away from the house. She clung desperately to the windowsill, barely managing to hang on. The water had risen so much that Natalie couldn't feel the ground underneath her anymore.

She was treading water now, completely at Reuben's mercy.

Inside the house, Natalie's mother was sinking under the weight of Tía, whose face was the only thing above water. Natalie tried to crawl back inside, but her mother waved her off.

"Don't!" her mother yelled. "You'll be trapped!"

Mama handed Churro out through the window instead. The little dog was barking—always barking!—but Natalie took him in her right hand and held him close to her chest, up out of the water.

Mama pointed away from the house.

"Go!" her mouth said. "Get out of the storm!"

Natalie shook her head, the driving rain mixing with her tears.

"No!" she cried. "I won't leave you!" But then another wave came and lifted her, and her hand slipped from the windowsill.

"No!" Natalie cried again, swallowing another mouthful of the foul water. She tumbled and turned, trying to stay upright, trying to keep herself and the little dog from drowning.

"I love you, mija!" her mother yelled. Or at least that's what Natalie thought she heard as she and Churro were swept away down the street.

THE SIERRA NEVADA, CALIFORNIA

PART 2

GOING NOWHERE

Akira looked up in a daze. Something had hit her side of the car. *Another car*, she remembered groggily. And then something had punched her in the head.

An airbag. Airbags had burst from the dashboard and the doors, knocking everybody around as much as the crash.

Akira and Sue had been pushed into the middle of the seat, and they helped each other up as Akira blinked away the fog in her brain.

"Dad?" Akira said, her tongue thick in her mouth. "Are you okay?"

In the front seat, her dad stirred. So did Daniel. Everybody seemed to be all right.

Akira's dad clawed at the airbags that surrounded him, trying to see. "Can we move?" he asked.

Daniel punched at the gas pedal, but the engine had stopped. He tried the ignition.

"It won't start," he said.

Akira pushed her airbag out of the way. The car that had hit them was right outside her window. Its airbags had gone off too, and she couldn't see inside.

Just seconds ago they'd escaped the fire. But now Akira saw flames spreading through the forest around them. The fire leapt from tree to tree, almost like a squirrel. It was mesmerizing to watch.

Hot cinders bounced onto the car that had run into them and settled in, smoldering on its surface. Akira suddenly remembered the other car they'd seen. The one burning in the ditch. How long until the car that hit them caught on fire?

How long until *their* car caught on fire?

"Dad!" Akira cried. "We have to get out!"

TRAPPED

"We can't leave the car," said Daniel. "We'll die out there."

"The car in the ditch caught fire," Akira told them. "Ours will too!"

Sue sobbed next to her. It was blazing hot and hard to breathe.

"Akira's right. We have to get out," Akira's dad said. "Let's go!"

He threw open his door, and brown smoke poured inside. Akira squeezed her eyes shut and choked.

Daniel got out on his side, letting in more smoke. "Sue, let's go!" he called.

Akira unbuckled her seat belt and tried to open her door, but it wouldn't budge. What? No! She yanked on the handle again and again and looked out the window. The car that had hit them was blocking her door.

Akira's dad opened Sue's door and leaned inside. "Akira! Get out!" he cried.

"I can't! It's blocked!" Akira told her dad. "Sue, we have to go out your side," she said.

Sue stayed where she was, clutching her shoulder and crying. She shook her head. "I can't," she sobbed.

Akira huffed. Whatever was wrong with Sue, there was no time to talk her down. Akira unbuckled Sue's seat belt, and the two dads pulled Sue out through the door.

Akira crawled out right behind her and winced. Leaving the car was like walking into an oven. Hot air blasted Akira in the face, and she choked on a lungful of heavy smoke. The woods all around them were alight with scorching, blinding flames.

Akira's father pulled her close, and she felt her desperation and fear echoed in his embrace.

"The other car!" Daniel cried. "Nobody's gotten out of it yet!"

"Stay here on the pavement," Akira's dad told her and Sue, and the two girls watched as their dads hurried to help whoever was inside.

Sue wobbled, and Akira helped her stand. Sue's left arm hung limp, and she grimaced and clutched at it with her other hand. She was clearly more hurt than Akira had thought.

CHOOM! A flaming tree on the other side of the street exploded from the inside out, startling Akira and Sue and making them cry out.

The tree began to tilt, and then fall, and—*Crick. Crack. SHOOM!*—it crashed into the road, separating the girls from their dads.

THE HUMAN PINBALL

"Dad!" Akira screamed.

"Dad!" cried Sue.

Akira tried to lead Sue around the burning tree, but she couldn't find a safe path through the flames. Glowing orange cinders swirled in the wind.

"Akira! Sue!" they heard their dads cry, and Akira squinted to see through the branches of the burning tree. Their dads were together, their arms around an old couple, helping them stand. The people from the other car.

"Dad!" Akira cried. "I can't get back to you!"

Another tree fell behind them, and Akira and Sue ducked and scrambled away from it.

"Akira, run! Get somewhere safe!" her dad yelled.

"No!" Akira cried. She couldn't leave her dad. Where would she go? How would she and Sue survive the fire?

"Just get out of the fire, then head for home!" Akira's dad yelled. "You know the way!"

"I can't!" Sue screamed. "Dad!"

"You can do this," Sue's dad called back, his voice strangled with anguish and smoke. "Stay together. Everything's going to be all right, Sue. I love you."

"No! Dad!" Akira cried again.

"I love you, Akira!" her dad called.

Another tree *woomphed* down behind them, and another,

and there was no more time for debate. Akira grabbed Sue's hand and pulled her away.

Get somewhere safe, Akira's dad had said. But what was safe in the middle of a wildfire? Not even the pavement was free from the fire anymore. Burning branches and tree limbs filled the road, and Akira and Sue tripped and stumbled as they ran. Akira could barely breathe, let alone see.

Akira squeezed her eyes almost all the way shut and put her free hand out to feel where she was going. She felt heat to her right, and went left. She heard crackling and popping to her left, and went right.

Behind her, Sue cried out in pain. Akira looked back and saw the arm Sue had been clutching dangling unnaturally by her side. She was hunched over, like she was sick to her stomach. Something was definitely wrong with Sue, but they couldn't stop. Not yet.

Akira plodded forward, trying to get them someplace where there was no smoke, no fire. But the smoke and fire were *everywhere*. Akira ran into a burning pine tree and bounced away, crying out in pain from the sting of the flames. She bumped into another tree and pinballed through the heavy smoke and heat, Sue staggering along behind her.

The forest floor crackled and smoldered under their feet, and Akira stopped. *Oh no*, she realized. *We've left the road and we're in the forest!* She spun, trying to find her way back to the safety road, but it was gone. Lost in the smoke.

Akira picked a direction and pulled Sue with her. They kept dodging flames until at last they stumbled into a small clearing in the woods full of smoke, but no fire.

"Dad?" Akira called, bending double and trying to catch her breath. "Are you there? Can you hear me?"

"Dad?" Sue tried.

They heard the crackle and pop of somebody walking toward them through the dry pine needles on the forest floor, and the girls looked up hopefully. But it wasn't their dads.

It was Morris. The crackling and popping was the sound of the fire slowly advancing on them through the woods as it ate up tree after tree after tree. It was like the wildfire was playing some horrible game of hide-and-seek with them.

"Come on," Akira said wearily, taking Sue's hand. "We're not beat yet."

BAD SIGNALS

Akira and Sue found another small clearing where the smoke wasn't as thick and there wasn't any fire. Not yet, at least.

Sue collapsed onto the ground, and Akira slumped down beside her, glad for a moment's rest. They were both gasping for breath and covered in sweat and scratches and burns.

Sue closed her eyes and clutched her injured arm while Akira tried to get her bearings. They had left the road and run uphill into the forest, but where were they now? How far had they run?

"Dad?" Akira called again, her throat ragged.

No one answered.

"Dad?" Sue yelled, hacking and coughing.

Still no answer.

"We're going to die," Sue moaned. "The fire's going to eat us up, and we're going to die."

Akira shook her head. She refused to believe that.

"We're not going to die," she wheezed. "Do you have a phone?"

Sue shook her head and wiped away a tear. "I dropped it in the wreck."

Akira still had hers. She pulled it out and tried to call her dad, but he didn't answer. Or couldn't. Panic seized Akira's throat, making it even harder to breathe. The wind was hot and strong, and gusting in their faces. How long until Morris blew hot embers into the clearing and chased them away again?

Akira tried her mom's cell phone, and she listened to it ring and ring and ring with growing despair.

"Akira!" her mother cried, answering at last. "Oh, thank goodness you're alive! Where are you? What happened?"

Akira sagged with relief. She quickly told her mom about meeting Sue and Daniel, about the harrowing drive through the fire, and her and Sue getting separated from their dads.

"Don't worry about your father. He knows these mountains like the back of his hand," her mother said. Akira could hear the panic in her voice though. The doubt. "You have to focus on *you* now," her mother said. "You have to————————"

"Have to what?" Akira said, sniffling. "Mom, you're breaking up."

"Akira, I'm looking online," her mother said, her voice going in and out. "There's one big fire, but ———————— fires all over the mountains around you too, maybe started ———————— or sparking electric lines. The smaller fires are ———————— and the bigger fires are joining up to make one massive megafire. ———————— in every direction, but you can make it home if you————————"

"If I what?" Akira said. "Mom? Mom, are you there?"

Akira pulled the phone away from her ear and looked at the screen. The call had disconnected.

TAG, YOU'RE IT

Akira tried her mom again, but an automated voice told her the call could not be completed as dialed. She was getting no signal bars at all now.

Akira lowered her head. She and Sue were truly alone.

"What did she say?" Sue asked.

"She was cutting in and out," said Akira. "But it sounds like there's fires all around us, combining into one big megafire."

Sue's eyes went wide and she got a far-off look, like she was about to go catatonic.

"We can stay out of the fire's way," Akira said, trying to calm her down. "I can get us back to my house."

Akira noticed again how Sue was holding her shoulder. "Are you hurt?" she asked.

Sue nodded. "I can't move my arm."

Akira slid over and took a look. Sue hissed as Akira pulled the sleeve of her T-shirt back. There was no cut and no blood, but something about her left shoulder didn't look right. It was lower than her other shoulder, and not as round.

"My dad and I were going camping once when his horse threw him and he dislocated his shoulder," Akira said. "I think that's what this is. It was probably your seat belt that did it."

Akira remembered how much pain her father had been in when he fell. If it hurt as bad as all that, Sue was one tough cookie.

"You need ice on it. And a sling. My dad showed me how to make one from an extra shirt." One more thing her dad had taught her, Akira thought. "For now, just take your shirt off and put it back on with your injured arm inside instead of through the sleeve," she told Sue. "That'll keep your arm from moving around."

Akira helped Sue stand up and rearrange her shirt.

"How can you be so calm about all this?" Sue asked.

Akira *wasn't* calm. This was supposed to be her day away from everything. The day she recharged her batteries. She hadn't gotten to do that, and now she had a wildfire to deal with, *and* somebody she had to take care of and talk to. She was freaking out inside. She just didn't feel the need to show every emotion all the time, especially with someone she didn't know very well.

Akira sighed. If she was going to be lost in a wildfire, Akira wished it was just her and Dodger, and nobody else.

"There," she said when they had Sue's shirt fixed. "They can put your arm back in its socket at the hospital in Cooperstown. That's the same direction as my house. If we don't find some-body to help us before that, my mom can drive you. You think you can make it?"

Sue still frowned with pain, but she sniffed and stood up a little straighter. "Yeah," she said. "I've been through worse."

Akira couldn't hide her surprise at that. *Is she talking about when she got those scars?* Akira couldn't *not* see them now—three half-inch parallel lines on Sue's forehead. But Sue didn't say anything more, and Akira didn't ask. Sue would tell her when and if she wanted to.

A red-hot ember floated down to the dry brown pine needles at their feet, and Akira watched as the pine needles caught fire with a *whoomp*.

Tag, thought Akira. *You're it.*

It was time to move.

Akira steered Sue away from the fire, and they fell into the slow, clumsy rhythm of a three-legged race.

Sue grunted. "Do you know where we are?"

"Not exactly," Akira admitted. "I'm taking us back up to the top of the mountain. Then we can look for a clear path to my house down the other side."

It was an old trick her father had taught her. When you're lost, get higher to get some perspective.

As they walked, Akira looked back at the orange flames that filled the valley behind them. Morris was gaining on them. They needed to be moving faster. *Could* have been moving faster, if not for Sue. The other girl kept clutching her midsection with her good arm, and Akira wondered if Sue didn't have a couple of fractured ribs to go with her dislocated shoulder. There was no way to know until they got her to a hospital, but Sue was moving at the loping pace of a bear.

A rumble echoed down the mountainside and Akira froze. A tiny rock hit her, and she flinched. Then another rock hit her. And another.

She knew what this was.

"Rockslide!" Akira cried.

THE NEW NORMAL

Akira dragged Sue behind the closest pine tree. She'd seen rockslides up in these mountains before, but here? Now? With Morris nipping at their heels? It was like nature itself was trying to kill them.

Akira hugged Sue close, waiting for the earth to come sliding past, but it fell on their heads instead. Tiny rocks like rain.

Thunder boomed, making them both jump, and Akira suddenly understood.

This wasn't a rockslide. *It was a hailstorm.*

Akira and Sue ducked, trying to protect themselves. The tree's branches helped a little, but the hail still hurt.

"That explains the wildfire, I guess," Akira said.

"The hail does?" asked Sue.

"Lightning strikes from the storm," said Akira.

"But it wasn't raining before," said Sue.

"Dry thunderstorm," said Akira. "We get the lightning, but not the rain."

Sue nodded. "When we moved to Fresno, the city told us we were only allowed to water our lawn on Saturdays, and never during the day," she said while the hail beat down on them. "We got this postcard telling us not to leave the water on when we brush our teeth, and to fill our bathtubs only half-full or take five-minute showers. That's not normal, is it?"

Akira thought about that. California had been in a drought

for ten of the thirteen years she'd been alive. Her father said it was just part of nature's cycle. But if they had drought conditions more often than not now, didn't that make droughts the new normal?

Sue looked at her sideways, and Akira realized she'd never answered her out loud. She grimaced. She had a bad habit of not talking enough—which was part of the reason she didn't have any close friends besides Dodger.

"Does dry lightning cause *all* the wildfires?" Sue asked.

"No," Akira said, remembering to speak this time. "Mostly it's people. Sometimes it's sparks from our electric lines that start wildfires. Sometimes it's people burning trash." She paused. "One time it was a woman boiling bear pee to drink it."

Sue gave Akira a dubious look.

"It's true," Akira told her.

Sue cracked up, and Akira laughed with her. It felt wrong to laugh when they were in so much danger, but they both needed the release.

The hail stopped as suddenly as it had begun, and Sue and Akira stepped out from under the tree. It had grown darker and smokier while they'd waited out the storm.

"Well, while we're standing around talking about it, Morris is just getting closer," Sue said. "Come on. Let's get the hail out of here."

Akira snickered in spite of herself. "If we don't, there'll be hail to pay," she said, trying to be funny again.

Sue guffawed, and Akira smiled. Maybe having Sue with her wasn't the worst thing in the world after all.

A DAY OFF

Akira and Sue limped through a patch of California lilac and white firs, the fire hissing and growling somewhere behind them. The sounds made Akira imagine all kinds of horrible things. Dodger and Elwood running through the burning forest. Her dad, surrounded by fire. Were he and Sue's dad all right? And what about the old couple from the car? Were they all picking their way through the smoky forest like Akira and Sue, or had Morris caught them up in his fiery jaws and—

Akira shook her head. She couldn't think like that.

Akira looked at Sue. The normally chatty girl had gone quiet. Usually Akira would have been fine with that. People talked too much as it was. But Akira worried that Sue being quiet meant she wasn't doing well.

What would Akira's father do right now? Make small talk, of course. But how? What did people talk about when there wasn't anything they *had* to talk about?

"So . . . why did your family move to Fresno?" Akira asked at last.

"Hunh? Oh. I'm a competitive swimmer," Sue said. Sue's voice was tight with pain, but Akira was secretly pleased at her own success in making small talk.

"Part of the reason we moved here was because our little town only had one pool," Sue went on, "and it wasn't even Olympic-sized."

"You're going to the Olympics?" Akira asked, impressed.

"No, no," said Sue. "I mean, I'd like to, but that probably won't happen. I might be good enough to make a college swim team though. Get a scholarship. That would be awesome. It's a lot of work though. I have swim practice twice a day, almost every day. Today was my day off," she said sadly.

"Mine too," said Akira, and she felt another pang of loss for her peaceful Saturday morning ride among the monarchs.

"I do love swimming though. I could be in a pool all day, every day," Sue said. "The town I came from was really small. Like, just sixteen kids in my whole grade level. It was kind of hard to get away from everybody, unless you went off by yourself in the country. That's not really for me. So I learned to disappear in the pool. When I'm in the water, it's like . . . the rest of the world just falls away, you know? Like, it's just me and my thoughts."

"Yes!" said Akira. "That's exactly what I love about riding Dodger. That's where I want to be, every day, all day. On my horse, riding the trails. Nothing else really matters."

Sue nodded. *She gets it. She really gets it*, Akira thought, and she smiled. The last person Akira had felt this close to was Patience, the college student her parents had hired as a babysitter when Hildi was born. Akira had been nine then and didn't really need a babysitter, so Patience had become more like an older sister to her. Patience had given her space, but when Akira wanted to talk, she'd really listened, and understood what Akira was trying to say. And boy, talk about somebody who wasn't afraid to argue with her dad when he went off about climate change!

Akira hadn't thought she'd ever find a friend like that again. But maybe Sue was somebody who could be a real friend when all of this was over.

Sue stumbled on a rock and cried out in pain, and Akira caught her before she could fall. They stood together for a moment, Akira hanging on to the injured girl while Sue bent over and tried to swallow the pain. Akira couldn't imagine how she was doing it.

"I'll be okay," Sue grunted. "Just give me a second."

Sue used her good hand to pull her hair to the other side of her head, and Akira saw the three pink scars on Sue's forehead again. She'd thought they were only half an inch long, but this close up, Akira realized the scars were only the beginning. Sue's hair hid the worst of it, and Akira pulled away and gasped as she saw what lay underneath.

FOLLOW THE NOSE

Under Sue's hair were three lines of raised, angry welts that ran like long, thick fingers across her scalp.

"What happened to your head?" Akira whispered.

Sue pulled herself up and used her good hand to comb her hair back over her scars. "I don't like to talk about it," she said, looking away.

Akira held up a hand in apology. But what could have caused an injury like that, with three long, parallel scars? Akira was dying to know, but she didn't want to press Sue, especially now.

Sue lifted her nose and sniffed.

"I smell food," she said.

"You can't smell food," Akira told her. The only thing Akira could see, feel, smell, or taste was the bitter gray smoke that hung in the air.

Sue breathed in deep and quick, and immediately fell into another coughing fit. But even as she bent over double, she raised her good arm and pointed off into the smoke.

"I smell meat," she said around her coughs. "Not meat, but charcoal. Cookout."

That could be the forest fire turning trees and houses into charcoal, Akira thought. But the fire was *behind* them. So who was having a cookout with a wildfire marching toward them?

A cookout meant people, at least, and they needed any help they could get.

They followed Sue's nose, the fire popping and cracking below them. Minutes later a dark, shadowy shape loomed ahead in the smoke, and as they got closer, they saw what it was. A two-story house! One of the many private homes that dotted the mountainside. And it wasn't on fire.

Without a word, Akira and Sue picked up their pace. There were no cars in the driveway, and the front door stood open.

Akira knocked and called inside. "Hello?" she rasped. "Is anybody here?"

Nobody answered.

Ordinarily, Akira would never have walked into a stranger's house without an invitation. But this wasn't an ordinary situation.

She and Sue exchanged a look, and pushed their way inside.

POOL PARTY

Smoke drifted in through the open door, and Akira closed it behind them. The light switches didn't work, and the smoky house had a ghostly emptiness to it.

"Hello?" Akira called again.

No response.

She and Sue moved through the house. There was a living room with couches and a TV. Bedrooms with half-made beds and clothes on the floor. A game room with a pool table and beanbag chairs and another TV. It was creepy walking around a stranger's house and peeking into their lives while they weren't around. A little exciting too.

"Do you see any phones?" Sue whispered.

"No," said Akira. "They must not have a landline." Akira pulled out her phone to check it again, but it still said no service. She fought down her panic and followed Sue down the hall.

As they looked into the rest of the rooms, Akira got the strangest feeling that she had been here before. But who did she know who lived in a big expensive house like this?

"Nova!" Akira cried.

"What?" Sue asked.

"Not a what, a who," said Akira. "A girl my age named Nova lives here. I finally remembered. I came to a birthday pool party at her house when we were in the same fourth-grade homeroom." She and Nova were in different classes now and hung out with different people, but they still waved hello to each other in the hall.

"Nova?" Akira called. "Nova, are you here?"

"I think everyone's gone," said Sue. "They probably saw the smoke and got out."

Akira nodded. "Let's find the kitchen."

The kitchen was as big as two rooms in Akira's house combined. Akira ran first to the refrigerator, where she found cans of soft drinks for her and Sue. They guzzled the drinks down, quenching their ragged throats.

"Oh hail yes," said Sue, and Akira giggled.

When they were finished, Akira raided the cabinet drawers.

"What are you looking for?" Sue asked her.

Akira held up her find triumphantly. "Aspirin!" She and her dad always carried aspirin with them when they camped overnight in the mountains, just in case.

She shook two pills out of the bottle and handed them to Sue. "Take these. Hopefully they'll help with the pain."

Akira's dad had also taught her to use ice to reduce any swelling. The power was out, but the freezer was still cold and the ice in it hadn't melted. Akira found a heavy-duty Ziploc bag with some frozen leftovers in it, dumped the food out in the sink, and filled the bag with ice.

"Here. Hold this on your shoulder," she told Sue. "I'll see if I can find something to make a sling."

Akira ran back to Nova's room and grabbed a sweatshirt, a pillowcase, and a pink backpack. She realized suddenly how weird it was to be going through another girl's room and grabbing things, and she stopped. She was acting like it was the end of the world and Nova was never coming back, but that wasn't true. Once the fire was out, Nova's family would come home like the three bears and find that some Goldilocks had been drinking their sodas and stealing pillowcases from their beds.

Akira rooted around in Nova's desk for a pen and paper and quickly scribbled a note to Nova, apologizing for raiding her house and promising to pay her back for everything.

Oh. Should I ask how they're doing? Akira wondered.

PS I hope you and your family are okay, she added.

Back in the kitchen, Akira opened drawers until she found a roll of duct tape. She made a sling for Sue out of the pillowcase and helped her slowly ease her dislocated arm into it. Next she took the ice pack, stuffed it into the sweatshirt, and duct taped it all around Sue's arm, shoulder, and neck.

When she was finished, Sue looked like a monster with one shoulder way bigger than the other.

"Sorry," Akira told her. "But now you don't have to hold the ice to your shoulder the whole time."

"Thanks," Sue said. She shifted around as much as she could without hurting herself, but the ice pack didn't come off. "Where'd you learn to do all this?"

"My dad taught me," said Akira, and an ember of worry smoldered in her stomach as she wondered again if he was okay. "Does the ice pack sting?" she asked Sue.

"No. I like the cold," Sue told her. "I'm kind of a polar bear."

Akira filled the backpack with water bottles she found in the pantry, and dumped in the apples and bananas that sat in a fruit bowl on the counter.

"Can't we stay?" asked Sue.

Akira pulled the backpack on and shook her head. "We need to keep moving. Stay ahead of the fire. That's why Nova and her family are gone. We've hung around too long as it is."

The house was on an electric well pump like hers, and Akira used the last of the water from the faucet to wet down hand towels they could tie around their faces to keep out the smoke. When she was done, Akira surveyed her handiwork and nodded. Her dad would be proud.

Akira suddenly heard the sound of sloshing water and froze. Sue heard it too. They stood and listened, not sure what they were hearing. There was more splashing, and . . . was that the sound of someone *laughing*? Akira got goose bumps. Was somebody here with them after all?

"Did you say you came to a pool party here?" Sue whispered.

Akira remembered the burning charcoal smell that had led them to this house. Someone wasn't really swimming and having a cookout in the middle of a wildfire, were they?

Akira heard the strange laugh again as she hurried to the back door. *No—not a laugh*, Akira thought, her heart skipping a beat. *It couldn't be. Could it?*

Akira threw open the back door and stopped dead in her tracks.

There wasn't a person splashing around in the pool. It was a *horse*.

Akira's horse.

"Dodger!" Akira cried.

CHURCHILL, MANITOBA

BAD TO THE BONE

Owen landed on his back with an *oomph* **that took his breath** away, and he slid to a stop. When his eyes refocused, he saw Momma Bear right above him, rising up to her full height on her back legs.

Owen snapped into a fetal position—chin to his chest, arms folded tight over his head, knees tucked all the way up to his stomach—and tried to disappear. The big polar bear didn't care. She gave a low, mean *rawr* and swatted at him with one of her claws, shredding the sleeve of his parka and raking long, deep gashes in his arm.

Owen cried out in agony and rolled over, clutching his bloody, stinging arm to his chest. Through his panic and pain, he saw something green and red rise unsteadily from the ocean of white snow in the distance. *It's George!* he realized with a flicker of hope. George was alive!

But wait—he was staggering *away* from Owen and Momma Bear as quickly as he could.

George wasn't coming to help him.

As much as it broke his heart to be abandoned, Owen understood. He hadn't been paying attention, and he'd come between a momma bear and her cub. Thanks to his obliviousness, he and George had been ruthlessly mauled.

If one of them escaped, it deserved to be George.

CHOMP. Momma Bear bit down hard on Owen's leg, and he howled in pain. A horrible, violent shudder went through him as he felt the unimaginable sensation of the polar bear's teeth grinding on his bone. The pain was almost impossible to endure, and Owen felt himself losing consciousness. He gave up trying to fight it and went limp, playing dead. Why not? He was dead anyway.

As his vision blurred, Owen saw the big momma bear rise up on her back legs for one final strike.

PAKOW!

The booming sound startled Owen awake and made Momma Bear flinch. She looked back over her shoulder, and Owen looked with her.

It was George!

Owen couldn't believe it. George looked like he was about to fall over. His ski mask was torn and his black hair stuck up in tufts and his head and face and parka were covered in blood. But he was holding the bright silver shotgun they had packed in the snowmobile, the one that was loaded with explosive cracker shells meant to scare off bears.

The shotgun Owen was supposed to have been carrying to protect them.

"Go on! Get!" George yelled. He cocked the shotgun—*ch-chik*—and fired it in the air again—*PAKOW!*—and this time Momma Bear moved. Her front paws thumped to the ground and she tore off toward a low hill, where Owen saw her cub hiding among the rocks. She put herself between George and her cub, and—*PAKOW!*—George fired the shotgun in the air again for good measure.

In the blink of an eye, the momma bear and her cub were gone over the hill, blending in again with the snowy terrain.

Owen lay back in the snow, panting. His heart was racing, and his breath came in great, deep, painful gasps. He had almost *died*. George too. He could see that as George staggered closer. The skin of George's scalp was torn, and there was a glassy look in his eyes. And Owen hadn't noticed it before, but George was holding the shotgun awkwardly. His right hand was on the trigger, but he carried the weight of the forestock on his left arm. His left hand hung uselessly underneath, either strained or broken from his fall.

George couldn't have aimed well enough to hit the polar bear even if he'd been trying.

"We have to get out of here," George said, his voice thick. "She could come back."

Owen knew he was right. Some bears did that, even if you scared them off. And he and George would make good meals for Momma Bear and her cub. The bears probably hadn't eaten much in the five months they'd been waiting for the sea ice to re-form.

George helped Owen up as best he could. They leaned on each other as they hobbled back to the snowmobile, both ready for another attack and neither one sure how they would survive Momma Bear round two.

LIKE A BOSS

Owen punched the emergency stop button on the handle of the snowmobile, and the engine sputtered out. The snowmobile glided to a stop, and he slumped off the seat, taking George with him as they *flumped* into the snow. Owen didn't know how far they had ridden, or even what direction he'd taken them. He'd just put as much distance between them and Momma Bear as he could before his exhaustion had overtaken him.

Even so, Owen's heart was still beating madly in his chest. *They had been attacked by a polar bear.* Yes, it had happened to people up here in Churchill before. But it always happened to somebody *else*. Never to *you*.

Owen could barely lift his head, and his right arm and left leg were on fire. But if he was in bad shape, he knew George had to be worse. George had saved them both with the shotgun and the cracker shells, but he'd passed out during their frantic escape on the snowmobile. It had been all Owen could do to steer *and* keep George from falling off at the same time.

Now it was up to Owen to make sure they didn't die out here.

Grunting in pain, Owen climbed to his knees and lifted the seat on the snowmobile to access the storage compartment underneath. There was a first-aid kit at the bottom, and luckily it was still stocked with bandages and antiseptic wipes and Tylenol. Owen swallowed a couple of the pain relievers himself, hoping they would do something for his pounding headache and help him focus.

Owen's wounds were still oozing blood and screaming in pain, but George was unconscious. He had to come first.

Owen pulled George up into a sitting position against the snowmobile. George's eyes were closed and his head lolled lifelessly, but Owen could still see the slow, steady rise and fall of his friend's chest. That gave him hope.

"Stay with me, George," Owen said. "This is gonna hurt."

Very gingerly, Owen pulled his friend's torn ski mask off his head. It was crusted with blood and hair, and was sticky as it came away.

Owen took one look at what was underneath and shuddered. George's head looked terrible. How was he even alive?

Owen poured a little water on the wound from one of the bottles they'd brought with them, and as the blood washed away, he was relieved to see that the gash looked worse than it really was. Even so, his best friend had taken a really good whack from that bear. Enough for him to still be unconscious. *Maybe he has a concussion*, Owen thought. There was no way to know. Not until he could get George to the health center.

Owen cleaned the rest of the wound as well as he could with water and antiseptic wipes. After he'd wrapped his friend's head in bandages, he tried to wake him up.

"Yo, Cheese. Wake up, man," he said, gently shaking George's shoulder.

"Not . . ." George muttered, his eyes fluttering.

"Not what? Come on, dude. You have to wake up," Owen told him.

"I'm not—" George said, his words mushy like wet snow. "I am not the cheese."

Owen laughed with relief. If George was making jokes, he was all right. Or would be. He got his friend to drink some water and take some Tylenol, and slowly George began to come back to his senses.

"Dude," Owen told his friend. "You looked like a *boss* back there, face and hands all bloody and scaring off that polar bear with a shotgun."

The shotgun I was supposed to be carrying, Owen thought. The guilt still weighed on him like a heavy coat, but if George was thinking the same thing, he didn't say it.

"I *was* a boss," said George, his tongue still thick. "You have to tell all the girls back at school."

Owen laughed again. "I will, dude. I will."

Owen shifted in the snow and hissed in pain. That seemed to wake George up more than anything, and he lifted his head off the snowmobile.

"That polar bear tagged you pretty good too," he said. "Let's see."

George pulled back Owen's torn pant leg and sleeve, and then it was George's turn to gasp.

SWISS CHEESE

Owen hadn't had a problem looking at the gash on George's forehead, but he couldn't bring himself to look at his own injuries.

He sucked in a breath against the pain. "Is it bad?"

"Let's just say that *you* are now officially the cheese," George told him. "As in, the *Swiss* cheese."

Owen spent the longest minutes of his life clenching his stomach against the pain as George cleaned and bandaged his wounds. When George tipped his leg up, blood ran out of Owen's boot like cranberry juice from a cup.

"We need to get you to the health center," George told him.

"You too," Owen said.

The health center was where you went for everything from a little cough to getting mauled by a bear. But it was all the way back in Churchill. They had a snowmobile, but neither of them was in much condition to drive.

"Maybe we can call the Mounties, get them to fly us out of here in a helicopter," George said. The Mounties were the Royal Canadian Mounted Police. Still blinking dully, George shifted himself around to look for his phone in the seat compartment. "Where are we?" he asked.

"I don't know," said Owen. He'd stopped on a wide, flat spot with no rocks sticking up out of it, but other than that he had no idea.

"Well, did you go north? East? South? What?"

"Dude, there was a *polar bear*," Owen protested. "You were unconscious. My leg was falling off. I just got us on the snow-mobile and drove. I didn't care where."

"Well, how is anybody supposed to find us when—"

CRACK.

The ground suddenly dropped a few centimeters underneath them.

George and Owen froze.

CRICK. CRACK.

The ground tilted, and the snowmobile slid slowly away from them, finally stopping with a little wobble.

"Did you . . . *did you drive us out onto a frozen lake*?" George whispered. In the heart of winter, every lake in the region would be frozen solid. But now, in October, the ice could still be thin in places.

"*I don't know!*" Owen hissed. "I just drove until I couldn't sit up straight anymore!"

CRACK.

The ground beneath them jerked lower again, and this time there was no doubt. They had both been out on the tundra enough to know when they were on thin ice.

There was no telling how deep the water was underneath them. Because the frozen permafrost was just a half meter beneath the active layer of soil, all the water on the tundra stayed near the surface. That meant that a lot of the lakes in the region were shallow enough to stand in. But no matter how deep it was, there was no way they were getting the heavy snowmobile out again if it fell in. And neither of them would survive very long out here if they took a dip in freezing water.

George and Owen looked at each other and knew what the other was thinking without having to say it.

They had to get themselves and their snowmobile off this ice as quickly—and as *carefully*—as they could.

ON THIN ICE

They didn't start the snowmobile up for fear that just yanking on the starter cord would break the ice underneath their feet. Instead Owen and George set the first-aid kit back inside the seat and, grunting and straining from their injuries, pushed the snowmobile as gently as they could toward what they hoped was the edge of the lake.

"I can't believe you drove the snowmobile out onto a lake," George said.

"*It's covered in snow,*" Owen whispered. "And *you're welcome*, by the way, for getting you out of there when you were unconscious."

"And *you're welcome* for saving you from the polar bear."

They were both tense and anxious. Owen knew that was why they were testy with each other. Slowly, slowly, the snowmobile crept along. Neither of them was in any shape to be pushing anything, but they had no other choice.

"I've never been so scared of anything in my whole entire life as when that Momma Bear attacked us," said Owen. "I was sure we were gonna die. I would have, if you hadn't fired those cracker shells."

"And I'd be a goner if you hadn't yelled at her and made her come at you," George said. "And you got me out of there when I was gonna pass out. You didn't leave me behind."

"Of course not," Owen said.

They looked into each other's eyes and nodded. They always had each other's backs.

Owen held up a fist, and George bumped it.

Owen kept searching the horizon as they pushed the snowmobile, looking for polar bears. He wasn't going to make the same mistake as before and be caught off guard.

"So, I realize this isn't the best advertisement for Churchill right now," Owen said.

"I don't know," said George. "You could put this on a postcard. 'Getting wrecked by a polar bear in Churchill, Manitoba. Wish you were here!' Bet we'd sell a ton of them."

"Seriously though, I don't want you to add this to the list," Owen told him.

"What list?" asked George.

"All the reasons you don't want to live here anymore," Owen said. "It's like you're looking for things to add to the list."

George stared at the ground and didn't say anything. Was he mad? Frustrated? About to pass out from pain again? Owen couldn't tell.

"I just don't want you to leave, man. You're my best friend in the whole world," Owen told George. "We're a *team*. We're Mac and Cheese!"

George shook his head. "I told you, I am not the—"
CRICK. CRI-CRACK.

The ice buckled underneath the snowmobile, and Owen and George froze as a thin layer of water pooled at their feet.

They were sinking into the lake.

THE ICE NEVER FORGETS

They were on another thin patch—so thin that lake water was already seeping through.

"We have to back up. Go a different direction," George whispered.

Owen and George pulled the snowmobile away from the cracking ice and made a difficult Y turn in the snow.

After they'd turned around, George had to take a minute before they started pushing again. Owen wasn't in much better shape. His arm and leg throbbed with pain, and his boot was leaving a red trail in the snow.

"You good?" Owen asked.

George nodded. "Of course. You?"

"Couldn't be better," said Owen.

They were both lying and they knew it, but they got moving. Together they pushed the snowmobile toward a rise that had to be the bank of the lake. Owen huffed and panted and sweated inside his clothes. Pushing the snowmobile wasn't easy when they *weren't* injured. Now it was grueling. Both of them needed to be lying in cozy hospital beds right now, not straining themselves out here in the wind and snow.

Owen scanned the horizon again. No polar bears.

When he looked back, he saw George starting to fade again.

"George, stay with me," Owen said. "Talk to me. Tell me

something your dad taught you about the ice." George's dad loved learning the old ways people used to survive up here before there were trains and planes and snowmobiles. Ways that had adapted and changed over time, and were often still useful and meaningful today.

George blinked and tried to focus. "My dad says that if it's minus twenty outside, people nowadays figure it's safe to go out on the ice—even if last weekend it was sunny and fifteen degrees *above* zero. But that ice, it's not going to be as thick as they think it'll be. *You* might have forgotten it was warm last weekend, but the ice never forgets."

"You bet your ice it doesn't," said Owen.

George started to laugh, and he closed his eyes and hugged his stomach.

"Don't," said George.

"Come on. Get your ice in gear, Cheese," Owen said.

"Stop," George said, laughing harder. "It hurts."

Owen was snickering now too, and they took a much-needed moment to laugh it out.

Owen lifted his goggles to wipe the tears from his eyes. When he got his goggles resettled on his face and looked up, he froze.

"*George.* George, stop," he whispered. "There's another polar bear!"

BIG BOY

A huge polar bear stood on its hind legs on the other side of the lake, sniffing the air. Owen glanced at the trail of blood behind him and winced. Polar bears could smell a seal from miles away, he remembered.

And bleeding eighth graders too, I guess.

George crept around to Owen's side of the snowmobile, keeping his eyes on the bear the whole time. It wasn't Momma Bear this time—it was a full-grown adult male. He would have been fasting for months while waiting for the sea ice to re-form, but he was still twice as big as the bear that had wrecked them before.

"Is he the same one from the tundra buggy this morning?" George asked.

"No," said Owen. This bear had been through the wars, as Owen's dad liked to say. He had a long scar down one side of his face that just missed his eye, and one of his ears looked like something had taken a bite out of it. Otherwise, he was a big, strong adult bear—as majestic as he was scary.

Owen didn't understand. What were so many polar bears doing this far inland? It was the end of the polar bear season. The sea ice had re-formed. The bears should be out on the ice hunting seals, not here hunting human beings!

"We do it right this time," George said quietly, and Owen nodded. They couldn't afford not to.

George leaned forward and patted around inside the seat compartment until he found the silver shotgun. Owen went next, feeling for the box of cracker shells. Neither of them took their eyes off the polar bear for a second.

Owen found the orange box of shells and held it open as George reloaded the shotgun. The shotgun held six shells at a time, and George fed in three new shells to replace the ones he'd fired to scare off the Momma Bear and her cub, bringing them back up to six.

The big bear thumped back down on all fours and began to circle them. Owen had seen polar bears do the same thing to the tundra buggy. It was how the bears investigated something new, spiraling in toward it to assess the threat.

"Just back away slowly," George said, gripping the shotgun.

Owen put down the rest of the cracker shells and backed up with him. As the polar bear circled in closer to the snowmobile, Owen and George spiraled farther away, always keeping the bear in sight as they backed up.

"He's a big boy, isn't he?" George said quietly. "Maybe he'll fall through the ice."

"Probably not," Owen said. "A polar bear's wide paws distribute its weight as it walks."

George looked sideways at Owen. "Dude, where was all this polar bear knowledge *before* we got surprised by two of them?"

Owen stumbled as they backed into a low ridge and fell on his butt. They were on solid ground! That was something. But they still needed their snowmobile. And right now, the big bear had his nose buried in the seat compartment, snuffling around for food.

The polar bear found some crackers Owen and George had brought with them and ate them up, box and all. Next he devoured a package of jerky, and chased it down with an entire plastic jar of peanut butter.

"Interesting choice," said Owen. "I would have paired the peanut butter with the crackers, but okay."

The polar bear stuck his nose back inside the seat compartment, and George grabbed Owen's arm in horror when he saw what he pulled out next.

The polar bear had found the brownies.

A POLAR BEAR ATE
MY SNOWMOBILE

"Noooo. Not the brownies," George moaned as the big polar bear scarfed them down. "Your mom's brownies are *life*."

"You know, if you move away from Churchill, you won't be able to eat them anymore," Owen said.

George looked sideways at Owen, his eyebrows even higher than usual. "Are you really worried about me leaving Churchill right now, when there's a polar bear using our snowmobile as his own personal picnic basket?"

Owen shrugged.

The polar bear swished his big paw around inside the storage compartment, looking for something else to eat. Owen winced as shotgun shells and a hatchet and his mobile phone tumbled out onto the snow.

"Maybe he'll leave us alone now that he's eaten all our food," George said.

"Um, with polar bears, it's not survival of the fittest but survival of the *fattest*," Owen told him. "They can eat a hundred-kilo seal in one sitting."

George sighed. "Your polar bear facts are really starting to depress me."

Owen was sure the polar bear would come for them next, but instead he opened his mouth and took a big bite out of the seat cushion.

Owen blinked. "He's—he's eating our snowmobile!"

George and Owen watched in stunned silence as the big polar bear ripped away another piece of foam padding and chewed on it.

"You know, it's weird, but polar bears love to eat plastic and stuff," George said matter-of-factly. "My dad told me he saw a polar bear eat the cushions off a sofa once."

"Dude, I don't care about somebody's sofa right now," Owen whispered. "He's eating our only mode of transportation."

When the seat cushion was totally gone, the polar bear moved on to the handlebars, gnawing on them like a dog working a bone.

Owen nudged George. "Shoot a cracker shell!" he told him.

"No! The sound might crack the ice and the snowmobile will fall in."

"It's not going to matter if he tears up the snowmobile so bad we can't drive it!" Owen told him.

George huffed, but he must have decided Owen was right. He took a step forward and raised the shotgun high into the air.

"Let's go, bear! Get!" George called.

PAKOW!

The cracker shell was designed to be louder than an actual shotgun shell, and Owen flinched at the sound. So did the bear. He lost his balance on the snowmobile and knocked it over, driving the other end of the handlebars into the ice like a harpoon.

Crick—CRACK—SPLASH! The snowmobile and the polar bear suddenly dropped through the surface of the ice together, and freezing water sloshed up out of the huge hole.

Owen and George gasped. Everything they had except for the shotgun and the parkas on their backs had just sunk to the bottom of the lake.

A few seconds later, the polar bear's head popped up out of the water and he snorted. *Polar bears* are *great swimmers*, Owen remembered.

George grabbed Owen by the arm and pulled him away.

"Dude, we have to get out of here while he's in the water," George whispered. "Run, ice hole. Run!"

MIAMI, FLORIDA

PART 2

SWEPT AWAY

No! Natalie thought in a panic, watching her house disappear in the rain. *Mama! Tía Beatriz!*

Natalie tumbled and turned in the water, cursing the squirming dog in her hand. *Stop fighting, Diablito!* she thought. Natalie's feet weren't even touching the ground. Water sloshed in her gasping mouth, and she choked as she kicked and thrashed. She had to find someplace up and out of the water. Somewhere covered and out of the rain and wind.

Natalie swam for the houses on the far side of the street, but Reuben pushed her back. She tried to kick up higher, but Reuben pulled her lower. She tried to grab on to a half-buried stop sign, but Reuben spun her away. Natalie screamed into the wind. She couldn't remember feeling so helpless. So exhausted. No matter what she tried to do, Reuben made her do something else. And all while blaring that train whistle roar—*BWAAAAAAAAA*

BWAAAAAAAAAAAAAAAA—like he was reminding her who was boss.

A refrigerator floated by, and Natalie grabbed at it, hoping to cling to it like a log, but it spun in the water and sank at her touch.

She didn't see the stove that followed the refrigerator until it slammed right into her. Bright pain shot up and down her side and she cried out, swallowing more gray seawater. The swirling storm surge pulled her under with the stove, and Natalie had to let go of Churro so she wouldn't take him with her. She kicked and fought, turning upside down and round and round in the water until she didn't know which way was up.

I'm going to die was all Natalie could think. *I'm going to die.*

Her head shot out of the water, and Natalie gasped and coughed, dizzy and disoriented. Reuben's attacks on her felt personal now, like this was some kind of game the hurricane was playing with her. First he had knocked down the wall of her house. Then he had swept her out into the street. Now he was batting her around like Churro playing with a squeaker toy.

Churro! Natalie was sure she had lost him. She treaded water, turning and squinting through the rain, and was surprised when she spotted him. But what she saw didn't make any sense.

Churro was standing *on top* of the water as he floated down the street.

HITCHHIKERS

Natalie swam toward Churro. How was he standing on top of the water, but still moving?

As she got closer, Natalie's hands struck something hard under the water's surface. She ran her fingers along it, feeling its contours, and she understood. The storm surge was carrying a car down the street, and Churro had hitched a ride on top of it.

Churro crouched low, his legs splayed out for balance. The wind pushed him back and forth on the top of the car, and he shivered in terror.

"Hang on, Churro!" Natalie cried.

She pulled herself along the car's roof rack, keeping her body in the water. Reuben tried to yank her away, lashing her face and hands with stinging rain, but Natalie hung on, working her way around the car until she could curl her legs up on the trunk.

With something finally underneath her, Natalie pulled Churro into a protective hug.

"I'm here, Churro," Natalie said. Churro couldn't have heard her above the wind, but for once he didn't bark at her or growl, nestling into the shelter of her arm instead.

BOOM! Something electrical exploded in a shower of sparks a block away and made them both jump. Natalie watched as the wind stripped the gutter off a house, as easy as peeling the skin off a banana. Trees snapped and went flying away into the darkness.

Street signs folded flat around their poles. And the water—the water was almost up to the eaves of the one-story houses that lined the street. Natalie's thoughts flew back to her mother and Tía Beatriz, trapped in the house. What if they didn't find a way out before the water reached the ceiling?

Something thumped inside the car beneath her, and Natalie looked down at the back window. A white, lifeless human face stared back up at her, and Natalie screamed.

There was a drowned woman inside the car!

Natalie turned away and retched into the water. She tried not to look, tried not to think about the body, but she could still feel the dead woman's eyes on her. She glanced down again—she had to, she couldn't help it—and saw the dead woman's body was mashed into the space where the window and the ceiling met, her head twisted sideways at an unnatural angle like something out of a zombie movie.

Natalie shuddered uncontrollably. She had to get off this car. And not just because of the dead woman inside.

All around her, Natalie recognized the familiar palm trees and traffic light poles of the six-lane Okeechobee Road.

Oh no. No no no, Natalie thought.

The highway wasn't the problem—it was what was just *across* Okeechobee Road that scared Natalie.

Reuben was pushing her toward the canal.

Fifteen feet deep and miles and miles long, Miami's canals funneled freshwater from the Everglades and rainwater from regular storms through the city and out to the sea. But Miami's canals were places you definitely did *not* want to go swimming.

Every year, the city pulled lots of cars and trash from the canals. Dead bodies too.

But there was something even scarier in the canals.

If Natalie and Churro didn't get off this car, and fast, they were going to go swimming with the alligators.

THE DROWNING HOUSE

Thunder boomed, and the lightning illuminated a row of houses along the side of the road. As the darkness returned, Natalie caught the flicker of light in one of the second-story windows. Candles! Which meant someone was in there. Someone she could take shelter with.

"Hang on, Churro!" Natalie cried.

She pushed off into the swirling water, trying not to think about the pale, lifeless face watching her from the back window of the car. Who was the woman? How had she been caught in her car when the floodwaters came? Had she been on the way home, or trying to make one last, desperate attempt to flee the city? Whatever the reason, that car—and the canal on the other side of Okeechobee Road—would be the woman's last resting place until someone could fish her out.

Natalie just had to make sure she and Churro didn't join her.

Natalie held the little dog up out of the water as much as she could. He wasn't thrilled to go back into the storm surge, and he was growling again—growling and shivering with fear at the same time. *Chihuahuas*, thought Natalie.

Natalie struggled toward the house, kicking and flailing. The rain and wind blasted her. The water rose and fell. But this time Reuben worked with her, not against her. The storm surge was already higher than the front door, but as the water ebbed,

Natalie was able to grab on to the top of the doorframe, take a deep breath, and swim in through the open door.

When Natalie came up out of the water inside, her head was only a foot away from the ceiling. She panicked in the tight space, thinking again about Mama and Tía Beatriz drowning as the water rose in their one-story house. But this house had a way up, a way out, if she could only find the stairs.

Natalie spun around in the darkness, still treading water. The room she found herself in was a washing machine full of all the things that had filled the house. Magazines, clocks, clothes, pots and pans, sofa cushions, video game controllers, hair-brushes, books—they all swirled around in the dark, foamy water that pushed and pulled through the open front door and the broken windows.

And the water was still rising.

"We've got to get out of here before we're trapped!" Natalie told Churro, and he barked in response.

It was dark and close, but Natalie thought she saw stairs on the other side of the room. She turned to float on her back, put Churro on her chest, and used her hands to pull herself across the ceiling.

The water in the room rose and fell, rose and fell, but always rising more than falling. A floating basketball bumped into her. Something prickly and spiderweb-like brushed her leg. Natalie's breath came in quick, frantic gasps, and she hurried her pace.

Suddenly Churro jumped off her chest and into the water.

"No! Churro! Wait!" Natalie cried out, turning to try and see where he was.

There—Churro was splashing toward a rectangular opening in the ceiling. The stairs!

Natalie spun around so she wasn't on her back anymore and swam like a frog behind Churro.

"Go, Churro! Go!" Natalie yelled.

Churro made it to the top step, half in, half out of the water, and turned to bark encouragement at Natalie. A few seconds later, she found the stairs herself, and she crawled up after the little dog and collapsed onto the carpet of the second floor.

"Good heavens!" said a woman's voice. "Marcus, Javari, pick her up. Get her away from there."

Gentle hands lifted Natalie, and she let herself be carried down a narrow hallway.

Two teenage Black boys propped her up against the wall in between electronics equipment they must have saved from downstairs. Their eyes were full of amazement and concern for the girl who had washed up on their stairs. The man and woman Natalie took to be their parents crowded in close behind them.

"You all right?" the father said. "How'd you even get down there?"

Natalie broke into exhausted tears. "¡Mamá! ¡Tía Beatriz! Tengo que volver con ellas," she sobbed.

"I'm sorry, honey. We don't speak Spanish," the mother said.

Natalie blinked. She hadn't even realized she was speaking Spanish. It was her first language, and Natalie sometimes found herself falling back on it when she was frightened or confused.

Natalie switched to English, and her whole story came gushing out. The wall collapsing, the water rising, escaping through the window with Churro, being swept away down the street.

"I have to go back for them," Natalie said. "Mama and Tía Beatriz. They're drowning in our house!"

"Calm down. You're safe now, honey," the mother said. "But I'm sorry. You're going nowhere 'til this storm is over. None of us are."

Natalie swallowed a sob, but she knew the woman was right. She'd barely survived being out in water the first time. There was no way she was getting back to her mother and Tía Beatriz any time soon.

A LITTLE SPACE

The woman's name was Anne Evans. Her husband was Derek, and their two sons were Marcus and Javari. Anne was taller than Natalie's mother, with curly hair and a friendly smile. Her husband, Derek, was a head taller than his wife. He was very fit and had a black beard the same length as the short hair on his head. Marcus and Javari were both long-limbed and good-looking. Javari wore his hair in a buzz cut, and Marcus, the older brother, had a temp fade. The family all had the same dark brown skin and the same kind, worried look in their eyes.

Javari in particular was really cute. Under different circumstances, Natalie might have blushed and looked away. But there was no time for that now.

"I'm N-Natalie, and that's Ch-Churro," Natalie said, her teeth chattering. Churro shook water off himself, then bared his teeth and growled at the Evans family. Friendly as always.

"Javari, give the girl your hoodie. She's freezing," his father told him.

Natalie didn't realize how much she was shivering. The water hadn't been cold, exactly, but it wasn't body temperature either, and she'd been in it for a long time. She gratefully accepted the hoodie and slipped it on, and Anne brought her a bottle of water.

"Give us a little space," Anne said, and shooed the men into one of the bedrooms off the hall.

She didn't know how Anne knew, but as soon as the others

were gone, Natalie's tears came, and she couldn't turn them off. Tears of grief for her mother and Tía. Tears for the dead woman in the car. Tears for herself, battered and bruised and so maddeningly helpless.

Natalie pulled Javari's hoodie over her head and drew her knees up to her chin, embarrassed to be crying in front of a stranger. But it didn't bother Anne. She sat down beside Natalie and put an arm around her, letting Natalie cry into her shoulder.

"Get it out, hon," Anne told her. "It's a lot."

Churro barked at something—*Rrrrr-rar-rar-rar-rar-rar!*— and Natalie dragged the sleeve of the hoodie across her nose and tried to see what he was on about now.

It was the water. Another wave crashed in the room below, and water sprayed up through the stairwell, sloshing on the upstairs carpet.

The water was still rising.

Churro barked and backed away, and Natalie watched in horror as the storm surge rose past the second floor and began to flood the hallway.

Anne stood quickly. "Boys!" she called over the howling winds. "Get these things up on a bed, quick!"

Marcus and Javari and their dad hurried back into the hall and were stunned to see the floodwater lapping at the top of the stairs. They hurriedly snatched up electronics and took them into one of the bedrooms, and Natalie got up to help.

By the time they were finished, the water was up to Churro's knees.

Natalie picked Churro up and backed away, shaking her

head. "It just keeps coming," she muttered. "It's too big. It's too much."

Anne took hold of her shoulders and looked her in the eyes. "It's all right, Natalie. We're going to be okay."

But we're not going to be okay, Natalie thought. There were already three inches of water on the floor. *On the second story.*

The Evans men came sloshing back into the hall and stared incredulously at the rising water.

"I don't believe it," Derek said. "The water's never come this high before."

Suddenly the floor shifted underneath them, and they all threw their hands out to brace themselves against the wall. Natalie and Javari shared a wide-eyed, disbelieving look.

They were dreaming. They had to be.

The floor underneath them shuddered and lurched again, sloshing water back and forth across their feet, and this time there was no doubting it.

The house was moving.

RISING WATER

Natalie hugged Churro tight and backed up against a wall. The storm surge was tearing the Evanses' house away—and them with it.

"We gotta get out of here!" Derek shouted over the roar of the storm.

"*Where?*" Anne yelled back.

"The downstairs is totally flooded!" said Javari.

So much water was coming up from below that it wasn't even splashing anymore. It was just rising, rising, rising, like a bathtub filling with water. The dark, murky storm surge was up to Natalie's calves.

No, thought Natalie. *This can't be happening. Not again.*

"Out a window?" Marcus yelled.

"No," Natalie said, snapping out of her trance. She remembered her battle with Reuben and knew she wouldn't survive a second round. She was too exhausted, and the storm just seemed to be getting stronger. "We can't get in the water," she told them. "Can we get up on the roof?"

It wasn't the greatest idea, Natalie knew. On the roof they'd be exposed to the full fury of Reuben. But the house lurched again and the floor tilted sideways, and they all knew they had to do *something*, and fast.

"There's a skylight in our bedroom!" Derek hollered. "Javari, get your baseball bat."

Derek and Anne led the rest of them to their bedroom, sloshing through almost a foot of water. Natalie suddenly thought how strange it was that she was walking around making plans with people she'd just met, but they were all in this together now.

Nobody was a stranger in a storm.

Derek and his eldest son pushed the bed under a small plastic skylight in the ceiling, and Javari came back with a metal bat. Natalie held Churro in her arms and watched as Derek hopped up on the bed and jabbed at the skylight with the bat until it broke. *Whoosh!* Rain and wind blasted in through the hole, and Natalie turned away from the spray.

Derek knocked away the rest of the plastic, and then his dad joined him up on the bed.

"You go first, and help the others from your end!" Derek told his son.

Marcus nodded, and Natalie watched as Derek helped him up and out of the hole.

Derek took Anne's hand for her to go next. "Our money!" she yelled, trying to pull away. "Our IDs! All our birth certificates and things!"

"We have to leave it!" Derek told his wife.

Natalie flashed back to putting all her family's valuables and personal mementos up high, to keep them out of the water. Their family photos. Her great-grandparents' love letters. Her weather journals. The box of friendship bracelets Shannon had made her. *And Mariposa*, Natalie realized with a gasp.

They were all gone now.

Derek lifted Anne up to Marcus on the roof, and motioned for Natalie to go next. She handed Churro up first, and he growled and barked at her and Marcus and the storm.

"I know, Churro, I know," Natalie said. "I don't want to go back out there either. But we have to."

Seconds later it was Natalie's turn. Derek lifted her up and Marcus pulled her through, and suddenly Natalie was in the storm again. Rain stung her and the wind tried to sweep her off the roof, but Anne was there to grab her hand. She pulled Natalie in close, and they hid as best they could in the lee of a solar water heater.

Natalie took Churro from Anne and zipped him up in her hoodie, wrapping her arms around him to keep him safe. Churro poked his head out and barked at the hurricane, but Natalie couldn't hear anything except the roar of the storm, couldn't feel or taste or see anything but the lash of rain and the brutal wind. Reuben was a total assault on her senses.

Javari and Derek joined them at last, but there was barely enough room for all of them behind the solar panel. Derek yelled something, but his words were lost in the storm.

Beneath them, the roof shuddered and tilted.

The storm surge was ripping the house off its foundation.

Natalie and the Evans family all looked at each other with terror in their eyes. They weren't safe here. But where could they go?

Natalie squinted through the storm. It was pitch-black outside, but the lightning strikes were so fast and so frequent they looked like strobe lights. On, off. On, off. On, off. Natalie could see other rooftops in the brief moments of full light, but they were all too far away, separated from her and the Evans family by wide, raging rivers of floodwater.

Natalie felt Churro shift in her hoodie, and she looked down at him. He was still barking furiously, one tiny dog against the biggest, baddest hurricane Miami had ever seen, but his focus had shifted. He was yapping at something new, something Natalie could now see floating toward them on the two-story-high storm surge.

Something that might be the answer to all their prayers.

ALL ABOARD

It was a boat!

The strobing light from the storm made it look like it was in a stop-motion video, but a small sailboat was definitely coming down the street-turned-river toward the Evanses' house.

Natalie couldn't believe it. Miami was a boat town, but all the marinas were way out on the ocean.

But if the ocean's come to us, why not a sailboat too? Natalie thought wildly.

The mast was torn away and dragged behind it in a tangle of ropes, but the boat looked like it had a small cabin. If they could get inside it—

Natalie poked Anne and pointed to the boat, and she saw the woman's eyes light up. Anne nudged the rest of her family, and Derek grabbed hold of the solar heater's struts and signaled for them all to hold hands. Derek anchored them at one end while Anne, Natalie, and Javari stretched as far as they could in the middle for Marcus to be able to reach the water.

The boat drifted closer, closer, until at last it bumped into the house. Marcus lunged for the railing, but missed.

"Grab it! Grab it!" Natalie screamed, Reuben swallowing her words. The wind and waves knocked the little boat around, began to push it away from the roof.

Marcus tried again, but the railing was just out of his reach. He wasn't going to be able to catch it! Natalie panicked, watching their one chance at escape drifting away. She stretched her arms out as far as they could go, just barely holding on to Javari's and Anne's fingertips . . .

And Marcus had it! He had the rail of the boat in his hand.

One by one Natalie and the Evanses slipped and slid down the roof and climbed on board, and within moments the wind had already pushed them and the sailboat yards away from the tilting house.

Derek pointed to the cabin door. Natalie was closest, and she held Churro tight as she climbed down the steps. The door was unlocked, and Natalie crawled inside and sagged with relief at the bottom of the stairs, thankful to be out of the storm again.

Churro poked his head out of her hoodie and barked, and Natalie looked up in surprise.

There were other people on the boat!

REFUGEES

A middle-aged Latina woman and her two small children, a boy and a girl, were huddled on a U-shaped bench at the far end of the cabin. They looked as wet and exhausted and frightened as Natalie, and just as surprised to see her as she was to see them.

"Hola," said Natalie.

"Hello," the woman said.

Natalie was about to say something more when the Evans family climbed down into the cabin behind her. Natalie moved toward the new family, and they made room for her on the bench. There was a small bed behind the stairs and a narrow space down the middle of the cabin with a stovetop and sink. Counting Natalie and the four Evanses, plus the mom and her two little kids, the eight of them filled the tiny space.

Derek was the last one in, and he turned to his family with a dazed look.

"Our house," he said. "I just saw it tear away and slip under the water. It's gone."

The Evans family sat in stunned silence.

I was just in that house, and now it's gone, Natalie thought. Had the other three walls of her own house been carried away? Or her roof again?

Was anywhere safe from this hurricane?

"Sorry," Natalie said at last to the woman with the two little kids. "We saw your boat come by and we jumped on it."

"It's not ours either," the woman said. "We hitched a ride when our house flooded, like you." She looked down, as though seeing something else in her mind's eye. "I came over from Cuba on a raft in the '90s," she said, hugging her children tight. "I'm an American citizen now. I never thought I'd be a refugee on a boat again."

Natalie nodded. There were a lot of Cuban Americans in Hialeah, and she went to school with more than a few kids whose parents had fled Cuba themselves when they were children.

Natalie never thought she'd be a refugee either.

The sailboat struck something in the water—a car? A street sign? What was left of the Evans house?—and there was an awful screeching sound. The little boat shuddered and swayed, and then they were past whatever it was and only the hurricane battered them.

The little boy reached out a hand to pet Churro, but the dog growled and snapped at him.

"Sorry," said Natalie. "Churro's not too friendly."

"He's scared, Iván, just like us," the boy's mother told him.

"Iván," Anne said. "Is he named after the Hurricane Ivan?"

"No," the woman said with a small smile. "For my best friend when I was a girl. This is my daughter, Valentina, and my name is Isabel."

Natalie and the Evans family slowly came back to life and introduced themselves.

The storm raged outside, and the little sailboat rocked and bumped into things as Reuben played with it. But they were safe. For now.

"Hurricane Ivan. That was the year Marcus was born," Derek said. "First big one I remember was Andrew, 1992."

"I was in Cuba for that one," said Isabel. "My abuela died in that storm." She was quiet for a moment, then looked back up. "But I was here in el norte for the others. Opal. Charley. Ivan."

"Jeanne. Then Dennis," Derek remembered.

"Katrina hit us on the way by," said Marcus.

"And Wilma," said Javari.

"Irma," Natalie said, adding her own most memorable storm. "Then Michael."

It was a list almost every South Floridian knew by heart and could recite like a mantra. The names of the worst hurricanes. The ones that had killed the most people, done the most damage. All within their lifetimes.

And it was getting worse, thought Natalie. Not only was climate change making hurricanes come earlier and stay later and get more intense, as she'd told Tía Beatriz that morning, but there were *more* hurricanes than ever before. Last year there had been thirty named storms—the most ever—and for two years in a row they had run out of names and had to start using Greek letters instead.

Natalie thought about saying all that, but this didn't seem like the right time.

Everybody was quiet, and after a while Natalie noticed the rocking of the boat seemed to steady out.

"Maybe the storm's letting up," Natalie said. But that didn't make any sense. They could still hear Reuben rampaging outside, as loud and angry as before.

"No—it's not the storm. Look!" Isabel gasped, pointing at the floor.

There had been water in the boat before, but now it was up over Natalie's shoes. Her feet were already so wet, she hadn't noticed.

"It's the boat!" Isabel cried. "The boat is sinking!"

THE SIERRA NEVADA, CALIFORNIA

THE HORSE IN THE POOL

Sue looked over Akira's shoulder. "There's a horse. In the pool," she said.

"Yes, *my* horse!" Akira cried, running outside.

Nova's family had closed the pool for the season, shielding it with a blue plastic cover to catch leaves. What the cover had caught instead was Dodger. Akira's chestnut gelding lay on his side, half in and half out of the water as the pool cover sagged under his weight.

"What's he doing here?" Sue called, following Natalie to the pool.

"He must have come up the mountain trying to get back home, and he ran out across the pool cover without realizing it was flimsy plastic," Akira said.

She dropped to her knees at the edge of the pool. Dodger was shivering uncontrollably, but was otherwise stock still, his eyes spinning this way and that in a panic.

"It's okay, boy. I'm here," Akira told him. "Stay calm. I'm going to get you out."

Akira scanned the pool and its cover, trying to figure out exactly how she was going to do that. The plastic tarp was held in place by long straps that attached to the concrete patio all around it. Maybe if she released some of the straps, let him down gently . . .

"Akira, look!" Sue cried, pointing.

Akira turned to see red embers from the wildfire landing on the roof of Nova's house and setting it on fire. More glowing coals drifted down and smoldered in the dried leaves around the pool.

Akira's heart stopped. Morris was almost on top of them!

They all might have been safe jumping in the water and letting the wildfire sweep past them, but there was an arbor over the pool. It was made of wood, and like everything else in Morris's path that was made of wood, it would catch on fire. And if it collapsed while they or Dodger were still in the pool . . .

"We have to get him out of here!" Akira cried.

Akira worked as quickly as she could to unhook the straps of the pool cover. Sue helped as much as she could with her one good hand.

KRISSH! KRISSH!

Akira flinched as windows on Nova's house shattered from the fire. They didn't have much time. She and Sue released enough straps on the pool cover to lower Dodger all the way down, and at last he stood on his own four legs.

Now Akira just had to get her horse to climb out of the water and into the path of a fire.

Akira ran around to the shallow end of the pool, shed her heavy pink backpack, and jumped in with all her clothes on.

"*Woo!*" she cried. An icicle chill shot up her spine, but Akira forced herself to wade deeper into the chilly water.

Dodger shook his head at Akira and whinnied, happy to see her but still afraid.

"I know, boy," Akira said, keeping her voice low and steady. "It's okay. I'm going to get you out of here. Just hold still. That's right."

Akira grabbed Dodger's reins out of the water. He still had all his tack on him from the trail ride—his reins, saddle, stirrups, bridle, and bit.

"Just look at me," Akira told him. "Don't think about that fire."

Dodger couldn't understand what she was saying. Akira knew that. It was the tone of her voice that mattered. Her manner. The confidence she didn't really feel, but was faking for Dodger's sake. Because he couldn't see what Akira saw right behind him—

Nova's house was now totally on fire.

YOU CAN LEAD A HORSE TO WATER

"Akira!" Sue cried, backing away from the burning house.

Akira nodded to let her know she saw it, but kept looking straight at Dodger to not break eye contact.

"All right. Come on, now. That's a good boy," Akira said, tugging gently on his reins.

Dodger loved to swim. Whenever they got close to the lake near Akira's house, he would not-so-subtly pull her off course toward it, trying to go for a dip. Akira always had to wear clothes she was okay getting wet in, because every trip out that way ended up in the water. But now was definitely not the time.

"Come on, boy," Akira said, trying to stay calm. She just needed to get him moving toward the shallow end, away from the fire.

RAUAR-RAUAR-RAUAR. WHOOMF. SHHHHHH. Morris sounded like a gigantic beast chewing on glass as it ate up Nova's house. The heat was intense, even yards away. Red-hot embers floated down into the pool, sizzling as they hit the water.

Up above them, the arbor caught on fire.

"Akira," Sue said, low and scared.

Akira panicked. "Come on, now, Dodger!" she cried. She tugged on his reins, but Dodger didn't budge. Akira's feet went out from under her on the slick pool bottom instead, and—*SPLASH*—she got dunked in the chilly water. She popped back up a second later, glaring at Dodger as she shivered and gasped for breath.

You can lead a horse to water, Akira thought, *but you can't make him get out again.*

"Here, horsey!" she heard Sue yell, and Akira turned to see Sue holding up one of the apples from the backpack.

Dodger saw it too, and he nearly knocked Akira over hurrying up the pool steps to get it.

"Yes! Good horsey," Sue said. Dodger devoured the apple, and Sue giggled reflexively as his lips tickled her hand.

Akira trudged up out of the pool to join them, water streaming from her soaked jeans and shirt and hair.

"Oh, sure," she said to Dodger. "You'll get out of the pool for food, but not to save your own skin."

Dodger shook himself, spraying Akira and Sue and making them yelp. Then he rubbed his face against Akira and snorted affectionately, and all was forgiven.

Akira wrapped her arms around Dodger's head and returned the nuzzle.

"I was so afraid you were dead," Akira whispered. "I'll never leave you again, Dodger. I promise."

Dodger gave her the quiet little nicker he saved just for her, and Akira smiled.

"I love you too," she told him.

KRICK-CRASH!

Both girls jumped as the burning arbor fell into the pool, collapsing right where Akira and Dodger had been standing just moments before. Dodger reared up and backed into a portable grill beside the pool before Akira could grab his reins. The grill tipped over and fell, spilling smoking charcoal and burnt steaks all over the patio.

"Told you I smelled food," said Sue.

A few yards away, the trees that surrounded Nova's yard began to burst into flames.

"Time to go!" Akira cried. "Get on Dodger. We're riding now."

She helped Sue work her way into the saddle, then put on the backpack and climbed up behind her. Akira reached around Sue, took the reins, and with a click of her tongue and a squeeze of her legs, they took off into the dark, smoky woods, Morris roaring angrily at their escape.

BURNING RAVIOLI

All the color had been sucked out of the world.

Akira and Sue rode Dodger along the shoulder of a road through lifeless gray trees. Brown electric lines hung low in the smoky air, and a thin layer of ash covered everything like snow, muting sound as well as color.

This was what the world looked like after Morris passed through.

"I thought the fire was behind us, not in front of us," Sue whispered.

Akira didn't understand either. She'd found the two-lane road soon after escaping Nova's burning house and had taken it up the mountain, past more driveways and homes. But the wildfire had always been *following* them. How had it gotten out in front?

"Maybe this fire wasn't Morris," Akira said, talking low. Something about the burned-out landscape made them both quiet. "The lightning may have started fires in lots of different places."

But if that was the case, they weren't so much ahead of the fire as . . . *in* it. And if there were multiple smaller fires, that meant they could run headlong into a wall of flames any minute.

Akira kept Dodger at a slow walk rather than a trot. Little fires burned in the underbrush, and trees smoldered. It was so hot that the moisture was all gone from the kitchen towels they had tied around their faces, and Akira and Dodger were almost completely dry from their dip in the pool.

A driveway angled off the road, and they saw the empty shell of a big two-story house that had been caught up in the fire and collapsed in on itself. It was still burning. Akira hoped there hadn't been anyone inside when the fire swept through.

"Have you ever burned a pot of ravioli on the stove?" Sue asked.

"I— What? No," Akira said.

"We did it in science class," Sue said quietly. "You put the ravioli in a pot of water and turn on the heat. If you leave it on long enough, the water boils. That's usually when you take the pot off the burner, drain the water, and eat the raviolis. But if you leave the pot on the burner, the water will keep boiling and boiling until it all evaporates. Then there's just raviolis left. If you keep the heat on and don't add any more water to the pot, all the moisture gets sucked out of the raviolis, and they shrivel and burn. That's California," said Sue. "Only, the raviolis are the houses and forests, and instead of leaving the stove on at an even temperature, somebody's been turning the heat up a little bit more every year."

Akira hadn't done that experiment, but her science teacher had done a simple one that explained why it was getting hotter. Mrs. Tally had taken two jars and put thermometers in each, then covered one with aluminum foil and left the other open. Then they turned on a heat lamp, and watched as the jar with the aluminum foil lid got hotter than the one with no lid on it.

"That aluminum foil lid is the greenhouse gases that are

trapping heat in our atmosphere," Mrs. Tally had explained. Some trapped heat was good—plants and animals needed heat from the sun to survive. But trap too much, which humans were doing by burning fossil fuels, and everything started to overheat.

That was climate change.

Dodger took a little hitch in his step, and Sue grunted. Akira knew she was trying to swallow the pain, but every time Dodger hit a rough patch, a little breath of agony escaped her lips.

"Are you okay?" Akira asked.

"I'll make it," Sue whispered back.

Akira wasn't so sure about that. They weren't to the top of the mountain yet, and she had no idea how far they had left to go.

Akira pulled out her phone to look for a signal, just in case. But there was still nothing.

Dodger took another awkward step, and Akira looked down to see what was wrong. Dodger was walking normally, but every time he tried to lift a leg, he paused for a second, like he was having to pull his hoof out of mud.

Akira gasped and quickly steered Dodger into the ditch alongside the road.

"What is it?" Sue asked.

Akira stopped Dodger and pointed behind them, where a line of horseshoe marks left indentations in the ashy road.

"The asphalt's so hot it's melting! We were sinking into it!" Akira told her.

Sue nodded wearily, as if that was to be expected. "Melting roads. *That's* normal."

She knew Sue was being sarcastic, but it made Akira think of her dad. He would have said the melting road was normal and meant it, coming up with some argument to explain it away.

Akira shook her head. Her dad was wrong, and the longer Akira stayed quiet about it, the longer she went without doing something to fix it.

Akira kept Dodger in the ditch to stay off the burning asphalt. As they rounded a small bend, a low dark shape appeared in the smoke up ahead.

"It's a pickup truck," Sue whispered. "Or what's left of one."

She was right. The truck was grayish brown like everything else, and lay slumped and broken on the road like the skeleton of a dead animal. The windows, the headlights, the paint, the tires—they were all gone. Burned away by the wildfire. The metal rims of the wheels had sunk three inches into the melting asphalt, and the truck ticked and popped and smoked, still hot from its incineration.

Dodger snorted in displeasure, sensing the wrongness of it all, but Akira brought him closer so they could see inside. The whole interior of the truck was gone—the seats, the upholstery, the steering wheel, the dashboard. Everything was just a heap of ugly, messy, black-and-gray ash.

And sticking up out of it all were the leathery black mummies of the three people who'd been inside when the fire caught them.

IF, IF, IF

"Oh God," said Sue, and Akira turned away and retched into the road.

Seeing the burned bodies made Akira remember the terror of being inside Sue's car after the accident, when the fire was closing in on them. If they hadn't been able to get out, if the fire had been faster, or they had been slower, if they hadn't been able to run away—

Akira wiped her mouth with the back of her hand. Where was her father? Where was Sue's dad? Were they off in the gray woods somewhere like this, gnarled and burned and—

"Go. There's nothing we can do for them," Sue said, her voice anguished. "Go!"

Akira gave a quick squeeze of her legs to Dodger, and they trotted away. Akira was relieved to move on, but she knew the image of those dead people would haunt her forever.

Two more cars emerged from the smoke ahead. Both had been reduced to slumping metal skeletons the same way as the pickup truck had been. One car held two people—a driver and a passenger leaning toward each other like they had been holding each other when the fire caught them. The other car had four passengers, two in the front and two smaller passengers in the back. They were all dead. Burned beyond recognition by the wildfire.

Sue cried. Akira didn't know what to do. What to say. She didn't want to look, but she couldn't *stop* looking. She'd never seen dead bodies before. Not in real life. In TV shows and movies, no matter how horrible the dead people looked, you always knew they were fake. Here, now, there was no escaping the awful reality of what Akira was seeing. Hearing. Smelling.

"*Akira,*" Sue said, like she'd been calling her name a few times already. "Akira, we have to go. There's nothing we can do for these people."

Akira tore away her gaze and nodded. "Sorry," she said. "I just—"

"I know," said Sue, and Akira got Dodger moving again.

Dodger usually kept his right ear back to listen to Akira and his left ear tuned in to what was going on in front of him, but now both his ears flicked forward and focused on something up ahead of them. Akira couldn't see or hear what it was yet, but she had learned to pay attention to Dodger's signals. She stiffened, ready for anything.

A moment later Akira heard what Dodger heard, and then she saw it: A big four-door pickup truck was driving slowly down the road.

Somebody else was alive in all this desolation.

A WAY OUT

Akira and Sue waved frantically at the truck.

"Hey! Help!" Akira cried.

The truck pulled to a stop beside them. It was so tall that the woman in the driver's seat sat just a little lower than Akira and Sue on the back of Dodger. The woman was blond and petite and wore jeans and a long-sleeved denim shirt. She rolled down the passenger window and leaned toward them with a frantic look.

"Have you seen a man in an SUV?" she asked. "Brown hair, blue eyes, a couple feet taller than me?"

Akira thought back to the other cars they'd passed, but all of them had had more than one person in them, and none of them were SUVs.

"No," Akira told her. "I'm sorry."

Tears ran down the woman's face. It looked like she'd already cried a lot today.

"I was at the grocery store when the fire came," she said. "My husband called me. Told me he could see fire. That he was getting out. But the phone stopped working and I haven't heard from him since. I went up to the house, and it's—"

She didn't finish. She didn't have to. Akira and Sue had seen the burned-out houses all along the road.

"There are so many burned-out cars on the road," the woman said, sobbing again. "And I can't tell if one of them is ours. If one of them is him."

Akira swallowed hard, trying not to cry. She didn't know what to tell this woman. How to comfort her. There was no sense telling her everything was going to be all right. How could it be? Her house had burned down and her husband was missing.

"We're looking for people too," Akira told her. Akira and Sue described their dads, but the woman hadn't seen them.

"I'm sorry," the woman said. "Are you two all right?"

"I am, but my friend's not," Akira told her. "She's got a dislocated shoulder, and maybe a couple of broken ribs. I'm trying to get her to the hospital in Cooperstown."

The woman glanced away for the briefest of moments and seemed to come to a decision. She looked back at them and nodded. "Get in. I'll take you."

Akira's heart leapt, and she could feel Sue sag with relief.

"What about your husband?" Akira asked.

The woman sniffed and dried her eyes with a tissue. "I don't know where he is. But you're right here, and you need help," she said. "Now come on."

Akira hopped down off Dodger and helped Sue dismount while the woman came around the front of the truck. Together, Akira and the woman got Sue up into the passenger seat of the pickup.

"My name's Vicki, by the way," the woman said, and Akira and Sue told her their names.

"You go on ahead. I'll follow you on Dodger," Akira told Vicki once they had Sue buckled in.

Vicki blinked, then shook her head. "Oh, honey, you can't. I drove through a lot of fire to get here. I thought I was going to end up like those people back there in those cars for a little while. You'll never make it through on a horse."

Akira wrapped her arms around Dodger's muzzle and hugged him close.

"But I can't leave him," Akira said. "Not again."

"He'll be all right, I'm sure," said Vicki. She put an arm around Akira's shoulder. "Now come on. There's fire all over the place up here. You have to go back with us."

"Akira, you have to come," Sue told her. "This is our only way out."

Akira wanted to go with Sue and Vicki. Wanted to get as far away as she could from Morris, as fast as she could. But that meant leaving Dodger behind. She couldn't do that again.

Could she?

Akira's stomach tied itself up in knots.

What should she do?

CHURCHILL, MANITOBA

NANUQ

Owen and George moved as quickly as they could across the snow, Owen's good arm draped over George's shoulder to take the pressure off his injured leg. The polar bear hadn't seen them slip away from the lake, but that didn't mean he couldn't smell them and track them down. Both of them kept looking over their shoulders and scanning the horizon, but so far the only things Owen had seen were small clusters of gray rocks and bent dwarf spruce trees.

Owen suddenly stopped, and George had to stop with him.

"My tips!" Owen cried out in despair. "I lost the tips the tourists gave me from the tundra buggy."

George blinked like someone waking up from a deep sleep, then frowned.

"*That's* what you're worried about now? Losing your tips?" George said, shifting his weight to keep them both up. "How

155

about *our phones*, Owen? Our flares? My snowmobile? I think I would rank all of those things *above* the handful of cash you got as tips from the tundra buggy."

Owen pouted. "I'm just saying. If I still had my tips, I'd be closer to having my own snowmobile."

George only grunted at that, and they got moving again.

They were headed north, back toward Hudson Bay. When they hit the water, they'd turn west to get back to Churchill, using the familiar landmarks of the *Ithaka* and Miss Piggy to guide them. It wasn't far, but they had to make it by nightfall. If the sun went down on them, they would lose their compass, their light, and, most importantly, what little warmth they had.

And they did *not* want to spend the night out on the tundra without shelter or heat.

"That polar bear back there, he can't even *feel* the cold," Owen said. "Polar bears have like four inches of blubber. They're so good at retaining heat they don't even show up when you film them with infrared cameras. They're like arctic ninjas!"

"Thank you, Mr. Wikipedia," said George.

"That one I learned from the Weather Lady who comes up here every year," said Owen.

"My grandmother used to tell me stories about polar bears," George said. "The Inuit call him Nanuq, and in the stories he can fly, and disappear into thin air, and hear things miles away. My grandmother told me not to say Nanuq's name out loud, or he would come in the night and steal me away."

"Dude! You just said his name!" Owen cried.

"It's only a story," said George. "But it shows you the respect the Inuit people have for Nanuq. To them, he's more than a source of fur and food. He's a great hunter and survivor. He's a symbol of who they are as a people. They believe that when a polar bear enters an igloo, it turns into a human, and when it leaves, it turns back into a bear."

"That's spooky," said Owen. "What if polar bears do that in every house and building?" His eyes went wide. "Wait—what if some of the people we know are actually polar bears?"

Owen thought for a minute about people he knew who might be polar bears in disguise. The old guy outside of town with all the sled dogs. The grouchy guy at the snack canteen. His fourth-grade teacher *for sure*.

"Remember that girl who got attacked by a polar bear on Halloween?" George asked.

"Suzy Tookoome," said Owen. She was a legend.

"When we were in kindergarten, she was always eating glue and chewing on erasers," George remembered.

"Ooh! Ooh!" Owen said, pointing at the bandages on George's head. "And she liked to sneak up behind people and whack them on the back of the head!"

George nodded. "Suzy Tookoome was *definitely* a polar bear."

"Right? That explains so much!" Owen cried. He felt like he was seeing the world in a whole new way. "Do the Cree tell the same stories about polar bears?"

"No. We've never had the same spiritual connection to polar bears as the Inuit," said George. "We have caribou and moose, which are a much bigger deal."

That made sense, Owen thought. The Cree now mostly lived south of Churchill, while the Inuit lived more in the north up in Nunavut, where the polar bears spent most of the winter.

As they walked, a light snow began to fall. The sky was slate gray, blending to white at the horizon. A wide, flat plain ahead of them looked suspiciously like another lake, and they gave it a pass.

George slipped a little in the snow, and he frowned. "This snow feeling mushier to you? Wetter?" he asked.

Hunh. Now that George mentioned it, the snow *did* seem more slippery, like the first snowfall of the season. Which was weird, because it had been snowing in Churchill since the beginning of October.

George started to wobble. "I need to sit down for a second," he said.

Owen quickly steered them to a cluster of rocks, and they slumped against them. George put his head all the way back, his head still clearly hurting, and laid his injured wrist across his chest. Owen checked his own bandages. They were soaked with blood and stung to touch.

Owen sucked in a breath as he repositioned himself. It was impossible to find some way of sitting that didn't hurt. "I'm sorry about your snowmobile," he told George. "If I had my own snowmobile, of course, we wouldn't be stuck here. We'd have a *second* snowmobile we could ride home."

"You are never going to own your own snowmobile," George said, his eyes closed.

"What are you talking about?" said Owen. "I know I lost the tips in the lake, but—"

"Owen, even if you had all that tip money, it would be gone by next week," George told him. "Every dollar you get is like a polar bear when the sea ice comes. It can't wait to leave."

Owen was offended. "That's not true!" he protested.

"How much money, right now, do you have saved up to buy a snowmobile?" George asked.

Owen went quiet.

George opened one eye to look at him. "What's that?" he asked. "Oh, wait, you have *zero* dollars saved up. Because three weeks ago, you bought a new video game. The week after that, you spent all your money on candy."

"Which I shared with you!"

"And last week," George went on, "last week, you spent all your tip money on new clothes for your digital avatar in the video game you bought three weeks ago. That's not even a real thing, and you spent money on it!"

"People were making fun of me for still wearing the starting outfit!" Owen protested.

A wolf howled in the distance, and Owen and George both sat up.

"We should get going again," George said.

"Yeah," said Owen. He was still feeling defensive about the money thing, but he'd have to argue with George about it later. It was bad enough that a polar bear might be following them. They didn't need a pack of wolves hunting them too.

THE BURNING TUNDRA

Owen kept scanning the horizon for Nanuq as they walked.
He didn't spot a polar bear, but there were plenty of other things
for a careful observer to notice.

Tourists always thought the tundra was a cold, lifeless des-
ert, but Owen knew better. So did George and everyone else
who lived up here. You could see it in summer, when the land
was a riot of lingonberries and crowberries and cloudberries,
mixed in among the moss and tiny orchids and the reddish-
purple sweet vetch.

But even now, when a blanket of white covered everything,
there was life above and below the snow. Arctic foxes and hares
and round, puffy birds called willow ptarmigan that were
brown in summer and turned white in winter. Ground squirrels
and hamster-like lemmings that carved tunnels in the snow.
Wolverines and wolves and snowy owls. Polar bears were just
the biggest, baddest, most obvious part of the food chain.

Owen and George steered away from another frozen lake
and headed for a small stand of low trees. There was something
odd about them, and as the boys drew nearer, Owen understood.

All the trees were burned black. They were leafless and dead.

"What happened here?" Owen asked.

"Don't you remember the wildfires from last summer? The
smoke?" said George. "You could see it all the way in town."

Owen frowned. He remembered the smoke making the

sky hazy and the air harder to breathe. He'd heard people talk about wildfires, but he hadn't really thought about what that meant. Wildfires in the tundra were almost unheard of. It was always too cool and too wet for fires to start in the wild, even in summer. So how had all these trees burned?

George and Owen walked through the charred trees with a quiet reverence, as though they were walking through a battle-field with hundreds of fallen soldiers.

And then Owen screamed as he fell through a hole in the snow.

WHAT HAPPENS
IN THE ARCTIC

Owen's first panicked thought was that he was falling into the icy depths of a lake. Even if he survived, even if he could claw his way out, he would be so cold and wet he would get hypothermia and die.

"Ahh! Help! *Help!*" Owen cried.

Owen heard George laughing, and he stopped yelling and thrashing around.

Owen *hadn't* fallen into a lake. He'd fallen into a smooth round hole in the ground that fit snugly between the roots of one of the burned-out trees. And the hole was only waist deep.

George bent double with laughter, like he was about to bust a gut.

"Stop laughing and help me out," Owen told George. "I think the bite on my leg reopened."

He was right—the drop into the hole had got him bleeding all over again. Owen grimaced as George pulled him out of the hole and redid his bandage. When he was done, they lay back in the snow and closed their eyes, achy and exhausted.

"What did I fall into?" Owen asked.

"Some kind of den," George told him. "It's big, but it looks empty."

"Oh, I know where we are!" said Owen. "This whole grove is filled with polar bear dens. We brought the Weather Lady here to see the mommas and cubs come out last spring."

George sat up quickly, worried about another momma bear encounter, but Owen waved away his concern.

"They're long gone," Owen told him. "The mommas and their cubs come out of their dens in the spring and head straight for the bay to start looking for food. After posing for the polar bear paparazzi, of course." Owen and his parents made good money bringing people like the Weather Lady and her crew out to film the baby polar bears' first adorable steps.

George lay back down. "Well, it wasn't an ice hole, but your mom was right. You did fall in a hole," he said.

Owen laughed, but he really wanted to cry. He was hurt, he was tired, and he was scared. He'd give anything right now to have his mom and dad scolding him for not paying attention. At least that meant they'd be together. He wasn't really that far from home, but he'd never felt so disconnected from his family.

"We gotta get going," George said.

"Yep," said Owen.

Neither of them moved.

"So, we don't need to tell anybody that I freaked out when I fell into an empty polar bear den. Right?" said Owen.

"Listen," said George. "What happens in the Arctic stays in the Arctic."

"That's what I'm talking about," said Owen, and they wearily tapped each other's fists.

FLAMING FARTS

George and Owen knew they had to get home before the sun went down, and they reluctantly pulled each other up and got moving. They avoided other clumps of blackened trees just in case they stumbled into more holes, but each time Owen saw a burned-out denning site, he felt a pang of sadness.

The Weather Lady had told him that momma bears were very particular about where they had their babies. The bears came back to dens that had been around for centuries, in part so they didn't have to spend time and energy digging new dens each year. They needed all that energy to survive for seven months underground without eating or drinking anything while they had their babies and nursed them.

What would happen when the pregnant momma bears came back and found all these dens destroyed by wildfires? What if the momma bears had to spend all their baby-growing energy digging new nests? Would there be a year with a lot fewer polar bear cubs? With none?

Owen was so lost in thought he didn't see the flat, ice-covered bog ahead of them until George changed course to go around it.

"Oh, we brought the Weather Lady here too!" Owen said, recognizing the spot. "She did this really cool thing for the cameras where she held a torch down low and punched a hole in the ice with a stick. Then—*woomph!*—the trapped air exploded in this huge fireball."

"The air under the ice blew up in a fireball?" George asked.

"Yeah. She said it had to do with farts or something," said Owen.

George raised his eyebrows again. "What, like fish farts?"

"It was something like that, but not exactly," Owen said, trying to remember. "She said the farts go up into the atmosphere and spread out all over the world, and I thought it was funny that people in Florida or California or wherever were breathing in Canadian farts."

"Hunh," said George. "I guess what happens in the Arctic *doesn't* stay in the Arctic."

Owen stumbled on the edge of the bog, and the ground crumbled. The wall of the pond broke away, and water gushed down the hillside.

Owen stood and watched, incredulous, as the entire pond drained away in less than five minutes.

He didn't understand. How could the permafrost have given way like that? Usually you needed a jackhammer to dig into permafrost, but this ground had disintegrated just from Owen walking on it.

"Well, any more habitats you want to destroy before we get back to town?" George asked.

Owen narrowed his eyes, and George cracked up.

"That's it!" Owen said, pulling off one of his mittens and throwing it on the ground. "I call an insult contest."

"Really?" George said. "You want to do this right here and now?"

"Yes," said Owen. "I'm calling you out, George Gruyére!"

George narrowed his eyes right back.

"All right, Owen Mackenzie," said George, throwing one of his mittens on the ground next to Owen's. "Challenge accepted."

THE INSULT CONTEST

Owen and George picked up their mittens and circled each other as best they could with their various injuries. This was probably the stupidest time to do this, but George had had one too many laughs at his expense, and Owen couldn't let that stand.

"You look like something I'd draw with my left hand," Owen told George.

"Oh, we're getting right into this? Okay," said George. "Calling you stupid is an insult to stupid people."

"I love what you've done with your hair," said Owen. "How do you get it to come out of your nostrils like that?"

"I would explain it to you, but I don't have any crayons with me," said George.

Insult contests were an ancient Inuit tradition that was still practiced today. They were like rap battles. The aggrieved parties each wrote funny songs about the other person, dissing them in as many ways they could think of. Then they performed their songs in front of the whole community. Sometimes the first person to make the other one lose his temper won. Sometimes their friends and family decided whose jokes were funniest, and that person was the winner. It was a way of having a duel without anyone getting hurt.

When Owen and George had first learned about Inuit insult contests in school, they had immediately created their own version of the game, studying up on jokes and disses to use on each other. In their version, the first person to make the other one laugh was the winner.

"The thing you need to ask yourself, *Mr. Cheese*," said Owen, "is do you want people to accept you as you are, or do you want them to like you?"

"You're gonna go far in life, Owen," said George. "And I hope you stay there."

"Listen," said Owen, "if I wanted crap from you, I'd squeeze your head."

"I'd give you a nasty look for that one," said George, "but I see you've already got one."

"You're so ugly, nightmares have dreams about *you*," said Owen.

"You're so ugly that when your mom dropped you off at school she got a fine for littering," said George.

"You couldn't pour water out of your boot without instructions on the heel," said Owen.

"You know everything about polar bears except how not to get *eaten* by one," George said.

"Well, maybe I wouldn't have gotten eaten by one if I didn't have to save your butt from getting *swatted* by one," Owen said.

"Maybe I wouldn't have been swatted by one if *the person riding shotgun on the snowmobile had actually remembered to bring the shotgun*," George said.

That one cut close to home, and Owen reared back like he'd been slapped.

"You don't *think*, Owen," said George. "You did every one

of the things you told the tourists on the tundra buggy not to do." He counted them off on his mittened fingers. "You didn't check your surroundings for polar bears. You got between a momma bear and her cub. You turned your back on a polar bear and tried to outrun it."

George was breaking the rules of their insult contest and not letting Owen have his shot, but he was fired up now.

"Then you didn't pay attention and drove the snowmobile onto thin ice," George went on.

"I was trying to get us away as fast as I could!" Owen protested.

George ignored him and kept listing his faults. "You walk out in front of cars in a town with, like, ten cars in it. You talk about saving up for a snowmobile, but you spend your money as soon as you get it. You can't remember the name of the Weather Lady who comes up here *every single year* to take a personal tour on your tundra buggy. You see the smoke from wildfires in the tundra but don't even stop to think about what might be burning."

Owen blinked back tears, and his hands balled into fists inside his mittens. He and George glowered at each other, their breaths coming out hot and fast from their noses like two polar bears squaring off in a fight.

"Oh yeah?" said Owen. "Well, why don't we talk about how you suddenly hate everything about Churchill?"

George gave him a don't-go-there look, but it was way too late for that.

Owen made his voice high and whiny. "It's too cold. There's

too many bugs. There's too many tourists. There's no movie theater. There's no roads in and out of town. There's no *girls*." Owen threw his hands in the air. "What the heck, George? Churchill's always been enough for you before. You know, *besides* the fact that your grandparents and all your aunts and uncles and cousins and your best friend live here."

George looked away so Owen wouldn't see him crying. "You think I *want* to leave Churchill?" George said, sniffing. "Owen, my dad just got laid off from the port."

NEWFOUNDLAND

Owen reeled. Everything George had said about him still cut to the quick, but his concern for his best friend came first. *George's dad lost his job?*

"Why didn't you tell me?" Owen asked.

George looked overwhelmed. He put his one good hand behind him to try to find a rock to sit on, and Owen hurried over to help him.

When George was settled, Owen collapsed beside him.

"He got his two weeks' notice five days ago," George said, peeling off his snow goggles so he could wipe his eyes.

George's dad was a longshoreman. He got paid good money to load and unload cargo from the big Panamax ships that docked at the Port of Churchill. But a few years ago, the Canadian government had stopped using the port to ship grain out to the rest of the world, and things had only gotten worse since then.

"There aren't enough ships going in and out anymore," said George. "Mom and Dad are talking about moving to Newfoundland, where Dad can get another shipping job. They've been trying to make the best of it. Talking about all the benefits of living somewhere else, all the hassles of Churchill we'll be leaving behind. I've been doing my best to get on board." He wiped his eyes and nose again, smearing snot on his parka. "I know it's already hard for them, and I don't want to make it harder. But I don't want to leave. And I know they don't either."

"Maybe the port will start shipping out more grain or oil or something," Owen said, grasping for any kind of answer. "There's less and less sea ice every year. Maybe if it gets hot enough, the Northwest Passage will open up and suddenly Canada will be shipping lots of stuff to Russia and Japan."

George laughed and sniffed. "That's a hell of a thing, isn't it? How bad is it when you're hoping global warming will save your dad's job?"

Owen blinked. He hadn't thought of it that way. He'd just been focused on him and George. Not the bigger picture.

I never do think, do I? Owen thought. His parents were right. And so was George.

Owen was still trying to figure out what to say to George when he felt a strange tingle, like he was being watched. George must have felt it too. He frowned and blinked and looked around.

They both saw it at the same time: an arctic ninja, almost invisible as he moved against the white hill a few dozen meters away.

Nanuq was back, and he was stalking them.

MIAMI, FLORIDA

PART 3

THE SINKING SHIP

Natalie watched in horror as water filled the floor of the sailboat.

"Whatever we hit before—whatever made that awful scraping sound," Anne said. "It must have torn a hole in the bottom of the boat!"

Nowhere is safe, Natalie thought, rocking in her seat. *Nowhere is safe!*

Isabel's son and daughter started to cry, and she hugged them close. "We have to get out of here before we sink!" she told everyone else.

Derek peeked out the cabin door and came back dripping wet.

"There are buildings all around us," he told them. "Some are just the roofs of houses buried in the water, but I can see the shadows of taller buildings. If we run into one of those, maybe we can jump out. But we have to be ready to move."

Isabel got her children up from the bench to join the Evanses by the door.

Churro shivered inside Natalie's hoodie, and she shivered right along with him. Natalie couldn't move. Couldn't think. She couldn't go back out into the storm again. She couldn't.

Isabel put a hand on her shoulder. "Natalie, we can do this. Together. Come on," she said, helping Natalie stand. "This will all be over mañana."

They waited long, tense minutes. The boat rocked and creaked. Water sloshed at their feet, getting steadily deeper.

Will I ever be somewhere the water isn't *rising?* Natalie thought.

Derek and Marcus looked at the ceiling of the small cabin, listening. Waiting. Anne's lips moved in prayer. Javari stared at the wall beside Natalie's head. She noticed for the first time that he was wearing a Miami Hurricanes basketball jersey, and something about that made her want to laugh. Isabel sang softly, holding her daughter's hands in hers as she clapped out a rhythm. The water rose.

Natalie's mind drifted to Mariposa, the fantasyland she had created when she was little. Mariposa used to be a place of retreat and solace for her, but all she could think of now were the maps and papers of Mariposa, swirling, ruined, in the dark water that had come crashing through the back wall of their house. Were Mama and Tía Beatriz still alive? Had they found somewhere safe to hide from the storm? How would they ever find each other when this was all over? Where would they live?

Natalie closed her eyes and crumpled. How could she put the broken pieces of her world back together again?

THUMP. SCRAAAAAAAPE.

Natalie looked up. The sailboat had run into something. This was their chance to escape!

THE PINK FLAMINGO

Derek took a quick look outside and came back excited.

"We hit the balcony of an apartment building!" he cried. "Marcus, come quick and help me grab the rail!"

The two of them scurried up and out, then called for the others to follow. Javari and his mother went next, then Natalie.

Outside, the storm was as bad as ever. Bits of trees and debris swept by, cutting and lashing at her. Natalie tried to stay low, holding Churro inside her hoodie with one hand and the tangled ropes of the boat with the other.

The apartment building they'd hit was like a thousand others Natalie had seen in Miami—rectangular and boxy and three stories tall. Windows and doors that normally opened out onto an exterior walkway were boarded up, but the walkway itself was protected by the building's flat roof and guarded by a metal railing. Even if they couldn't get into one of the apartments, the walkway would be someplace out of the rain.

At the end of the walkway, concrete steps disappeared into the choppy gray storm surge, leading down to the second- and first-floor apartments. Apartments that were already underwater.

We're docking a boat on the third-floor balcony of an apartment building, Natalie thought. It was all so impossible.

Derek and Marcus were already on the concrete walkway. Derek held the sailboat's railing while Marcus helped people off.

Anne went first, slipping and almost falling off the narrow boat deck before Marcus and Javari caught her. Natalie waved Isabel and her children up out of the cabin to go next, and Isabel handed her son and daughter across to Marcus before climbing over the railing and taking shelter with Anne near one of the boarded-up apartments.

SHUNK. WHACK.

Natalie ducked as a satellite dish came crashing into the boat and flew away, followed by a dented metal trash can lid.

Reuben was going to let them off this sailboat, but he wasn't going to make it easy.

Javari pointed at Natalie—her turn. She crouched low, holding Churro tight inside the hoodie, and inched her way toward Javari's outstretched hand.

Out of the corner of her eye, Natalie saw something big hurtling through the darkness of the storm, and she turned in time to see what it was.

A giant pink fiberglass flamingo statue was tumbling straight toward her on the wind.

Natalie only had a heartbeat to duck before—*WUMP. THUMP. CRUNCH!*—the flamingo statue smashed into the the boat. The impact ripped the boat's railing out of Derek's hands, and Natalie fell to the deck as her world went spinning, bumping, thrashing out of control.

In the chaos, Natalie saw Javari fall in the water. She reached out for him, screamed his name into the word-stealing wind, but he was gone. Or she was. The boat whirled away from the apartment building, away from the stretching, yelling Marcus and

Derek, and in seconds they and all the others had disappeared in the dark, pounding rain.

"No. *No!*" Natalie cried. "Come back!"

She had finally found someone to help her, found a safe place to hide from Reuben, and now she and Churro were alone again. Alone and lost in the storm.

FELLOW TRAVELERS

Natalie clung to the boat railing, knuckles white with fear. Inside her hoodie, Churro trembled. Sideways rain pelted them. The roaring wind ripped at them. The sailboat tried to throw Natalie and Churro like a wild horse.

It was too much. Reuben was attacking her in so many different ways, Natalie didn't even know where to start. All she wanted to do was crawl back inside the boat and hide until it was over, but she couldn't even do that.

The boat she was clinging to so desperately was sinking.

Natalie scanned the horizon, looking for someplace safe. Vague black shapes loomed in the distance, silhouetted by flashes of lightning. Were they more apartment buildings? She couldn't tell.

Something moved against the whitecaps on top of the water, and Natalie's heart caught in her throat.

An alligator was swimming by just a few feet away.

Natalie wouldn't even have seen the alligator if she hadn't been searching the darkness for some way to escape, but she saw it now—and it saw her. One of the alligator's glassy, beady eyes met hers as it glided by in the water, and Natalie held her breath. Churro saw the alligator too and growled, and Natalie quickly clapped a hand over the little dog's mouth.

Luckily the gator didn't seem particularly interested in them. Or in the slithery thing Natalie saw swimming by in the water next, going in the same direction. Something that frightened Natalie even more than the alligator.

A Burmese python.

Another denizen of Miami's canals, the huge snake was easily twelve feet long, with a spotted green-and-brown body as thick as Natalie's leg. In her imaginary world of Mariposa, Natalie had turned the ugly, monstrous pythons into dragons and sent brave knights out to slay them. In reality, the only things in nature that were a match for these snakes were their mortal enemies, the alligators.

But this alligator and this Burmese python didn't seem to want to eat each other. Or Natalie. Or Churro. They all had a bigger problem to contend with.

Hurricane Reuben.

Even so, Natalie kept a watchful eye on both the gator and the snake as they swam past.

Lightning flashed, and through the rain Natalie saw a square, shadowy island up ahead with a couple of small, rectangular structures on it. No, not an island, she realized. It was the rooftop of a two-story building that was otherwise completely underwater. It wasn't as good a refuge as the three-story building had been, but it would have to do.

THUMP. SCRAAAAAPE. The wind pushed the boat against the building.

Heart in her throat, Reuben roaring in her ears, Natalie climbed to her knees and grabbed the short wall along the top of the roof. The boat turned and twisted in the water, and Natalie held on tight to the building as the sailboat dragged away underneath her. Her legs fell into the churning storm surge, but she found enough strength to pull herself up and over the ledge. She and Churro tumbled into a puddle of water about three inches deep on the roof, but there was solid ground beneath them for the first time in forever.

Natalie was so exhausted she laughed and cried at the same time.

"We made it, Churro. We made it," she said. She was sure he couldn't hear her over the roar of the hurricane, but it didn't matter. She could tell from the way he collapsed onto her chest that he was as relieved as she was.

They still had to find somewhere out of the wind and driving rain. She had seen little buildings on the roof, hadn't she? A stairwell, maybe, or a storage shed.

Natalie worked her way wearily up onto her hands and knees—just in time for a wave to crest the edge of the roof and crash into her. Natalie tumbled along the rough rooftop, trying to grab hold of something, anything, and then suddenly the solid ground underneath her was gone and she was underwater again.

GOING FOR A SWIM

No—not back into the water!

Natalie kicked and thrashed, trying to grab the edge of the roof before she was swept away. She swallowed salt water, but there was another sharp taste there too. *Chlorine?* Natalie choked and gagged. She was lost. She was drowning. And then at last her hands found what she was looking for—the edge of the roof. But it didn't feel like the rough, low wall she'd climbed over to get here. It was smoother. Rounder. It felt like—

Like the edge of a swimming pool.

Natalie came up gasping for air and realized where she was. Reuben hadn't knocked her back into the storm surge. She was in a rooftop pool!

Churro kicked and clawed inside Natalie's hoodie, and she quickly unzipped it and pulled him out where he could breathe. The little dog hacked and coughed, but he seemed okay. Natalie just hoped he hadn't swallowed too much water.

Through the sweeping rain, Natalie saw a ladder sticking up out of the pool, and she kicked her way toward it. She was most of the way up the ladder and out of the pool when she felt Churro wriggling in her hand. He was barking at something behind her.

Natalie turned to see what it was and almost had a heart attack. There was a manatee in the pool.

Natalie cried out and fell back onto the rooftop. Manatees

weren't dangerous, but seeing this one here, now, *in the pool on the roof of a building*, was totally surreal.

Natalie stared at the creature. The manatee was *huge*. Natalie was just under five feet tall, and the sea cow was twice as long as that—and wide enough to swallow her whole, if it hadn't been a plant eater. Its gray skin was covered with blotches of green-and-brown algae, and scars from years of encounters with motorboats crisscrossed its back.

The manatee raised its fat snout out of the water to breathe and sniff at her, and Natalie felt a sudden kinship with it. She and the manatee were alike, she realized. Reuben had destroyed both of their homes, and then dragged them here to this rooftop to be stranded in the storm.

And none of what had happened was their fault, but they still had to deal with it.

Churro barked at Natalie, breaking the spell the manatee had on her. Churro was right. They had to go find shelter out of the storm.

"Goodbye, manatee, and good luck," Natalie whispered.

Natalie crawled away from the pool, trying to stay as low to the ground as she could while hugging Churro to her chest. She went for the nearest thing with four walls and a roof—a little storage shed by the pool. Natalie reached up and opened the door, then cried out and ducked as Reuben ripped the door off its hinges and sent it flying away in the storm.

Natalie crawled inside anyway, squeezing in between beach balls and Styrofoam coolers and pool noodles that floated in the floodwater. She hid in the back corner of the shed and wrapped herself around Churro, shaking and shivering and wondering how long she was going to have to survive here until the storm ended.

And then, just when Natalie thought things couldn't get any worse, when she thought Reuben had done everything to her he possibly could, Natalie felt water drip onto her face and looked up.

The roof was lifting off the little shack.

No. Not the roof, she thought. *Not again.*

Natalie's tears turned to anger. A fire burned inside her, and her arms shook.

She had had *enough.*

"No!" she screamed. "*No!* Irma took my roof, and you took my wall. But you can't have this!" she yelled at Reuben.

She knew it was hopeless. That screaming at a hurricane was like Churro barking at every single thing that frightened him. But she couldn't help it. She was tired of feeling so overwhelmed. Of not barking back.

"Stop it! Stop it right now!" Natalie screamed at the lifting roof. "Go away, Reuben!" she cried. "You leave us alone!"

And suddenly, to Natalie's surprise, he did.

THE SIERRA NEVADA, CALIFORNIA

PART 4

UP AND OVER

"I can't go with you," Akira told Sue and Vicki.

Akira looked longingly at Vicki's pickup truck, and its promise of instant escape from the wildfire. It was surprisingly hard to leave Sue too. But Akira couldn't abandon her horse.

"I left Dodger once before," Akira said, "and I promised I'd never do it again."

Vicki tried to talk her out of it, but Akira's mind was made up. She gave Vicki her number and her mom's number though, and asked Vicki to call her mom with an update when she got a signal.

Sue gave Akira her number too. "So we can see each other again, come hail or high water," Sue told her.

Akira laughed. She'd thought before that Sue might be somebody who could become a real friend, and she was sure of it now. Maybe even a best friend. And Akira still hadn't gotten the story of what those scars on her head were all about.

"You can count on it," Akira told her. "If not, all hail's gonna break loose."

Sue smiled.

"And if you see my husband—" Vicki said, but couldn't finish.

The smile left Akira's face. She nodded, understanding.

Akira sat in her saddle and waved as the pickup truck disappeared into the smoke. When it was finally gone, Akira let out a quick, anxious breath. Her heart was beating a million miles a minute.

"It's just you and me now, Dodger," Akira said. Dodger whinnied, and she patted his withers. "Let's get over the mountain and get home."

Akira turned Dodger off the road and ran him as quick as he could go through the woods and up the mountain. The blackened, burned trees eventually gave way to live ponderosa pines, and then to untouched bearclover and white alder, and at last she and Dodger were back among the monarchs again. The giant sequoias. Right where they'd started that morning.

The dry stuff on the ground here hadn't burned, which surprised her. Not that it would hurt the monarchs if it did. As her dad liked to remind her, these giant sequoias had lived through the worst the world could throw at them for a hundred human generations, and they would live another hundred more.

Her dad also liked to say *When you're lost, go higher to get some perspective.* So that's exactly what Akira had done.

And her dad was right. From up here on the mountaintop, Akira could see everything—including her house, down the other side of the mountain. There was smoke between here and there, but Akira didn't see the glow of flames. Was the smoke she was seeing from the Morris Fire on the other side of the mountain? Or had lightning strikes started other, smaller wildfires on this side of the ridge too? There was no way to tell.

Akira put a hand to the soft, dry bark of a sequoia. She wished she could stay, but while the giant sequoias would survive if Morris swept through, she and Dodger definitely would not.

"Okay, Dodger," Akira said. "Straight down the other side of the mountain, and home."

Dodger whinnied like he understood, and together they began picking their way back down the smoky trail.

Partway there, Dodger turned, trying to go sideways along the mountain instead of down it. Akira smiled. She knew what he was doing. There was a bald Akira and her dad liked to visit in that direction. The bald was a big, cleared field that had incredible views of the valley below, and of the giant sequoias above. Dodger must have figured she wanted to stop there.

"No, no, Dodger," Akira said, steering him back. "We're skipping the bald today."

Dodger's ears radared in on something in the underbrush, and Akira looked in time to see a flurry of little pikas running across their path.

Dodger pulled to a stop and went rigid. Akira didn't understand. It was unusual to see so many pikas at once, but that shouldn't have frightened him. So what was he scared of?

Akira waited, trying to see and hear whatever it was that had made Dodger tense up. But there was no sound except the hot, dry wind and the distant pop and crackle of fire.

"Okay, bud," Akira said. "Time to get moving again."

Akira squeezed Dodger's sides to urge him forward, but he wouldn't budge.

"Dodger, what are you doing?" Akira asked, and then a mountain lion burst out of the smoke and stopped right in front of them.

EXODUS

Akira froze, and Dodger froze with her. Akira's heart thumped so loud she could hear it.

The mountain lion on the path took one look at them, glanced back over its shoulder the direction it had come from, then took off running again, disappearing into the smoke.

"*Whoa,*" Akira whispered, letting out a breath. She had seen mountain lions before, but always in the distance, skulking by in the shadow of a ridge or hopping from rock to rock. She'd never seen one this close-up.

She was stunned it hadn't attacked them. Mountain lions were fierce predators, sometimes even hunting horses as big as Dodger. But this one hadn't given them a second look.

"Looks like we got lucky," Akira told Dodger.

And then, incredibly, Dodger turned to follow the mountain lion.

"Whoa, whoa, whoa! Dodger, we're going *this* way," Akira said, steering him back. "Why do you want to go that way? We just saw a mountain lion running that direction!"

Dodger followed her lead, but reluctantly. Akira frowned. Why was he fighting her so much?

A moment later, Dodger froze again as a small herd of bighorn sheep thundered past, going the same direction as the pikas and the mountain lion. Akira was so surprised she almost jumped out of her saddle, but like the other animals, the bighorn sheep barely noticed that she and Dodger were there. Or didn't care.

When the sheep were gone, Dodger wouldn't budge.

"Okay, what is going on?" Akira asked.

The wind suddenly shifted, blowing hot and fast from the direction all the animals had come from. Akira turned to look in time to see flames racing along the forest floor like a living thing, chasing after all the animals.

There was a wildfire on this side of the mountain!

The fire scampered up a pine, and—*WOOMPH*—the tree burst into flames. Akira flinched, and Dodger reared back.

WOOMPH. WOOMPH. WOOMPH. Another tree caught on fire, and another, and another, and suddenly the fiery predator was reaching out its burning paws for Akira and Dodger.

THE BALD

"I get it! I get it!" Akira cried, yanking on Dodger's reins and spurring him away from the fire. They plunged into the forest, branches scratching and whacking at them as they barreled through the pines and underbrush. Akira barely managed to hang on, until at last they burst out of the trees and into the knee-high brown grass of the bald.

Akira rode Dodger all the way out to the center of the clearing before finally pulling him up to a stop, both of them breathing hard. Dodger paced in a tight circle, and Akira turned frantically in her seat to watch as the wildfire roared up through the trees behind them.

Akira was about to yank on the reins again, to turn Dodger and keep running away from the fire, but the flames hit the edge of the bald and stopped. The fire burned a little way into the grassy field, but it seemed to like the taste of the pine trees all around it much better. Akira watched as the flames snatched first this group of trees, then that one, circling the round bald but leaving the interior of it untouched.

Akira shuddered, and Dodger whinnied in panic.

"I know, boy. I know. Just stay calm," Akira said, her heart hammering in her chest. Dodger was still dancing, still eager to turn and run, but he was a good horse and did as he was told.

In less than a minute, the blaze completely surrounded them.

Akira and Dodger were trapped in the bald, but safe. For the moment.

Akira slumped in her saddle. "I'm sorry," she told Dodger. "I'll listen the next time you're trying to tell me something."

Dodger snorted, as if to say, *You better.*

Dodger was still nervous. He spun in place, trying to put his back to the fire but always finding more fire in front of him. Akira knew they actually had a minute's peace, but there was no way to tell him. She got an apple out of her backpack to distract him instead, and ate one herself.

The bighorn sheep that had run past them were milling around on the far side of the bald. Did that mean the mountain lion was stalking around somewhere in the grass too? If it was, Akira hoped the mountain lion was more afraid of the fire than it was hungry right now.

The clearing let Akira see farther down the mountain, and she spotted another wildfire burning in the valley between the bald and her house. If the fire kept growing, or if the wind changed direction, Akira's house would be directly in its path. Akira felt her stomach clench up at the thought, and the bite of apple she was swallowing went down hard. Suddenly she wasn't very hungry anymore.

Dodger's ears swiveled toward something back down the mountain, and Akira turned to see.

Akira stared in surprise. She'd seen a lot of strange things today, but this might have been the strangest. A huge jet plane, like the kind you flew to other cities in, was coming down the canyon right toward them. It was flying way too low to be a passenger plane though. Big planes like that weren't supposed to be so close to the treetops. Goose bumps went up and down Akira's arms. Had the smoke from the wildfire somehow messed up the plane's equipment and made it impossible for the pilot to see?

Was the plane going to crash?

Akira held her breath, and Dodger danced underneath her, ready to run.

At the last second, the plane banked wide along the side of the mountain, showed Akira its belly, and then straightened out to go shooting along the front edge of the fire. Big doors opened on the bottom of the plane, and a ruby-red cloud of chemicals poured out, coating the green trees.

"Whoa!" Akira said. "It's a fire plane!" She thought they only used planes with propellers for this sort of thing, not jets.

The colorful fire retardant drew Akira's eye to the front line of the fire, and she saw a group of tiny figures using axes and bulldozers to fight the blaze in the valley. Cal Fire! They were trying to create a firebreak, a buffer zone like the bald where there would be nothing for the wildfires to burn. Akira couldn't imagine how exhausted the firefighters must be, wearing all that heavy gear and working so hard right next to the scorching blaze. Akira was bathed in sweat just sitting on a horse with the hot, bright flames fifty yards away from her.

Dodger trotted impatient circles in the middle of the ring of fire, and Akira did what she could to calm him. She couldn't blame him for being on edge though. She was nervous too. How long would it take the fire to sweep past them? What if the wildfire in the valley spread before they could escape, and blocked their way home?

Over the inferno's roar, Akira heard a low, even drone. She spun Dodger around in time to see another huge jet plane heading straight for them. Again it looked impossibly low, like it was going to hit the mountain. But this time the jet didn't swerve. It kept coming straight for Akira.

This one was coming to put out *their* fire.

"Dodger, we're saved!" Akira cried. "That plane's gonna cut us a path!"

BLASTED

The jet plane flew closer, closer, straight for the bald. Its big bottom doors opened, and bright red fire retardant came spilling out in a huge cloud. *Fwoosh.*

Akira pumped her fist in the air. "Woo-hoo!" she cried.

But the jet kept getting closer, and red stuff kept pouring out the bottom. Dodger turned this way and that, afraid of the coming cloud. Akira reined him in, hoping the deluge would stop, but it didn't. The mass of fire retardant wasn't just going to hit the fire—it was going to hit the bald too.

Akira turned Dodger to run, but too late. The bright red cloud hit them like a bomb—*WHOMPH!*—and blasted them with chemicals.

Every sense Akira had was overwhelmed by the stuff. It stung her eyes, went up her nose, filled her throat, thundered in her ears, and covered every inch of her skin. She coughed and retched—and then almost fell out of her saddle as Dodger reared up on his hind legs in a panic. Akira clung blindly to the reins, the saddle, Dodger's mane, anything she could to not fall off, and before she could stop him, Dodger thundered out of the clearing, carrying them both into the heart of the fire.

THROUGH THE FIRE

Akira couldn't talk, couldn't see, couldn't steer. All she could do was cling desperately to Dodger and pray she didn't fall off as the horse barreled through the burning woods. The blast of heat from the fire was immediate and searing. Akira felt it on her face, her arms, through her clothes. She bent low against Dodger's neck and held tight to his mane, her eyes squeezed shut against the glare and burn. Dodger squealed, high and frantic, a sound that tore at Akira's heart. She was as frightened and overwhelmed as Dodger was, but there was no comforting him, no calming him. Now that they were in the fire, they couldn't stop until they were out again.

Dodger thundered through the flames at a full gallop. Akira had no idea where they were going, and she doubted Dodger did either. Every inch of her radiated with burning heat, and her clothes felt like hot irons against her skin.

Akira felt her grip weakening, her butt sliding in the saddle. She was going to slip off. Fall beneath Dodger's pounding hooves. Be trampled and then burned alive in the fire.

And then suddenly—*WHOOSH*—they were out of the scalding heat, out of the roaring, crackling din of the inferno. They were free! Akira still had her eyes closed, still fought to stay in the saddle, but she let Dodger keep running, trusting him to take them both away from the fire as far and fast as he could.

When at last he began to slow, Akira raised herself up in the saddle. Her eyes were weeping from the fire retardant, and she barely got them open in time to see the tree branch in front of her.

THWACK. Akira took the blow right in her chest and flew off Dodger, landing flat on her back with a *thump*.

BURNED

All the wind went out of Akira. She gasped for air, writhing and clawing at the dry dirt and pine needles. *She was going to die.* She couldn't breathe and was going to die! She choked and gagged, and then suddenly her lungs worked again, and she sucked in great rasping breaths of smoky air. Akira coughed and shook, her heart threatening to hammer a hole in her chest.

When at last she wrenched her eyes open, Akira found herself staring straight up into the face of Dodger, who was coated all over in bright red fire retardant.

Dodger tilted his face and snorted impatiently at her, as if to say, *What are you doing down there on the ground?*

Akira held up her hand to tell him to wait, and saw that she was covered with the same sticky, gooey red stuff as Dodger. *Maybe that's what kept us from catching fire*, Akira thought.

"Ohhhhhh," she moaned. "I hurt like hail."

Akira chuckled through her pain at her joke. Sue would have liked that one.

She lay on her back, arms spread out wide, and listened to her body speak to her. A dozen places stung, some with scratches and bruises, others from the blazing heat of the wildfire. *First-degree burns*, Akira thought, remembering lessons her father had taught her. The equivalent of a bad sunburn inside and outside of her clothes. Painful, but manageable.

The underside of Akira's left arm was the worst. The fire

retardant hadn't hit that spot, and something there seethed and burned. She winced as she lifted it to see and then gasped. There was an egg-sized welt on her arm where the wildfire had laid a fiery paw on her. The skin was angry and pink, and was starting to blister and ooze.

Akira drew in a breath. *Second-degree burn.* The kind you got when you touched a hot stove or were scalded by boiling water.

Or were exposed to direct flames for more than a couple seconds.

Akira sat up with difficulty. She had to do something about the second-degree burn right now. The pain from it was already so intense she could barely see straight. But what did she have that could help? Just the aspirin, and the three bottles of water left in the backpack.

Akira poured a little of the water on the wound to rinse it, hissing as it touched her scalded skin. Her arm throbbed with blinding pain, and she felt her brain turning off. All she wanted to do was lie down on the pine needles and curl up into a ball and go to sleep forever.

Dodger nudged her with his muzzle, and Akira shook herself awake.

"You're right," Akira told Dodger. "I need to focus." This new fire could be on them any minute, and they needed to be moving.

Akira reached up and patted her horse's chin.

"Thanks, Dodger," she said.

Akira pulled off one of her shoes and socks, and soaked the

sock in water before wrapping it loosely around the burn. Her sock was hardly sterile, but at least it would soothe the pain and cover the welt. She would clean the wound properly when she got home.

If she got home.

When she was finished, Akira checked Dodger for injuries and burns. Besides some singed horse hair, he seemed all right. She worried that all the chemicals in the fire retardant couldn't be good for him, but at least it had protected him a little.

"And I guess it helps when your undercarriage is three feet off the ground," she said, patting Dodger's tummy.

Akira swallowed two of the aspirin and finished off one of the water bottles. She fed another bottle to Dodger, then used the last one to wash the fire retardant out of their eyes and off their faces as best she could.

"Now," Akira said when they were cleaned up, "where are we?"

They had ended up in the bottom of a ravine in between two slopes. But which slope led up the mountain, and which led down toward her house?

"When you're lost, get higher to get some perspective," she said to Dodger, quoting her father again. She looped Dodger's reins around a branch. "I'll be right back," she told him.

Akira picked the biggest pine tree she could and started to climb. It was slow going and painful with her burned arm, but eventually she rose above the low lake of smoke that filled the ravine.

From up here she could see the direction they needed to go

to get home. She could see the red-bombed bald she and Dodger had just fled too. But it was what she saw above the bald that made Akira almost lose her grip.

"No," she whispered. "It can't be."

High up on the ridge, at the summit of the mountain, the tops of the giant sequoias were on fire.

CHURCHILL, MANITOBA

PART 4

THREE LEGS, TWO ARMS, AND ONE BRAIN

Owen almost jumped out of his skin at the sight of the big polar bear sneaking up on them against the white of the snow.

"Go away, Nanuq! Back!" George cried.

PAKOW!

The sound of the cracker shell going off was deafening at close range, and Owen threw his hands up over his ears. Nanuq didn't like it either, and he loped off behind a low hill.

"How could something that big sneak up on us so quietly?" George asked.

"Arctic ninja," said Owen. "And I think he's going to keep stalking us."

"Don't polar bears prefer easier meals?" George asked. "He's burning up a lot of calories chasing us around."

"I think we *are* easy meals. Or at least I am," said Owen. He nodded at the ground, where his boot left a trail of blood.

"Holy crap, Owen," George said, immediately moving to support him. "Why didn't you say something?"

"You're hurt too," Owen said.

"Come on," George said. He slung the shotgun strap over his shoulder and let Owen lean on him to take pressure off his injured foot.

Owen and George had to turn their backs on Nanuq to keep heading home. That was a polar bear no-no, but they didn't have a choice. The sun was getting low, and they hadn't even caught a whiff of the bay.

"We're quite a pair," Owen said as they hobbled along. "Between us we only have three legs and two good arms."

"And one brain," George said.

It felt like something of an apology for their argument of a few moments before, and Owen chuckled.

"You know, it might not be the blood that Nanuq is following," Owen said. "How long has it been since you had a shower?"

It was a snowball insult. The kind they used to throw at each other in their insult contests, before things had gotten real. It was Owen's way of saying he was sorry too, and that he hoped they could go back to the way things had been between them before. George was his best friend in the whole world, and he didn't want to lose him. Not to Newfoundland, and not to his own thoughtlessness.

"It's true, I don't shower," said George. "I just roll around in the snow to stay clean, like a polar bear."

"Hey, that's a real polar bear fact!" said Owen.

"You're not the only one in Churchill who knows things about polar bears," George told him.

Owen smiled. They were good. At least with each other. He still didn't know how George was going to get out of moving away from Churchill though.

And he sure as heck didn't know how he was going to fix what was wrong with himself.

I'm not totally *oblivious*, Owen thought as they walked. He saw the permafrost walls of ponds and lakes crumble and flood. He smelled the wildfires on the tundra. He laughed at the Weather Lady lighting lake farts on fire. Pointed out to the tourists all the red foxes and orcas and grizzly bears that were pushing out native species because it was warm enough for the new animals to live here now.

He knew too that the polar bear season was getting longer and longer every year. Because it meant more money for him and his family.

What Owen wasn't doing was thinking about what any of that really *meant*. Crumbling permafrost lake walls were one thing, but what happened when it got so hot that the houses in town began to settle and sink into the softer soil? What would the momma polar bears do for dens when wildfires destroyed their ancestral denning sites? What happened when all the new animals in the north killed off the arctic foxes and belugas and narwhals and polar bears that already lived there?

And even though the warmer temperatures meant a longer tourist season, how long could the polar bears everyone was coming to see survive if they kept losing more and more hunting time on the sea ice every year?

The big picture. That's what he was beginning to see now. And the big picture was climate change.

Owen tried to remember everything the Weather Lady had said about the Arctic and climate change when they'd been out on the tundra last spring. It wasn't that the fish were farting, Owen remembered now. It was that warmer temperatures all around the world were melting the permafrost in the Arctic, and tiny microbes were feasting on the newly unfrozen plant material in the ground. It was the *microbes* that created methane—the farts—and methane was a greenhouse gas that trapped heat inside the atmosphere, making the earth hotter. And the hotter the world got, the more the permafrost melted, and the more the permafrost melted, the more the microbes feasted and farted, and . . . well, it wasn't hard to see how things could get out of control pretty quickly.

And like a really, really *good* fart—the kind you laid down in the corner of the classroom and watched linger and spread as people all the way up front wrinkled their noses and looked around for the culprit—the methane gas from the arctic permafrost was going all over the world.

What happens in the Arctic doesn't *stay in the Arctic*, Owen thought.

As they walked, Owen saw a few patches of ground here and there without any snow. Which was weird. Everything should have been covered in snow this time of year. The ground *had* been covered in snow, as far as the eye could see, just that morning. So what was with the bare spots he was seeing now?

Pay attention and think, Owen told himself. What did patches of ground without snow *mean*?

George tapped Owen's coat, snapping him out of his deep thoughts.

"Check it out," said George. "A hunting shack!"

Owen couldn't believe it. Up ahead was a little cabin like the one they had planned to spend the night in. It was the first sign of civilization they'd seen since tangling with Momma Bear, and they excitedly picked up their pace. Maybe there was someone inside who could help!

JIMMY'S PLACE

As they got closer to the one-room hunting shack, Owen's excitement dwindled. Even from a distance, he could see that its one window was broken, and a whole corner of the building had fallen in.

The exterior walls of the old, square cabin were unpainted plywood, and the part of the flat, slanted roof that was still standing was covered with black tar paper. Three wooden stairs led up to a small landing in front of the door, where the owners had left a piece of plywood with hundreds of rusty nails sticking up through it, pointy sides up. Owen knew what that was. Locals called them "polar bear welcome mats." They were designed to keep nosy polar bears from coming right through the front door.

In front of the cabin's lone window, Owen saw another polar bear prevention device: a ratty old couch. There was something about the springiness of couches that polar bears didn't trust, and they wouldn't walk on them. They sure liked *eating* them though. This couch had a bunch of big bites taken out of it by hungry nanuqs.

A hand-painted sign hanging on the front of the shack read JIMMY'S PLACE.

Owen and George pushed the door open and stepped over the polar bear welcome mat.

"Hello?" George called, but it was pretty clear to Owen that no one had been here in a long time. The inside of the cabin was small and spartan. There were two folding lawn chairs, a plastic bucket turned upside down to make a table, and a plastic milk crate nailed to the wall with nothing in it but empty tin cans and a couple of forks and spoons. The roof beams were so low Owen could almost reach up and touch them, and there was no sink, and no toilet.

Next to a long-disused wood stove in the center of the room was a wooden crate with a handwritten sign that read FIREWOOD: KEEP FULL. It was empty.

"Thanks a lot, Jimmy," said Owen.

Lighting the wood stove wouldn't have helped much anyway. Snow trailed down through the hole in the roof and collected in a small mound on the floor.

"Don't think we're going to find anything useful," said George.

"Think we should try to spend the night here, though?" Owen asked. "The sun's going to go down soon."

"Gotta say I'm not excited about that idea," said George.

Neither was Owen. But what choice did they have? They could be a half-hour walk from Hudson Bay, or three hours. Owen had no idea. And half a shack was better than none.

Something huffed and snorted outside, and Owen and George motioned to each other to be quiet. Owen crept over and peeked out the window, and his worst fears were confirmed.

Nanuq was circling the cabin.

CHEF NANUQ

Owen turned to George with big eyes and pantomimed chewing and clawing, and George immediately understood. They looked around quickly, trying to think of something they could do. Somewhere they could hide. George's face lit up like he had an idea, and he pointed to the hole in the ceiling. Yes! They could get away from Nanuq on the roof.

Owen picked up one of the folding chairs and quietly repositioned it under the hole. They went through a pantomime of "*You* go first," "No, *you* go first," until finally George lost his patience and steered Owen toward their makeshift ladder.

The folding chair was rickety, but Owen managed to get his head and his good arm up through the hole. George gave him a boost from below, and Owen hooked his arm around the stovepipe chimney on the roof and pulled. His clawed arm and bitten leg screamed in pain, but he made it up.

Owen lay on his back and panted for a few seconds, then turned and saw Nanuq coming straight for the cabin. *George!* Owen slid around on his belly, his arm and leg leaving red blood trails in the snow, and helped pull George through the hole.

"*Kick the chair over!*" Owen whispered.

George wriggled around, and Owen heard the *clack-clack-clack* of the folding chair collapsing. Now Nanuq couldn't use it to follow them up.

Owen pulled George the rest of the way onto the roof, and they flopped on their backs, breathing hard, but safe. A skiff of snow fell on them, soft and pretty against the darkening gray sky.

Crunch. Crunch. Creak. Owen heard Nanuq padding through the snow and stepping up onto the stairs at the front of the cabin.

Owen suddenly remembered the polar bear welcome mat they'd stepped over to come inside.

"Nanuq!" Owen hollered over the side of the roof. "Look out for the nails!"

George punched him. "Dude, what are you doing? If he stepped on that, he'd be too hurt to chase us, and we could get away!"

"Yeah, but that's just mean," said Owen. "I don't want to hurt him."

George shook his head and winced with pain. The bandages Owen had wrapped around George's head were soaked through with blood, just like the ones on Owen's arm and leg. They both needed a break. And a hospital.

Down below, Nanuq ignored the chewed-up bear couch and climbed in through the window. The flimsy little cabin rocked from the weight of the big polar bear moving around inside it, and Owen thought again about the Inuit story George had told him, the one about polar bears turning into people inside human houses. The way Nanuq was clattering around underneath them sounded almost like a person making dinner.

Owen felt a little tingle of magic at the idea. What if Nanuq *had* turned into a human being down there? If he didn't look now, he would never know.

As slowly and stealthily as he could, Owen slid back around to the hole and peeked inside the house.

PEEK-A-BOO

Nanuq was definitely a polar bear, not a person. He was huge and white, and stood on all fours, filling the little shack.

And he was looking right back up at Owen.

Their eyes locked, and Owen suddenly felt a connection as strong as anything he'd ever felt with his parents or with George. He understood at once why the Inuit would think that polar bears were human beings in disguise. There was something *there* behind those eyes. Something thoughtful and sensitive. Something intelligent.

Nanuq took a swipe at Owen with a claw, and Owen yelped and pulled away just in time to miss being slashed. Nanuq huffed and stood up on his back legs, and suddenly he was tall enough to stick his head right up through the hole in the roof.

George scrambled backward with the shotgun in his good hand, aiming it high over Nanuq's head. *PAKOW! PAKOW!* He fired off two cracker shells in a row, and Nanuq dropped back down on all fours.

Owen watched over the side as the polar bear burst through the hole in the corner of the shack, tearing off a bigger piece of the wall. The rickety little building groaned and shuddered, and Owen and George threw their hands out to steady themselves. The shack creaked and settled, but finally held, and Owen and George each let out a long, steamy breath of relief.

"Where is he?" George said, scanning the horizon. "We can't lose sight of him."

Owen crawled up to the top of the roof and looked over the other side. "I see him," he said.

"What's he doing?" George asked.

"He's pooping."

"Nice," said George.

"I think it might be a comment on our cracker shells," said Owen. "How many of those do we have left, by the way?"

"We had six to start, once I reloaded." George held up one of his mittens, presumably counting off on his fingers as he spoke. "I fired one at the lake, one right before we got here, two more just now. We have two left."

That wasn't good news. Worse, the two cracker shells might have scared the poop out of Nanuq, but they hadn't scared him away.

Nanuq finished leaving his Yelp review and circled the cabin again. The roof was slanted enough that Owen and George could see in one direction while still lying on their backs, and Nanuq chose that side of the cabin to nestle down on the snow where he could watch them back.

George gave Owen a look, and Owen knew his friend was wondering if he should try another cracker shell. He nodded and put his hands over his ears. If that bear wasn't going anywhere, neither were they.

PAKOW!

Nanuq jerked, got to his feet, rose up on his hind legs, and sniffed the air. He opened his mouth wide to show off his teeth, said *"HAROOF,"* and sat back down in the snow.

"Uh-oh," said George.

"Yeah," said Owen. If Nanuq had decided that the cracker shells weren't that scary anymore, they were in serious trouble.

Nanuq closed his eyes and laid his white paw over his black nose, making himself completely white. Owen and George looked at each other and snorted. If they hadn't been staring right at him when he did it, Nanuq might have been invisible against the snow. Now it just felt like he was a little kid covering his own face and thinking he was hidden.

"You chucklehead!" Owen yelled. "We can still see you!"

Nanuq didn't budge. Maybe he thought they'd forget.

"We could slip away while he's not looking," Owen whispered.

"Yeah, I don't think that's going to work," said George. He tapped his nose, reminding Owen of the polar bear's keen sense of smell. "And now we're down to one cracker shell. *If* he's even still afraid of them." George sighed and settled in. "Looks like we're just going to have to wait him out."

ROOF DREAMS

A light, thin snow continued to fall as dusk set in, and Owen and George tightened up their parkas and mittens. They had been almost too warm while they'd been walking, sweating inside their heavy winter clothes. Now that they were stationary, they both started to shiver.

"It's not really his fault," Owen said after a while. "Nanuq, I mean." Owen was trying to not only pay attention, but to *think* more. And now he was thinking about the polar bear lying in wait for them down below.

"Nanuq's not hunting us because he's evil or anything," Owen said. "He's just hungry."

"So am I," said George.

Owen looked down at Nanuq still pretending to be invisible against the snow. He remembered the look they'd shared, the intelligence in Nanuq's eyes.

"Yeah, but it's *our fault* he's hungry. Not me and you specifically, but everybody's. It's humanity's fault," Owen said, really seeing the connection for the first time. "We're the ones heating up the planet and making the sea ice melt earlier and come later. If there's no sea ice, Nanuq can't catch seals, which means he has to find his meals somewhere else."

"I get that," said George. "I just don't want his next meal to be me."

Owen nodded. Suddenly he remembered that time in third

grade when the *people* of Churchill had been stuck without a lot of food to eat. The spring floods had washed away the train tracks into town, cutting Churchill off from the rest of the world. Owen had been a little kid back then, so it hadn't been much more than an inconvenience to him. There hadn't been any new movies at the theater for a while, and the canteen at the town center had run out of his favorite candy. And it was actually kind of fun, in a way, because no train meant no tourists, which meant Owen's mom and dad had lots more time to play games with him and go exploring together all over Cape Churchill.

But Owen saw things differently now. The tracks washing away had exposed how tenuous life was up here in the north. Not just for the polar bears, but for the people too. With no train service, every single thing the town needed—every apple, every can of pop, every piece of lumber, every new shirt and pair of shoes—had to be flown in by plane, which cost a fortune. The price of living skyrocketed, and nobody was making any money. It took a year and a half for the tracks to be repaired, and in that time, a lot of people moved away. They couldn't survive in Churchill anymore.

"You think maybe we shouldn't be here?" Owen asked.

"Up on this roof?" said George. "Duh—yeah."

"No, I mean our town. Churchill. We build a city right in the middle of the polar bears' migration route, and then we spend all this time and money and energy trying to keep them out," said Owen. "But Churchill is in the *exact spot* where polar bears have come to sit and wait for the sea ice to form every fall for thousands of years. *Hundreds* of thousands of years. I mean, I don't know, maybe we should have built a town somewhere else? And if the Port of Churchill *does* actually do more business as the sea ice melts, it's just going to mean more people and more trouble for the bears. I hate to say it, George, but maybe your parents have the right idea."

Owen heard George shaking his head beside him. "People gotta live too," George said. "We just have to find a way to live together. *With* nature, not against it. I mean, we *are* nature."

Owen turned to look at his friend. "Dude. That is deep. Did your granddad teach you that?"

"No," said George. "I heard it from that survivor guy on TV who peed into a snake skin and then drank it."

"Nice," said Owen.

NORTHERN LIGHTS

Owen checked on Nanuq. He was still lying in the snow. Still hiding his snout with his paw.

Sneaky boogerhead.

"I'm going to say something," George said. "To my parents. I want to stay in Churchill."

Owen turned to look at George again. "I'm sorry I gave you crap for being down on Churchill. I had no idea your dad lost his job."

"No, you were right. I was being really negative because it made it easier to leave if I hated Churchill, you know? And I didn't want to rock the boat," said George. "But I have to tell my parents what I want, even if it seems hopeless."

"Yeah," said Owen. "And you and me will come up with some way you can stay."

"Deal," said George, and they lifted their mittens and gave each other a fist bump.

"Hey. Check it out," George said. He nodded in the direction they'd been walking when they'd found the shack. It was dark now, and the winter sky was alive with the twisting, dancing, ghostly green lights of the Aurora Borealis. The northern lights. They writhed in the air like giant spectral snakes. You could see them all the time up here in Churchill, but Owen never failed to be mesmerized by them.

"Awesome," said Owen.

"No, underneath that," said George.

Owen looked down. George wasn't talking about the northern lights. He was talking about the big rusty shipwreck lit up by the green light of the Aurora Borealis.

"The *Ithaka*. Hudson Bay!" Owen cried. Either he'd been too focused on Nanuq to see the bay before, or they'd needed the Aurora Borealis to illuminate it. He scolded himself for not paying attention, but he wasn't too hard on himself. The important thing was, they'd made it all the way back. They were so close to home. Churchill was just a little way off to the west.

"Dude. I'm freezing my ice off out here," Owen said. "We need to get going."

"I think we've got bigger problems," George said, and he sat up and pointed.

Owen gaped. Another polar bear as big as Nanuq—maybe bigger—had just come out of the darkness to join their little party.

MIAMI, FLORIDA

PART 4

HERE COMES THE SUN

Hurricane Reuben had stopped, suddenly and completely, like somebody flipping a switch.

Was Natalie dreaming? She held her breath and listened, but all she heard was the drip-drip-dripping of water. Outside the rooftop storage shed, the bright Florida sun shone in a cloudless blue sky.

Natalie looked down at the dog in her arms. Churro was frozen, as if he too couldn't believe it was over. And was that a look of fear in his eyes as he looked up at her? Fear of *her*?

Truth be told, Natalie was a little scared herself. She had barked at the storm, and the storm had tucked its tail between its legs and run away.

Natalie trembled as she got to her feet. She was shaking with exhaustion, buzzing with adrenaline. Her feet had trouble working, and she stumbled as she stepped out of the shed.

There was half a foot of water on the roof, and the manatee still floated lazily in the pool. But there was no wind. No rain. No hurricane. Just bright sun and blue sky and an eerie silence.

Natalie didn't know what to think. Shouldn't there be clouds? Rain? Even when a hurricane *missed* Miami, it poured for days.

Natalie held Churro tight and inched over to the edge of the roof. The street looked like a river, and she could see cars and boats stacked up against a flood control gate. And there, upside down and half-sunk at the top of the heap . . . was that the sailboat she'd been on? Natalie shuddered. She and Churro had gotten off just in time.

Natalie gave the pool a wide pass and glanced over the other side. Everywhere she looked, the city and ocean and swamp were all one. A few taller buildings stood up out of the floodwaters like castles with moats, and the tops of palm trees and electric poles sprouted from the water like mangroves. Cars and boats and parts of houses floated by. In the street-turned-canal, train cars were piled up like a giant child had left his toys out.

Natalie caught movement out of the corner of her eye and turned to see an older white man staggering out from his hiding place a few buildings away, gaping and staring in disbelief. A Latino family stepped tentatively out onto the balcony of another apartment building. A white family emerged blinking from a sixth-floor condo. A young Black man emerged from the small rooftop stairwell on top of a completely submerged building, followed by half a dozen people who'd taken shelter in there with him.

On a third-floor balcony across the street, a metal shutter

protecting a sliding-glass door rolled up, and a young Black woman with orange Bantu knots in her hair came out on her balcony to record a video with her phone.

Natalie didn't see the Evans family, or Isabel and her kids. She put a hand to her mouth, thinking again about Javari falling into the water, and prayed that Marcus and Derek had been able to pull him out.

Natalie had her own people to find. But where was she? How long would it take her to get back home?

Below her, the building's fire escape was slowly emerging from the retreating water. Holding Churro close, Natalie climbed over the side of the roof and onto the metal balcony.

"No! No, everybody get back!" the Black woman with the orange hair cried. She waved frantically at Natalie and all the other people who were leaving their hiding places. "Get back! Take cover!" the woman yelled. "The storm's not over!"

Natalie frowned. What was she talking about?

"This is just the eye of the hurricane!" the woman yelled. *"The storm is coming back!"*

ROUND TWO

Natalie felt dizzy. *The eye of the hurricane.* **Of course!**

She'd read all about hurricane eyes, but she'd never been in one. The eye was that round dot in the middle of the swirling clouds of a hurricane. It was the focus of the storm, the place the rest of the hurricane rotated around. The eye was always super calm, because the powerful winds circling the eye never made it inside.

Natalie wanted to kick herself. She'd been so ready for the hurricane to be over that she'd completely forgotten about the eye.

A few blocks away, the water receded rapidly, building into a massive wave—a towering wall of water and wind and rain that swallowed buildings and palm trees and electric poles as it advanced.

And it was coming right for Natalie.

Natalie remembered to breathe. Every instinct told her to get back onto the roof and hide. But Reuben had been about to tear the little shed apart before, and round two looked like it was going to be even worse. The shed wasn't safe, but where else could she go?

Natalie looked around frantically. The only things she could see were the metal fire escape she stood on and the young woman with the orange hair on the balcony across the street waving people back into hiding.

And the jumble of train cars between them.

The idea came to Natalie in a flash. The woman across the street had a metal shutter to cover her sliding-glass door. She was dry. She had a *phone*. Which meant she had a safe place to ride out the storm.

A safe place Natalie could share, if she could get there in time.

Natalie looked back at the advancing eye wall, and her fear turned to resolve. She was tired of feeling overwhelmed by Reuben, done with letting him push her around. She was sick of being swept along by the current without any say about where she was going or how she got there.

It was time to take charge.

Without another thought, Natalie stuffed Churro into her hoodie, zipped it up tight, and ran down the fire escape stairs into the path of the storm.

NO TIME

On the other side of the street, the woman with orange hair saw Natalie running down the fire escape and waved her arms in warning.

"No! What are you doing?" she yelled. "Go back!"

Natalie ignored her. The piled-up train cars formed a crooked path across the street. She could get from one side to the other without ever going in the water—*if* she could outrun the advancing eye wall.

Natalie hugged Churro tight inside her hoodie and hopped from the last fire escape step onto the first boxcar.

"You're not going to make it!" the woman cried. "Go back!"

No, thought Natalie. *I have to make it.* There was no time for doubt.

The train car's roof was slippery, but Natalie found her balance and ran right down the middle of it. She jumped from that car to the next and stumbled, falling to her knees. She glanced up at the storm. The eye wall was moving so fast! Faster than she'd thought.

Natalie got up and ran, her shoes echoing loudly on the metal roof of the train car. She was almost there—almost to the second-floor balcony below the woman with the orange hair. But suddenly Natalie realized there was no way to climb up the outside of the building. She had to get inside and find the stairwell up to the third floor, and the water was almost on top of her.

No no no, Natalie thought. *How am I going to get up to the third floor before the storm surge catches me?*

More water pulled away from the train cars, sucking up into the steep slope of the swell, and Natalie suddenly had her answer.

At the front of the woman's building, Natalie changed course. Instead of climbing over the second-floor railing and trying to get inside, Natalie turned and ran down the roof of another train car.

One that led straight into the oncoming wave.

PATIENCE

"No!" the woman up above cried.

The storm surge was on Natalie in seconds. She had a heartbeat to take a deep breath, and then—*WHOOMP*—the wave swallowed her and swept her off her feet. In the blink of an eye Natalie was as high as the third-floor balcony and rushing past. She threw out her hands, grasping desperately for the railing, and found it. Her fingers banged against the balusters, slipped, clutched the bars again, and hung on tight as the water tore at her, trying to rip her away.

Then, suddenly, the crest of the wave was past, and the water level fell.

Natalie started to fall with it, but a hand grabbed hers, and she looked up to see the young Black woman with the orange hair, bent over the railing to catch her.

The woman pulled Natalie up onto the balcony and held her close as Natalie coughed and retched and tried to get her breath back. Inside Natalie's hoodie, Churro coughed and squirmed, swamped but not drowned.

Reuben was back at full power now, and he hammered them with gale-force winds and driving rain and flying debris. The woman pointed to the sliding-glass door behind her and leaned in close where Natalie could hear her.

"We have to get inside!" her rescuer yelled.

Natalie nodded. They had to hold each other to keep from

blowing away, but she and the woman managed to slip through the door and pull the rolling metal storm shutter down.

When it was done, when they were safe, they collapsed on the carpet inside and lay there in the dark, trying to get their breath back. Churro squirmed to get free, and Natalie found just enough energy to unzip her hoodie before letting her hand flop back on the floor.

With all the raging indignation only a Chihuahua could muster, Churro ran to the metal shutter and barked furiously at the hurricane outside, even though he couldn't see it.

Natalie didn't even try to tell him to be quiet. She understood. She and Churro were in the safest place they'd been since the back wall of her house crashed in, and still the building shook. The metal storm shutter wobbled. Rain lashed the roof, and the wind roared. It was like Reuben was furious he hadn't been able to catch Natalie out in the eye of the storm, and he wanted to let her know.

"I've seen some wild stuff in my day," the woman said at last. "But that just about takes the cake." She sat up and looked at Natalie. "You hurt?"

Natalie gave a single, tired laugh. What part of her *didn't* hurt? She lifted her head to look at herself. Her shirt was blood-stained and torn, and she had cuts and bruises all over from her battle from Reuben. But there was nothing that couldn't wait.

"I'm all right," Natalie told her. She closed her eyes and put her head back down. "I'm Natalie, and that's Churro."

"I'm Patience," the woman told her. "Welcome to my newly oceanfront apartment."

HURRICANE ZOMBIE

Natalie was happy to lie with her eyes closed on the damp carpet while Patience got up to dry off. Churro eventually got tired of barking at the storm and climbed up to lie down on Natalie's chest. He had to have been as worn out as she was.

"I can't believe you made it across those train cars," Patience said, coming back. "Here."

Natalie dragged her eyes open. Up close, Natalie saw that Patience had arching eyebrows, gold hoop earrings, and a diamond stud in her nose. She wore a black hoodie and black jeans, and held a towel and a change of clothes out for Natalie.

Natalie almost cried. She had begun to think she was going to be soaking wet for the rest of her life.

Patience helped Natalie up and pointed the way to the bathroom. Patience's apartment was small, with a bedroom and kitchen all connected to the main living room, where a cluster of candles burned on a coffee table. As Natalie stumbled blearily to the bathroom, she noticed a television, a case full of books, walls covered with posters of anime characters, and a bright orange kayak in the corner. Everything else was a blur of exhaustion.

A few tea lights glowed on the bathroom sink, and Natalie pushed the door closed and started to peel off her wet clothes.

"Where's home for you?" Patience called through the door. "What were you doing out in the storm?"

Natalie told Patience the short version of her story while she dried off.

"Wow. I'm sorry about your mom and your neighbor," Patience said. "I hope they're okay. I don't have any signal on my phone, but when it comes back, we'll try to call them, okay?"

Natalie wrapped her hair in the towel and stared at herself in the mirror. She looked like something that had been dredged out of the canal. She was damp. She was cold. She was tired and bruised. But she was alive. How could she say the same for her mother and Tía Beatriz?

"You said you're from Hialeah?" Patience asked, still talking through the door. "That's miles from here. This is Liberty City. Edge of it, at least."

Natalie knew Liberty City. It was a mostly Black community between Hialeah and Little Haiti. She couldn't believe she'd traveled so far.

"You're safe now," Patience told her.

Am I? Natalie wondered. *Will I* ever *be safe? How much worse will the next hurricane be? And the next? And the next?*

When she was as dry as she was going to get, Natalie put on the oversized sweatshirt and sweatpants Patience had loaned her and walked back into living room. She felt like a zombie. She wanted to pass out and sleep for days.

"Curl up on the futon there and I'll get you some water," Patience told her. "You hungry?"

"No, thank you," Natalie said, but her quiet words were swallowed up by the shriek of Reuben outside. She shook her head instead and crawled onto the futon. It was so weird to be in a stranger's house. She felt like she should make small talk. Ask Patience who she was and what she did. But the howling wind made conversation difficult. And she was tired. So tired.

Natalie pulled a blanket on top of herself and closed her eyes, and in seconds she was asleep.

In her dreams, Natalie saw a giant, swirling white storm as though she were looking down on it from space. It swallowed up the entire peninsula, and when it was gone, South Florida had been entirely erased from the map.

THE SIERRA NEVADA, CALIFORNIA

PART 5

PERSPECTIVE

Akira's arms and legs went weak, and she fought to hang on to the pine tree she'd climbed. She couldn't believe what she was seeing was true.

The giant sequoias were on fire.

The monarchs' shaggy leaves, so high off the ground that normal forest fires never touched them, were burning like torches now. The Morris Fire's flames were so big, so intense, that they could reach the top of a giant sequoia tree, two hundred and fifty feet in the air.

Akira closed her eyes. Just that morning her father had been reminding her that giant sequoias couldn't burn. That they were adapted to survive wildfires. And they were.

But they were built to survive *regular* wildfires. Not wildfires like this.

Akira cursed and shook the top of her tree in anger. She felt so helpless. And so *stupid*. Her father had said that the earth could take care of itself. That this was all part of a natural cycle. But if the giant sequoias—trees that had evolved not just to *withstand* wildfires but to *thrive* in them—if the *giant sequoias* were burning, the cycle was broken.

Akira felt her pink, fire-burned skin glow hot with shame. She had never challenged her dad on climate change because she hated to argue. She liked peace, and calm, and quiet. But staying quiet was the same as agreeing with him, and while she said and did nothing, her world was burning.

Her dad always told her to get higher when she needed a better perspective on things, and now she had it. Nature wasn't just going to fix itself. Not this time. Human beings had broken it, and it was up to human beings to fix it.

THOOM. Something exploded in the valley behind her, and Akira turned to look. A giant orange fireball in the shape of a mushroom cloud was pouring thick black smoke into the air. Akira had never seen anything like it before, except in pictures of wars. Had one of the smaller wildfires blown up a gas station?

The same hard, hot breeze that swept Akira's hair away from her face cleared the hazy smoke away from the valley, and Akira sucked in her breath as she realized what she was looking at. She had thought that the fires on this side of the mountain were small. Isolated. But they weren't. They were connected. All of them. The fire that had chased her and Dodger to the bald and the fire that lit up the gas station were part of one big fire, stretching back through the valley and around the base of the mountain she had just crossed.

It was Morris. It had always been Morris. The fire she had escaped with Sue, the fire that was burning the monarchs above her, the fire in the valley below. The same gigantic megafire burned up and down and around the mountain, connecting both sides.

Through the smoke, Akira spotted the firefighters she'd seen before down in the valley. She watched as they gave up trying to cut a firebreak, abandoning their bulldozers and backhoes to the fire and running away.

"No. No!" Akira cried. She didn't want the firefighters to get hurt, but she didn't want them to quit either.

Without the firebreak to stop it, Morris was headed right for Akira's house.

CHURCHILL, MANITOBA

PART 5

POLAR BEAR
THROWDOWN

Nanuq sensed the other polar bear immediately. He was up on all fours now, and Owen watched as the two big bears began to circle each other warily. Nanuq hissed. The new polar bear growled. They got closer and closer to each other, slowly wagging their heads back and forth and holding their mouths open. Owen knew what was going to happen next: These two bears were about to *throw down*.

Owen was excited. He'd seen polar bears fight from the safety of his parents' tundra buggy but never up close and personal like this. In the summer, male polar bears sparred the same way George and Owen did in their insult contests—for fun, and not really trying to hurt each other. Things only got low-down and dirty when they were fighting over mates in the spring—or fighting over hunting territory in the winter.

"Nanuq must have wandered into Boomer Bear's yard, and he's telling him to get off his lawn," said Owen.

George looked at him. "Boomer? Really?"

"Tell me he's not a Boomer."

Nanuq and Boomer put their ears back, stood on their hind legs, and slammed into each other with a resounding *thump*.

"*Whoa*," the two boys said, watching them battle. Owen couldn't take his eyes off the heavyweight fight, and neither could George.

The two polar bears pushed and pawed at each other until Boomer pulled away and took a swipe at Nanuq's head. Nanuq fell on his butt, and Boomer pounced. The two big bears rolled around in the snow, grunting and snapping and growling, totally oblivious to anything else in the world.

"This is exactly the kind of distraction we need to escape," George whispered.

The two boys looked at each other and blinked stupidly. What were they doing sitting here watching when they could be running away?

"Let's boogie," said Owen.

George slithered through the hole in the roof first, and Owen followed. When he was halfway down into the shack, Owen paused to take one last look at the battling polar bears.

"Good luck, Nanuq," he whispered. "You show that bully who's boss."

SHADOWS IN THE SNOW

Owen and George hurried away from the cabin, leaving the fighting polar bears behind. The northern lights cast a ghostly green color over the white world ahead of them until dark clouds rolled in and it began to snow, making it hard to see. The boys trudged on in their three-legged formation, shivering and sweating at the same time.

They didn't talk as they hiked. They were both too tired, and they had to use all their senses to orient themselves. In the distance, Owen thought he saw Miss Piggy, the old graffitied cargo plane wreck, but it was hard to tell through the thickening snow. He hoped they were that close to home.

It suddenly occurred to Owen that so many of the landmarks around town were ruins. Miss Piggy. The *Ithaka*. The old abandoned radar facility that looked like two giant golf balls. The Prince of Wales Fort. They were all failed attempts to impose western civilization on the merciless, untamable Arctic. Did the same fate await their whole town? Maybe one day Owen's family would be leading tundra buggy tours through the abandoned streets of Churchill. Showing tourists the falling-down, graffitied buildings that had been surrendered to the snow and ice and polar bears.

A huge dark shape standing up on two legs appeared ahead of them in the swirling snow, and Owen and George pulled up short. *Not another polar bear!* thought Owen, but George clapped him on the shoulder and shook him excitedly.

"It's the inuksuk!" George cried.

Owen saw it now—the tall stack of stones in the shape of a person. The one tourists posed with, that pointed the way into town. They were almost home! Owen and George hugged each other in happiness.

An immense sense of relief at being so close to the finish line washed over Owen, and he wobbled. When all this was over, Owen planned to curl up under a big, heavy blanket on his couch and not come out for months and months, like a momma bear in her den.

"Come on," said George. "We're almost there."

Their three-legged march took on more urgency now. A minute later, something new began to take shape in the snowy darkness, and George and Owen slowed again. Owen was so exhausted he wanted to cry. If this was Nanuq—or worse, Boomer—he might just lie down in the snow and be done with it.

But whatever the shape was, it wasn't moving. George and Owen approached it slowly. Cautiously. And as they got closer, Owen finally understood what they were looking at.

BING, BANG, BOOM

The shadowy thing wasn't a polar bear. It was a polar bear *trap*.

Owen had seen traps like this all over town and knew exactly how they worked. The main part of the trap was a big, round metal pipe, like the ones that ran under roads to let creeks and streams pass underneath. One end of the pipe was open, with a big trap door suspended above it like a guillotine. The other end was covered by a sturdy metal grate with a big stinky hunk of meat hanging on it to lure a bear into the trap.

When a polar bear climbed inside and took the bait, the trap door on the front would slam closed, and bing, bang, boom, you had yourself a polar bear.

And since the whole trap was built on a trailer, all the DNR had to do was come around in the morning, hook the trap to a pickup truck, and haul their prisoner off to Polar Bear Jail.

"Holy crap! Look out!" George cried, and to Owen's surprise George climbed up inside the bear trap.

"George, what are you *doing*?" Owen asked.

Owen sensed something behind him and turned. There was Nanuq, as big as life and almost on top of them.

"Holy crap!" Owen cried, and he scrambled up inside the trap behind George.

George and Owen slid all the way to the back of the trap, near the stinky hunk of meat. They were safe from Nanuq for the moment, unless—

Thu-thump. Nanuq put his front paws up on the edge of the metal pipe and sniffed at it, like he was thinking about coming in after them.

"No no no no no!" Owen cried, and he reached up and yanked on the hunk of meat.

"No, wait!" George cried, but it was too late.

WHA-CLANG! The trap door at the front slammed shut, separating them from Nanuq.

George and Owen sat in the dark pipe and panted, their breaths coming out in quick, cloudy bursts.

"We're safe now," Owen said in between wheezes. "We're safe."

"Yeah," said George. "But now we're caught in a bear trap."

PART 5

SOLAVAYA

It wasn't a sound that woke Natalie, but the absence of sound.

Reuben wasn't howling anymore. Rain wasn't lashing the roof. Wind wasn't vibrating the windows.

Vague memories of her dreams haunted Natalie as she blinked and rubbed her eyes. Where was she? How long had she been asleep?

Natalie propped herself up and looked around. Saw a TV and a bookcase and anime posters. A kayak in the corner. Churro asleep at her feet.

On the table next to the futon was a framed photo of a young Black woman and an Asian American girl, posing in front of an enormous tree. Natalie recognized the woman in the photo.

Patience. She was in Patience's apartment.

The sliding-glass door to the balcony was open, and bright

sunlight spilled in from outside. Patience stood in the doorway, looking weary and sad.

"Hey," Natalie said, still groggy. "Sorry. How long was I asleep?"

"All night and half the morning," said Patience. "You were zonked."

"Is it over?" Natalie asked.

"In a way," said Patience. "And in a way it's just getting started. Come and see."

Natalie joined Patience on the balcony, and Churro got up to follow her. The wind was still blowing a little and a light rain fell even though the sun was out, neither of which was unusual for South Florida.

Otherwise, the city was completely unrecognizable.

Miami had been carved out of the swamp a hundred years ago, and now the swamp had returned. The Everglades to the west, the ocean to the east, the city in between, they were all one giant body of water. The few houses that still stood were tiny islands, separated not by streets but by wide brown canals.

There were boats in the new canals, but not in a way that could help. Reuben had cleared the coastal marinas of their sailboats and yachts and dragged them five miles inland and dumped them on their sides in parking lots. Cars and trucks were upended and swept up in piles like Matchbox cars. Trees were stripped completely clean of their leaves. Telephone poles were snapped in two, and downed power lines covered everything in a tangle of black silly string.

Natalie picked Churro up and held him close. How in the

world had they survived all that destruction? And how would they survive what came next?

"Adios, Reuben," Natalie said with venom. "Solavaya."

"What does that mean?" Patience asked.

"It's something my Cuban math teacher says when we finish our standardized tests," Natalie explained. "It means, like, 'good riddance.'"

Patience nodded. "Solavaya, Reuben," she repeated, and they shared a small smile.

Churro barked at the wreckage below, and Natalie turned to look. Someone was trying to climb up out of the water on a half-buried tangle of two-by-fours and sodden drywall.

"Hey!" Natalie called out to him. "Hey, are you all right?"

The man didn't move, and he didn't yell back. He just hung there on the pile of debris, motionless.

Natalie gasped and took a step back. That man wasn't climbing the wreckage. He was dead.

"Oh God," Patience said. She turned Natalie away quickly and steered her inside. "I'm sorry. I didn't see him before."

"My mom," Natalie cried. "Tía Beatriz—"

Patience hugged her close. "It's all right," Patience told her. "I'm sure they're safe."

Natalie couldn't believe that. But she couldn't *not* believe it either. Otherwise she would collapse right there on the floor.

"Is your phone working yet?" Natalie asked.

Patience shook her head. "There's still no signal. I'm sorry."

Natalie bit back a sob. She needed to talk to her mother. But how? When?

"You're not alone anymore, Nat," Patience told her. "I'm with you now. We're gonna get through this together, all right?"

Natalie nodded. "What about you?" she asked. "Is your family okay?"

"I grew up here, but my mom and dad got tired of all the hurricanes and moved us to California when I was in high school. They're still out there. They're fine," said Patience. "I'm the one who was fool enough to come back to Miami. I run a community food bank here in Liberty City. That's where I need to get to now. See if I can help folks."

"What, now? How?" Natalie asked. She saw Patience's kayak in the corner. Of course! That's how she planned to get around the city after the hurricane.

"Wait," Natalie told her. "You can take me in the kayak to look for my mom!"

"Oh, Nat," Patience said. "Take you to look *where*? You washed up five miles away from home. Your mom could be anywhere now."

Natalie swallowed. She knew Patience was right, but she was so desperate to find Mama and Tía Beatriz again. To be safe.

To be home.

Patience squeezed her shoulder.

"Best thing is to get you in touch with the Red Cross," Patience told her. "They'll be helping people find each other. And as soon as I get phone service back, you can call your mom. In the meantime, there's a lot of people in Liberty City who could use our help. This is only going to get worse before it gets better."

Natalie nodded. She was impressed that Patience could think of other people and not herself at a time like this. But it all felt so hopeless.

"The time to do something was *before* the hurricane hit," Natalie said, "not after it."

"Oh, I totally agree," said Patience. "We need to have ways to evacuate people in the path of a storm who can't afford to leave, or places they can go to be safe if they can't get out in time. We need to have warehouses full of emergency food and water and medical supplies *in advance*. And in between the hurricanes, we need to be working on climate change, because that's what's making all this worse in the first place."

Natalie was gobsmacked. Usually she was the one going on and on about climate change, and everybody else was telling Natalie to cool it. But Patience was *fired up*. Natalie got a little giddy thinking she might have met someone as passionate about all this stuff as she was. But it was hard to get truly excited about anything right now.

"But Patience, you saw what it's like out there," Natalie said. "We can't fix all that."

Patience nodded. "You're right. But we don't have to do everything, Nat. We just gotta do *something*."

PART 6

HOME

Akira's house was barely visible in the thick, dark smoke as she and Dodger galloped onto her family's property.

They had managed to stay one step ahead of Morris on their ride down the mountain, but from the hot wind at her back and the way Dodger's ears were constantly focused behind them, Akira knew the wildfire was close.

Akira's long, one-story house sat on a flat piece of land with a small red barn out back. Akira glanced at the fenced-in area outside the barn. There was Elwood! He'd made it back. Akira let out a whoop of joy. Now if only her father and Sue's dad had made it back safe—

Someone was in the front yard, wetting down the house with a hose, and Akira recognized her at once.

"Mom!" Akira cried. She pulled Dodger up short and jumped down. Her mother tossed away the hose, and they ran into each other's arms.

"Akira, I was so scared I'd lost you," her mother said, wrapping her up in a hug.

"Me too," said Akira.

"What happened to you?" her mother asked. She held Akira away from her and took in all her scrapes and bruises. "And what's this?" she said, peeling back the dirty sock she'd used for a bandage. "You're burned! We have to get this taken care of!"

"Mom, I never found Dad," Akira said, trying not to cry.

"He's here! He's inside!" her mother told her. "I'll put Dodger in the pen. Go."

Akira thought she might burst. She ran inside the house, and there was her father, lying on the couch. Akira shed her backpack and ran into his arms.

"Akira!" he said, his voice raspy. "I tried to go back and look for you, but the police were blocking all the roads in and out of the fire." He sobbed into her hair as he hugged her tight. "I hated to leave you. I was so sure you were dead."

"I thought you were too," Akira said, and now she was crying.

"Kira!" her little sister, Hildi, yelled, running into the room. She threw herself onto the pile on the couch and hugged Akira with the ferociousness of a four-year-old. Akira laughed. It felt so good to be together with her family again.

Their mother joined them a minute later. She'd brought the box of bandages and antibiotic ointments from the bathroom, and she pulled Akira into a chair to see to the burn on her arm.

"You smell like smoke!" Hildi told Akira.

Akira wiped away her tears and chuckled. She felt like

she was going to smell like smoke for the rest of her life.

"Did Vicki call?" Akira asked as her mom cleaned her wound. "Is Sue okay?"

"Your call was the last one I got. There's been no phone service ever since," her mother said.

Akira turned to her father. "What about Sue's dad and the people from the other car?"

"Daniel and I found somebody to take the old couple to the hospital," Akira's dad said. His voice was ragged, and he was clearly having trouble breathing. "Daniel went with them. The smoke really did a number on them," he added, then coughed.

"On you too," Akira's mother said. "Drink your water."

"Who's Vicki?" Akira's dad asked after taking a sip. "What happened to Daniel's daughter?"

Akira told them as quickly as she could about escaping through the burning woods with Sue, raiding Nova's house, and finding Dodger in the pool. She stopped occasionally to hiss as her mother dabbed ointment on her burn.

"Dodger went swimming in a pool?" Hildi asked, and she cackled at the thought.

"Sue and I found a lady named Vicki in a big truck, and she drove Sue to the hospital. I hope they're okay," Akira said. "After that I went higher, Dad, like you always told me. To get some perspective."

"That's my girl," her dad said.

Akira swallowed. She didn't tell him the other perspective she'd gotten, about him and climate change. This wasn't the time for that.

Akira winced as her mother finished wrapping her burn with a gauze bandage. "You're going to have to see a doctor soon, but you can relax," her mother said. "You're home now. You're safe."

The TV was on with the volume turned down low, and Akira saw live coverage of the enormous fire filmed from a helicopter. Suddenly it all came washing back over her. Running through the flames, finding the burned bodies, watching Morris wrap his fiery arms around the mountain . . . Akira closed her eyes. She was so tired. She wished she *could* relax. She wanted nothing more than to curl up on the couch with her family and never have to think about Morris again. But Akira knew she couldn't. Her mother was wrong. Akira *wasn't* safe. None of them were.

Akira stood up. "Mom, Dad, we can't stay here," she told them. "The wildfire is on the way. Cal Fire couldn't contain it. It's headed for our house!"

"Oh no!" Hildi cried, and she ran for her mother's arms.

"Akira, Akira," her dad said, raising his hand. "You're over-reacting. We're going to be fine where we are."

"What? No!" Akira said. "If we get in the car right now, we can make it, but we have to be fast. Where's the Go Bag?"

Like a lot of California families, the Kristiansens had a Go Bag at the ready if they needed to escape a wildfire or an earthquake. The bag held things like money and respirator masks and paper maps and a first-aid kit and copies of their important documents. Luckily Akira's family had never had to use their Go Bag.

Until now.

Akira's mom shot a worried look at Akira's father, but he shook his head.

"Akira, stop," he told her. "We live in fire country. We're prepared for this. The house is made of concrete, and we've got the generator running out back so we have electricity and water from the well. Your mom wet down the roof and the yard with the hose, and there's nothing burnable within a hundred feet of the house. We're good."

In the past, Akira would have accepted what her father told her. But not after what she'd seen. Not after what she'd been through.

"No!" Akira cried. "I've been out there. *You've* been out there," she told her father. "You've seen what's going on. It's worse than ever before, and we can't just close our eyes and pretend it's all going to sort itself out!"

Akira's little sister buried her head in her mother's shirt.

"Look. You're scaring Hildi," Akira's dad told her.

"She should be scared!" Akira yelled. "We should all be scared! Dad, the monarchs are burning!"

Her dad had been about to say something else, but he closed his mouth and frowned. "The trunks, maybe, but they're thick enough to—" he started to explain, but Akira cut him off.

"Not the trunks, Dad. The leaves and branches all the way at the top. *The Morris Fire is so bad it killed the giant sequoias.*"

Akira's mom and dad were speechless. Akira huffed. They didn't have time for this!

Akira ran to the last place she remembered seeing the Go Bag. It was still there, buried underneath boots and shoes on the floor of the front closet. Akira pulled the Go Bag out and picked up Nova's backpack.

"Get whatever else you need to take with you and get to the car," Akira told her family. "We've got to get the horse trailer hooked up so we can take Dodger and Elwood with us. But we have to hurry."

Akira threw open the front door and froze.

It was too late. Towering flames lit up the pine trees at the edge of their property like birthday candles, and her family's car and truck were on fire.

BLINDERS

"Oh my God!" Akira's mother cried. "How is the fire already here?"

Morris roared like a monster, and the blast of heat and wind made Akira throw a hand up and take a step back. The fire reached out toward the house with greedy arms, and embers pinged off the walls and windows. One of the embers landed on the rug in the entryway and set it on fire.

Akira threw the door closed and stomped out the flame.

"Do you believe me now?" Akira shouted.

Her mother stood with Hildi in her arms, and her father was sitting up. But they weren't moving. They knew they were in trouble but weren't *doing anything*.

Akira looked this way and that, trying to think. "I don't know where we go now. I don't know what we do!" she said. The time for doing something about the fire was *before* it got here, not after.

"We need to get in a pool, like Dodger," Hildi whined.

"Not a pool—the lake!" Akira cried. Of course. There was a lake about a quarter of a mile behind their house. Akira kissed Hildi on the head and raced to the windows that looked out on the backyard. The barn was already on fire, and Dodger and Elwood were running around their pen in a panic. But Morris hadn't completely surrounded the house. Not yet. They still had a chance, but they had to leave *now*.

"If we can get to the lake, we can swim out to the island," Akira told her family. "Come on. We'll be safe there."

"We're safe *here*," her father said, not moving from the couch.

"Lars, look at that fire!" her mother snapped. "Akira's right." She turned to Akira. "But we'll never make it to the lake on foot. The fire's moving too fast."

"We can ride on Dodger and Elwood!" Akira said. "They're still saddled up. Dodger's already been through the fire once, and Elwood will follow wherever he leads."

Akira's dad pushed himself up off the couch, wheezing from the smoke he'd breathed in escaping Morris the first time. Akira thought he'd finally listened to reason, but *still* he shook his head.

"Akira, you're just making things difficult. Let me get the hose," he said, coughing. "Ume," he said to Akira's mom, "get the fire extinguisher from the kitchen."

"The hose? *The fire extinguisher?*" Akira cried. "Dad, you have to be kidding! Morris is a *megafire*! It's too late for that!"

"The house isn't going to burn down, Akira," he said. "This has happened before. The fire will go around us, like it always does. We just have to wait it out."

Akira closed her eyes and fought back tears. She took a deep breath. "Dad, I don't know why you don't believe in climate change," she said, "and now is definitely not the time to argue about it. But for whatever reason, you've got blinders on when it comes to what's really happening out there, and it's going to get us all killed."

"*Akira,*" her dad said, his voice stern. But this time Akira's mom cut him off.

"We're going," she said. *"All of us,"* Akira's mom added, looking at her husband. "And that's final."

Akira's father looked like he was still going to argue, but Akira's mother hiked Hildi up on her hip with one arm and pushed her husband toward the back door with the other. Akira followed them with her backpack and the Go Bag.

The heat outside was like a physical assault, and they all staggered. The fire had moved to the trees along the sides of the property, and as Akira and her family watched, flames leapt from tree to tree to tree until the circle was complete. In the time they had taken to argue about it, the fire had completely surrounded their house.

"What do we do now?" Akira's mother cried.

Dodger and Elwood ran in circles in their pen, heads and tails up, ears swiveling, eyes darting back and forth. They were spooked so badly that Akira knew there was no way she could steer either of them calmly through the inferno. The horses would panic and throw them.

"Back into the house," said her father.

"No, look!" Akira cried.

She pointed to the roof, where red-hot embers had already landed and caught the asphalt shingles on fire.

"I don't believe it," her father whispered.

Akira huffed. There were those blinders again. Why did he refuse to see what was right in front of him?

"Blinders!" Akira said aloud. "Wait here!" she added, and she ran for the burning barn.

THOUSAND-POUND SCAREDY-CATS

"Akira, no!" her mother shouted, but Akira was already at the door of the burning barn. Akira put an arm up to block the heat radiating off the wood and stepped inside. The horses' blinders hung on a wooden wall that was turning black and buckling from the fire. Akira snatched the blinders and ran back out.

"Mom! Help me!" Akira cried. Her mother handed Hildi off to Lars and hurried over.

"See if you can get these on Elwood," Akira said, giving her mom a set of blinders. "I'll take care of Dodger."

Akira ran to intercept Dodger on one of his panicked circuits around the yard. "Dodger!" she cried, then caught herself. This wasn't going to work if she was freaking out too.

"*Dodger,*" Akira said more evenly, trying to calm her own panic. "Hey, boy. I just need to get these blinders on you. Can we do that? Huh?"

Dodger stopped running and stood a few yards away from Akira, his eyes still spinning wildly in his head.

Horses had monocular vision, which meant they looked at things separately with each eye, rather than together with both eyes like humans. And they could see up and down and forward and back, which made them really good at spotting danger. Almost too good. Add in the fact that horses did *not* like to be surprised, and you had thousand-pound scaredy-cats that saw danger everywhere. Blinders kept horses looking straight forward, and what they couldn't see everywhere else couldn't spook them.

"Dodger, I need you to help me and my family right now, okay?" Akira said, keeping her tone as steady as she could. "I need you to take us through the fire one last time. Can you do that?"

Dodger snorted. He tilted his head and gave her a look that stared deep into her soul, like he wasn't buying any of this. His look seemed to say, *Are you kidding me right now?*

"I know, I know," Akira told him, her heart thumping. Out of the corner of her eye, she saw her roof fully on fire. *Her house was on fire!* She felt herself starting to hyperventilate, and she fought down the terror that was threatening to swallow her.

She had to think of a way to get these blinders on Dodger, or they were all going to die.

UP IN SMOKE

Akira suddenly remembered the last time she'd tried to get Dodger to do something he didn't want to do—get out of Nova's pool. No matter how much she'd pulled and begged and whispered encouraging words, he hadn't budged.

Not until Sue had tempted him with an apple.

Akira smiled at the memory of her two best friends getting to know each other better. She quickly slid Nova's backpack off her shoulder and fished around inside, keeping eye contact with Dodger the whole time to make sure he didn't run away.

"Look. An apple, see?" she said, pulling one out. "Your favorite."

Even with the fire all around them, Dodger couldn't help himself. He stepped forward to take the apple from Akira's hand, and Akira held his bridle while she fixed the blinders into place.

"Always a sucker for an apple," she said, putting her head against his.

"Akira!" her mother yelled. She'd gotten the blinders on Elwood and was putting Hildi up in the saddle. "I'll ride with Hildi on Elwood. You and your father take the lead on Dodger. Hurry!"

Akira mounted Dodger and rode over to her father, who'd gotten masks for all of them out of the Go Bag. She helped him up behind her and put on her mask. Her father was having an even harder time breathing now, and she could feel him wheezing.

Akira turned Dodger toward the dirt trail. The woods all around it were a wall of flames. It was only a ten-minute ride down to the lake, but that was *without* a raging inferno all around them

"We have to be fast," Akira's mom said. "We can't stop for anything."

Akira nodded. She knew what it was like to ride through fire. She had the burns to prove it.

KISSSH! KISSSH!

The windows on their house shattered, and flames licked through the frames. Dodger danced underneath her, and as Akira fought to keep him under control she felt a sudden pang of loss for all the things she hadn't had time to take with her. Her favorite books. Her iPad. Her clothes. Her diary. Morris was eating up everything she had ever owned. Everything she was. And what about all her parents' things? Her father's anime collection. Her mother's jewelry box. The framed photos of her mother's ancestors, all the way back to when they'd first come to California from Japan. The clock her Norwegian grandfather had made. It was all on fire.

"I can't believe it," her father said again.

Maybe now you will, Akira thought. She kicked her legs, and off Dodger went, down the fire-edged trail.

A CLEAR PATH

The sunburn heat on the path was immediate and intense.
Entire trees were outlined in white-orange flame, and the forest
floor writhed, alive with fire. Only the dirt path straight ahead
of them was free of flames.

Akira heard Hildi cry out and wanted to look back, but she
had to keep her eyes on the trail.

"They're okay," Akira's father told her. "They're right behind
us. Keep going!"

Akira spurred Dodger on, and he broke out in a fast trot.
Without his height, without his speed, she and her father would
never have survived the dash through the fire. And Elwood was
doing the same for Akira's mother and sister.

Akira felt herself choke up. Dodger was putting himself
through this awful danger just because she had asked him to.
She patted his withers and told him what a good horse he was.
Whether he heard her over the roar and crackle of the fire, Akira
didn't know, but she thought he understood. The two of them
shared a connection that went beyond words and actions. It was
the purest connection Akira had had with anybody or anything
in her entire life.

Dodger could still see the flames ahead of them with his
blinders on, but his focus was on the flat dirt path that created
a narrow firebreak through the burning woods. For years Akira
and her dad had been keeping the path clear by moving fallen

branches and tree trunks to either side of the trail, but now those same trees and branches were easy fodder for Morris. They burned like kindling, creating a searing three-foot-high wall of flame on either side.

Akira's father hacked and coughed uncontrollably behind her, and the two of them bent low trying to escape the heavy smoke and the burning tree branches. Akira was bathed in sweat all over again, and her burns radiated with pain. How far had they gone? How much longer did they have to go? Everything looked different in the fire. All of Akira's old landmarks were gone.

Suddenly Dodger came to a stop, right in the middle of the burning path. Akira didn't understand. She spurred him on, but he wouldn't budge.

"Akira! What's wrong?" her mother cried. Because Dodger had stopped, Elwood had stopped too. Now they were all roasting in the searing heat.

"*Akira*," her father said, coughing so much he could barely speak. "*Make him go.*"

"I'm trying!" Akira called back. "Dodger, what's wrong?" she asked.

He couldn't answer her, of course. Akira looked all around, trying to figure out what was making him hesitate. The path ahead of them was clear. Everything else was blazing trees and burning ground and black smoke, but that's what the forest had looked like from the very beginning. Akira slumped in the saddle, feeling helpless and lost. What was Dodger trying to tell her that she didn't understand?

HORSE SENSE

Akira squeezed her legs and flicked the reins again, but Dodger wouldn't move.

Come on, Dodger! Akira thought. *We're burning up out here!* The heat was scalding them. Cooking them. Behind her, Akira could hear Hildi sobbing.

"Akira! Tell him to go!" her father cried.

"We have to move!" Akira's mom yelled.

I know, I know! Akira thought. She felt the flames growing hotter and taller as the seconds ticked away, but she didn't know what to do.

Akira was just about to give up when she noticed Dodger's ears. They were focused in on a big redwood up ahead. The tree was on fire, but so was everything else. There didn't seem to be anything special about it.

Akira didn't understand. The path ahead of them looked safe, at least as far as she could see. But Dodger was telling her they couldn't keep going on like they had before.

Like when all those animals ran by us on the way down the mountain, and I didn't listen, Akira thought.

Or when I try to tell my dad about climate change and he refuses to hear it, she realized with a start.

If Akira kept her blinders on, if she ignored Dodger and pushed on despite his signals, she would be as bad as her dad. Dodger was trying to warn her, the same way the earth was trying to warn them when the monarchs burned. *Something is wrong here. Danger. Change course.*

Akira thought again about the unspoken connection she and Dodger shared. She didn't know what Dodger and his horse sense knew. But Dodger trusted her, and she had to trust him back.

"Okay, Dodger, you've got the reins," she said, letting them go slack. "Tell us where we need to go!"

Dodger understood, and without another moment's hesitation he turned and plunged off the trail into the burning woods.

CHANGING COURSE

Without the dirt trail underneath them, Akira, her father, and Dodger were completely engulfed in flames. Fire licked at Akira's jeans, her shirt, her hands, her face. Behind them, Hildi screamed. Elwood had followed Dodger into the inferno.

"Akira!" her father cried. "What are you doing? Why did you leave the path? We're going to die out here!"

CHOOM! Akira flinched as something exploded with devastating force behind them. Dodger spooked and ran deeper into the burning woods, but Akira caught a glimpse over her shoulder of what it was that had frightened them. It was the redwood Dodger had been so focused on. The tree had spontaneously combusted, just like the one that had separated her and Sue from their dads, blowing apart from the inside like someone had set off a bomb.

As she watched, the top of the tree that hadn't exploded settled down on itself and—*Crick. Crack. SHOOM!*—fell right down on the trail, covering it in flaming wreckage.

If they had kept going down that path, if Akira hadn't listened to what Dodger was trying to tell her, they would all be dead.

Now they needed to not die in the fire.

"Hiyah!" Akira cried, kicking Dodger's sides. He was already galloping full tilt through the burning woods, but she wanted to let him know she was with him now, fully and completely. There was no turning back. No slowing down. Akira felt her clothes melting into her skin, felt the exposed parts of her skin blistering. Her father clung to her so tight she could barely breathe. Were her mother and Hildi still behind them? She hoped so, but couldn't look back. Akira held the reins, but it was Dodger who was taking the lead now, running on terror and instinct. She didn't even know if they were still headed toward the lake. All she could do was spur Dodger on faster. Faster.

A wall of fire rose in front of them, and Akira put her head down and slapped her heels against Dodger's side. "Go, boy! Go!" she cried, not knowing if he could hear her. It didn't matter. She knew he understood.

WHOOSH.

For a white-hot moment they were engulfed in flames, and Akira had the sense that every inch of her was on fire. That this was it. That she was going to end up like the people in the cars—a black mummy buried in the ash of the mountain forests she loved so much.

Then suddenly—*woompf*—they burst out of the fire and the ground fell away, and Akira went flying off her horse.

TAKING THE PLUNGE

Akira flailed, her arms and legs swimming in midair for a long, weightless moment until—

SHOOM.

Akira plunged into the iciest, coldest water she'd ever felt. The shock of it took her breath away. Water flooded into her mouth, her nose, her ears. Wrapped her up in its icy fingers and pulled her down, down, down until she thumped to the rocky bottom of the lake.

Akira kicked back up and burst from the frigid water, gasping and coughing. She spun as she treaded water, looking desperately for her father, her mother, her sister. Her mother came up first, then her father, with Hildi in his arms. They were alive!

And there were Dodger and Elwood, swimming along as calm as could be, like they were taking a dip after a hot afternoon on the trail. Akira laughed through a sob. *Dodger had done it. He'd led them safely to the lake.*

Akira turned back to look at the forest. Up above them, the ground ended with a six foot drop-off into the water. That's where they had gone flying. Everything beyond that point was a raging inferno of burning trees and black smoke and towering flames. That was what they had come through. What they would have been trapped in if Dodger and Elwood hadn't seen them through it and taken the plunge.

Akira could barely get her arms and legs to move, but together she and her family swam for the little island in the middle of the lake. Dodger and Elwood got there first, splashing their way up the short, rocky beach and shaking themselves off like dogs. Akira and her mother followed close behind, and they helped pull her father and Hildi onshore. When all four of them were safe, they collapsed near the edge of the water, hugging and crying and shivering violently from the cold.

Across the black water, the dark mountainside was orange with fire. As Akira watched, red embers floated out over the lake like fireflies. It might have been pretty, she thought, if it wasn't all so devastating.

The glowing embers drifted down slowly, gently, dying sizzling deaths on the surface of the water, and Akira got a sinking feeling in her stomach. All it would take was a strong gust of wind to carry more embers all the way to their little island.

"We're—we're not safe," Akira said, her teeth chattering. "Not even here."

She couldn't believe it. If they weren't safe from the fire here, on an island in the middle of a lake, where would they *ever* be safe? On the moon?

"We're going to—die of hypothermia before that," her mother said, still shivering uncontrollably.

Akira heard something thrumming above the roar and crackle of the wildfire, and she looked up. Against the smoky, moonlit sky, she saw a big two-rotor helicopter. It was coming down low to dip a big hanging bucket into the lake. Akira had seen Cal Fire using similar buckets to drop water on the fire.

Akira forced her legs to work and ran out into the freezing water. She jumped and waved her arms and yelled, and Hildi and her mother and father joined her. Akira was afraid the pilot wouldn't see them in time, but then a bright light on the helicopter clicked on and spotlighted them.

Akira and her family whooped and hugged each other with relief, and Dodger and Elwood pranced around them. The horses didn't understand what was going on, but were happy their people were happy.

"Stay where you are," the pilot said over a loudspeaker. "We'll come back and get you and the horses."

Akira wrapped her shivering arms around Dodger's head and put her face next to his. "You hear that, Dodger? You're going to fly in a helicopter!"

Dodger whinnied and nuzzled her face. Akira loved him so much. She was so glad she'd listened to what he was trying to tell her on the path.

The helicopter flew away, and Akira could hear the wildfire again, roaring and popping across the water. Morris was trying to tell them something too. He was saying that what was happening in the Sierra Nevada and everywhere else wasn't normal. That it *wasn't* part of the normal cycle of nature.

Akira's dad didn't want to hear that. She watched him hugging her mother and sister and she sighed, feeling the familiar tug of war in her heart. Akira loved her father. He was a good dad, and he cared about these mountains as much as she did. But he was dead wrong about what was happening to the world and what was causing it.

Akira hadn't said or done anything about climate change because she didn't want to ruin her relationship with her dad. But that wasn't her problem, she realized now. It was his. Akira didn't need to argue with her dad about climate change. She just needed to do what she knew was right. If her father didn't like that, that was on him.

Because she wasn't going to stay quiet anymore. Climate change was real and it was here, and Akira had to do something about it.

CHURCHILL, MANITOBA

PART 6

CAUGHT IN A BEAR TRAP

Owen looked around at their cold, cylindrical prison. A metal door locked one end shut, and a metal grate covered the other. There was no way out.

Owen shook his head. He'd been doing *so well*. Paying more attention. Until now.

"I'm sorry," Owen said. "I panicked."

George put a hand on Owen's shoulder. "No, man. I'm the one who crawled inside the bear trap. I wasn't thinking either. What did I expect Nanuq to do, leave us alone?"

A deep thrum vibrated through the bear trap—*THUMP-THUMP-THUMP-THUMP-THUMP*—and Owen felt a fresh rush of hope. He knew that sound. Everyone in Churchill did. It was a helicopter! Probably the DNR, out on polar bear patrol.

Owen and George crowded the metal grate. The helicopter was still a ways off, but they could see its searchlight cutting through the darkness, illuminating the falling snow. Had their parents sent the DNR out to look for them when Owen and George hadn't checked in?

George and Owen yelled and tried to work their hands through the squares in the grate to wave. But the holes were too small and the rotors were too loud, and a few minutes later, the helicopter thundered away without even knowing they were there.

George cursed, and Owen sagged. The momentary excitement had taken Owen's mind off the cold, but now he felt the wind and snow coming right down the metal pipe. Owen shivered uncontrollably. George felt it too, shuddering and folding in on himself to conserve heat.

"If we don't get out of here, the DNR's gonna find frozen Mac and Cheese when they make their morning rounds," Owen said through chattering teeth. "Come on. Let's try the door."

Together they crawled to the other end of the metal pipe, but there was no way for them to get at the crank that opened the trap door from the inside. The only other thing they found was a small door cut into the metal pipe and reattached with hinges. Owen guessed it was there for people outside the trap to be able to shoot the bear inside with a tranquilizer.

"Hey, it's open!" Owen said, lifting the little door with his hand. "And it's just big enough for one of us to squeeze through!"

"But where's Nanuq?" George whispered.

Owen crawled to the grate at the back again and scanned the dark, snowy tundra. He turned to George and shook his head. He didn't see Nanuq anywhere.

They waited, sitting as still and quiet as they could, but they heard nothing.

"Do you think he's gone?" George whispered.

"No. Do *you* think he's gone?" Owen whispered.

George shook his head. Neither of them was buying it. Nanuq was too clever. Too persistent. It was a trick. It had to be. But where was he?

There was nothing else for it. One of them was going to have to stick his head out the access hatch and take a look.

ARCTIC NINJA

Owen pulled off one of his mittens and held up a fist, and George immediately understood and did the same.

They shook their fists in unison—one, two, three, shoot!

Owen kept his fist tight for rock, and George covered it with paper. Owen rolled his eyes. They put their fists up again. One, two, three, shoot! Owen threw scissors, and George smashed them with a rock. Owen cursed silently, and George smirked. George always won at Rock, Paper, Scissors.

George scooted out of the way, and Owen crouched underneath the access hatch. He put his mitten back on, took a deep breath, and pushed the hatch up very, very slowly. When nothing happened, he squeezed his eyes shut and stuck the top of his head out of the hole. He expected Nanuq to be right outside, waiting to play Whack-a-mole with his head, but nothing happened.

Owen opened his eyes. It was dark out, and snowing harder than before, but he could see a few meters in every direction. There was no sign of Nanuq. It was like he had disappeared into thin air. *Wasn't that one of the Inuit stories about Nanuq?* Owen thought. He was beginning to believe it.

Owen dropped back inside.

"I don't see him anywhere," he whispered.

"Then we should go," George said.

Owen shook his head. Something about this wasn't right. "No. Not yet," he said.

George frowned. "Owen, Nanuq knows he can't get the last Pringles out of the can, and now he's gone. It's freezing, you're bleeding, I can't see straight, and we're right outside of town. We have to get out of here and get to the health center."

Owen sat back down. "No. You said it yourself. I don't *think*."

George looked even paler than he did before. "Owen, I'm sorry I said all that stuff in the insult contest."

"But you were right. About everything," Owen said. "It's like, I *see* things, but I don't think about what they *mean*. I've got to pay better attention. I've got to think about the big picture."

"Owen, I support your personal growth goals," said George. "But do you have to start *now*? What is there to think about here?"

"Polar bears can't disappear into thin air, no matter what the Inuit stories say," Owen told him. "So where did he go?"

"Underneath the trap?" George tried, but they both shook their heads. Nanuq was too big for that.

"No. Polar bears are arctic ninjas, remember?" Owen said. "So what do ninjas do?"

"Sneak around on rooftops. Kill people with throwing stars. Hide in plain sight," said George.

Hide in plain sight, thought Owen. He and George had the same thought at once, and their eyes went wide and their mouths formed Os of surprise and admiration.

"*He's out there in the snow with his paw covering his nose!*" Owen whispered.

CHILLIN' IN CHURCHILL

Hiding in plain sight. **George** and **Owen** had seen **Nanuq** do it before from the rooftop. That had to be what he was doing now. If they crawled through that hole right now, he'd be all over them in seconds and they would have nowhere to hide.

George put up a mittened fist, and Owen tapped it. "That's pretty good thinking for a white boy," George told him.

"Thank you," Owen said with a smile.

Now they just had to wait Nanuq out, and hope they didn't freeze to death first.

Owen and George settled in near the grate at the back. The metal was bitterly cold against Owen's back, even through his clothes, and the icy wind blowing through it threatened to turn him into a Popsicle.

George sat straight across from him, arms wrapped around himself and shuddering so hard Owen could hear his teeth rattle.

"Sure you don't want to give all this up?" Owen asked George.

George let out a little laugh. "Yeah. I mean, I don't need to be hunted across the tundra by a polar bear or go camping with you in a bear trap in the middle of a snowstorm ever again, but I'd still like to stay in Churchill. And I'm going to tell my parents that. If we ever get out of here."

Owen nodded and smiled.

Out of the corner of his eye, Owen caught the slightest hint of movement out in the snow. He grabbed George's foot and pointed.

Together they watched as Nanuq took his white paw off his black nose and stood up, shedding snow.

Owen and George silently pretend-boxed each other in excitement. They were right! That turd burglar had been sitting just a few meters away from them the whole time, pulling his toddler peek-a-boo trick. But Nanuq had run out of patience at last, and now he was turning and walking away into the snow.

"Dude!" George whispered.

"I know! Mac and Cheese for the win!" Owen said.

"Let's get out of here," George said.

"No, wait," said Owen.

"Not again! Owen, there's nothing to think about now. Nanuq is gone!" George told him.

"No, no. We're going," Owen said. "I just want to take something with us first."

DEAD MEAT

It was dark and cold and the snow swirled around them, making it hard to see. But Owen and George were out of the bear trap, and their fate was in their own hands.

And that fate was a big hunk of stinky meat.

Owen held the raw meat from the bear trap as far away from him as he could and turned his head away. The meat was stringy and gray with little streaks of pink in it, and it reeked like roadkill.

"Ugh. I think I just became a vegetarian," George whispered.

Owen hoped the hunk of meat would keep Nanuq busy long enough for them to stagger back to town without running into him again. Together they pushed the stinky thing up on top of the bear trap where Nanuq could see it and reach it. Neither of them knew how to reset the bear trap, and Nanuq was probably too smart to go inside it anyway.

Smarter than they'd been, at least.

"There you go, buddy," Owen said when they were done. "I know you're really hungry. Eat this instead of us."

"Okay. How do we tell him the meat's here?" George asked. "I mean, I know he can smell things miles away, but how do we know he's not headed for some trash can in town?"

"Nanuq!" Owen bellowed, banging on the side of the metal trap like it was a dinner bell. "Nanuq! Dinnertime! Come and get it!"

George slung the shotgun over his shoulder and dragged Owen away by his parka.

"*Are you nuts?*" George whispered. "I meant 'How are we going to let him know the meat's here *once we're gone.*' You're gonna get us killed!"

"What?" Owen said as they ran. "You know he's going to come back. Nanuq always comes back. Now there's something else for him to eat."

"Unless that meat's the appetizer, and we're the main course," said George.

Owen and George limped along on three legs again, breathing hard and not talking as they skirted the edge of a frozen lake. If they had to stop one more time, Owen wasn't sure he could get back up and start again. They had to get to town *now*, or it was all over.

Thump-thump thump-thump.

Owen and George looked at each other in a panic. That thumping—it sounded just like a polar bear running across the snow. But they'd left food out for him! Why hadn't Nanuq gone for the meat first? Or had he already scarfed it down and was now following the two boys who were bleeding *and* smelled like raw meat?

Owen shook his head. What an idiot he'd been. So much for paying attention and thinking big picture.

Owen staggered, throwing off their three-legged rhythm. He and George stumbled, slipped, and fell down face-first in the snow.

"Argh!" Owen cried. He was tired and hurt and about to be

run down by a polar bear, and now he had slushy, freezing snow down his pants too.

The sound got closer. *THUMP-THUMP-THUMP-THUMP-THUMP.*

Owen and George looked at each other with surprise and relief as they realized what they were hearing.

That wasn't the sound of a polar bear. It was the sound of a helicopter!

THE LAST
CRACKER SHELL

There was a helicopter somewhere right above them, but they couldn't see it in the snowstorm. And that meant it couldn't see *them*.

"Now! Shoot the last cracker shell now!" Owen yelled over the sound of the blades.

"What? No! There's no bear!" George cried.

"But maybe the helicopter will hear it," Owen told him. "Then they'll know where we are and they can rescue us."

Owen could see George doing the math in his head. "What if they *don't* hear us?" he yelled. "What if Nanuq comes back and we need that last cracker shell?"

Owen looked away. George could be right. What if he was just seeing what was in front of him, and not the big picture? Like when he watched the Weather Lady set pond bubbles on fire without thinking about what that meant for the rest of the world. Or how he'd only seen dollar signs in the melting sea ice, not the threat to the polar bears.

The thumping of the helicopter was starting to sound like it was going away from them. They had to make a choice.

Owen shook his head. It was dangerous to not pay attention and not think about the big picture, but it was equally dangerous to finally understand what was going on and not do something about it. Maybe worse.

"Do it, George!" Owen cried. "Do it now!"

George nodded. Owen put his mittened hands over his ears, and George pulled the trigger.

PAKOW!

The cracker shell was loud up close. But was it loud enough for the helicopter to hear over the sound of its own rotor? Owen wished they had a flare. The helicopter would definitely have seen that. But their flares were at the bottom of a lake, along with George's snowmobile.

Owen held his breath. He and George listened and watched the sky, hoping that any second now a helicopter would burst out of the snowstorm and see them.

THUMP-THUMP-THUMP-THUMP-THUMP.

"It sounds like it's getting closer!" George yelled over the echoing blades

"Then where is it?" Owen yelled back.

George shrugged. "Maybe it's circling us!"

The boys helped pull each other to their feet, and Owen spun around, searching the dark clouds for the helicopter. *Where are you?* he thought. *I can hear you, but I can't see you!*

Movement caught Owen's eye. He spun excitedly, only to have his heart catch in his throat.

"George!" Owen cried.

A polar bear was walking straight toward them out of the snowstorm.

George raised the shotgun and then sagged and lowered it as he remembered.

Nanuq was back, and they had fired their last cracker shell trying to signal a helicopter that wasn't coming.

SAY GOOD NIGHT

Nanuq had come back.

Nanuq *always* came back.

The big polar bear started to circle them, but they couldn't retreat any farther. They had a frozen lake behind them.

Think, Owen told himself. He ran through all the polar bear facts he'd memorized for the tundra buggy tour, but none of them helped here. The only one that came to him now was "If it's brown, lie down. If it's black, fight back. If it's white, say good night."

But I don't want to say good night! thought Owen.

George wrapped Owen's injured arm in his and waved the shotgun, trying to look big.

"Get, bear! Go on!" George yelled.

Owen waved his other arm. "Go away, Nanuq!"

Nanuq kept circling. Kept coming closer. Owen and George inched as far back against the frozen lake as they could go. Owen briefly considered stepping out onto the lake, but even if it didn't crack, a slippery block of ice was nowhere he wanted to be while trying to get away from a polar bear.

"Hey, hey!" Owen yelled, just trying to make noise.

"We're the ones who left the meat out for you!" George called. "We're your friends!"

"Yeah, I think he wants us to feed him again," said Owen. "Only *we're* the food now."

Nanuq opened his big mouth and made a popping sound as he cricked his neck. He was getting ready to rush them, and they both knew it. George held up the silver shotgun like a stick, and Owen looked around frantically for somewhere they could hide.

But there was nowhere to go.

THUMP-THUMP-THUMP-THUMP-THUMP—

Owen and George ducked as the helicopter burst out of the snowstorm behind them and flew right overhead. Its bright searchlight found the two boys first, then swung toward Nanuq. The big polar bear turned his head away from the light, but he stood his ground.

Owen felt like jumping for joy and collapsing to his knees all at the same time. They were saved!

A man in a Department of Natural Resources uniform leaned out of the helicopter with a hunting rifle in his hands, and the bottom fell out of Owen's stomach. He broke away from George and waved his hands, trying to get the man's attention.

"*No!*" Owen yelled. "*Don't kill him!*"

Suddenly George was beside him, waving the shotgun in the air. "*Don't shoot! Don't shoot!*" he cried.

The man in the helicopter didn't see them, or didn't care. Two puffs of smoke erupted from the barrel of the gun—*PAK! PAK!*—and Nanuq stumbled and fell.

CONNECTED

The shots from the helicopter were like bullets in Owen's heart. He fell to his knees in the snow, tears streaming down his cheeks. He didn't want Nanuq to hurt him or George, but he didn't want Nanuq to die either.

"It's not his fault," Owen sobbed.

George grabbed his shoulder and pointed. *"Owen, it's not bullets,"* he yelled over the sound of the helicopter's rotors. *"It's tranquilizer darts!"*

Owen looked and saw two silvery white tubes with bright red tufts on the end sticking out of Nanuq's side. The darts wobbled as the big bear stood up and lumbered away from the helicopter.

"They're just putting him to sleep to take him to Polar Bear Jail!" George told him.

Owen nodded with relief. He was embarrassed that he'd gotten so emotional. But he felt connected to Nanuq now, and he couldn't stand the thought of him dying. Especially if he was the reason the polar bear was killed.

George helped Owen to his feet. A few meters away, Nanuq was starting to feel the effects of the tranquilizer dart, and he paced around like his brain was getting foggy. The helicopter hovered, waiting for the polar bear to pass out.

Nanuq suddenly seemed to catch a second wind, and he charged straight at Owen and George again. There was no time for them to do anything but cling to each other and cry out. *He's so fast!* Owen thought. The DNR officer's rifle barked again—*PAK! PAK!*—but Nanuq was already on top of them. Owen and George dove together into the snow—

And Nanuq ran right past them onto the lake.

Of course! thought Owen. Nanuq was frightened and hurt, just like they were, and now he was doing what they'd been doing all along: running home. For Nanuq that was out onto the ice, onto the water, where the polar bear was king.

Owen and George watched as Nanuq loped out onto the snow-covered lake and—*crick-CRACK-SPLASH!*—the thin ice broke underneath him and he dropped into the water.

Owen breathed a sigh of relief, for him and George *and* for Nanuq. It was over.

Or was it?

Owen frowned. Something about this wasn't right.

Think, Owen told himself. *What's wrong with what I'm seeing?*

Owen looked away, playing the scenario forward in his head. Nanuq was tranqed, and he was going to lose consciousness before the helicopter could land and the DNR officers could fish him out of the lake. Polar bears were great swimmers, but they couldn't breathe underwater. If Nanuq was still in the water when he passed out and the DNR couldn't get to him in time—

Owen gasped.

"George," Owen cried. "Nanuq is going to drown!"

SAVE THE POLAR BEARS

Without saying a word to each other, George and Owen ran straight out onto the lake, their boots crashing through the thin ice and into the freezing water.

"STOP!" a voice boomed from the helicopter's loudspeaker. "GET OUT OF THE WATER! THE BEAR IS STILL MOVING!"

"Good!" George cried.

"It's not his fault!" Owen yelled, even though there was no way the helicopter could hear them. He and George understood though. They couldn't let Nanuq die. They were the ones who'd invaded *his* world, not the other way around.

Owen tried to pick up his feet as he splashed out next to Nanuq, but his big boots and snow pants were already full of water. He staggered, tripped, and fell hands-first into the icy lake.

"OH OWEN YOU DUMB ICE!" Owen yelled, popping back up again. "OH THAT IS COLD!"

George fell down onto his knees on the other side of the polar bear. "HOO HOO HOO HOO," he huffed as the freezing water filled his pants.

Nanuq didn't feel the cold, but that wasn't what was going to kill him. The polar bear was so big that he sat on the bottom of the lake, half-in, half-out of the water. He pawed sluggishly at the floating ice like he wanted to go even deeper, but the tranquilizers were already taking effect. His eyelids drooped, and his head sank below the surface. Air bubbles blooped up from his mouth and nose.

"GET OUT OF THE WATER!" the loudspeaker boomed again, but Owen and George ignored it.

"George, we have to get him turned around and pull him up onshore!" Owen cried.

The initial shock of the ice water had worn off, and now every part of Owen was on fire with the kind of burn you only felt from a bitter, bone-deep cold. He and George pushed and tugged on Nanuq with shaking, juddering hands, trying first to get him turned around, and then to pull him back to shore. But nothing was working.

"It's no use," George said, his teeth chattering. "This dude weighs five hundred kilos! We're never going to budge him."

Nanuq's eyes were closed all the way now, and no more air bubbles were coming out of his nose.

"We have to get his head out of the water," said Owen. He stumbled forward on his knees, his lower legs dragging behind like huge chunks of ice. They probably *were* huge chunks of ice by now. Owen had never been so cold in his entire life, and he had grown up in Churchill, Manitoba, the Polar Bear Capital of the World.

Owen put his good arm around Nanuq's head and lifted. Even in the water the polar bear's head weighed a ton, but then George was there on the other side of him, helping him lift. The two boys strained and grunted, and at last they were able to raise Nanuq's snout above the surface.

A mix of water and snot blew out of the polar bear's nose like a fire extinguisher. His breath sounded heavy and labored, but Nanuq was alive.

Owen slid his frozen legs underneath Nanuq's head, and George did the same, making a pillow for the polar bear to lie on. Ice-cold and exhausted, the boys slumped over Nanuq, their arms wrapped around him in a great big bear hug.

"Mac. Mac. Mac," George said, saying Owen's nickname with every panting breath he let out.

"What is it, Cheese?" Owen asked, panting just as hard.

"Look," George said, patting Nanuq's head. "I'm doing what you told me I couldn't do on the tundra buggy. I'm petting a polar bear."

It hurt to laugh, but Owen couldn't help it. He laughed so hard he cried, his tears freezing on his eyelashes.

Owen thought back to the tundra buggy, and the tourist who had asked about climate change. Owen had given him a careless answer and moved on to the fun stuff. But what if instead of telling the tourists a bunch of polar bear facts, he also talked about the melting ice and the crumbling permafrost and the momma bears losing their dens? Owen had people from all over the *world* on his family's tundra buggy. Why couldn't he show the visitors how awesome polar bears are *and* send them home fired up about saving them?

Because what was happening in the Arctic *couldn't* stay in the Arctic. The whole world had to know.

And if they saved the polar bears, maybe they could save the planet too.

The helicopter landed and two DNR officers ran toward them with a bear-sized stretcher.

Nanuq's eyes fluttered open for a second, and he let out an exhausted little *huff*.

"I know, man. I know," said Owen.

"You're gonna be okay now, buddy," George said, patting the big bear's head again.

"Yeah. Don't worry, Nanuq," said Owen. "We got you."

MIAMI, FLORIDA

PART 6

BROTHER'S KEEPER

Natalie and Patience paddled Patience's kayak through the quiet, flooded streets of Liberty City until they ran aground on dry pavement. Every part of Miami had been underwater during the hurricane. But most of Liberty City was a few feet higher than a lot of the other neighborhoods, which meant that as the water slowly receded, Liberty City emerged like an island from Lake Miami.

"Call it Liberty Island now, I guess," said Patience as they stepped out of the kayak.

Churro rode like a king in a palanquin in the kayak as Patience and Natalie carried it between them, picking their way through downed trees and overturned cars and unidentifiable debris. Natalie watched with sympathy as people dragged broken furniture and ruined carpets and sodden drywall from their shattered homes in the eighty-five-degree heat, tossing everything into growing junk piles in their yards. Natalie knew what heartbreaking, miserable work that was. She and her mother had done the same thing after Irma. It was like starting over every few years.

Is there anything left to save of my house? Natalie wondered. Were people in her neighborhood doing the same thing right now, or was Hialeah still underwater? Where were her mother and Tía Beatriz?

Natalie took a deep breath and tried not to panic. There was no way to know. Not yet, at least. Like everybody else wanting to hear if their loved ones were okay, Natalie was just going to have to wait.

Natalie and Patience came to a small cinder-block building with a long line of people outside it. As they set the kayak down next to a big garage door, Patience explained that her community food bank had been an auto mechanic's shop before she'd had taken it over.

"They used to change people's oil here," Patience told Natalie. "Now we change people's lives."

A sign up top read BROTHER'S KEEPER FOOD PANTRY.

"We collect food and necessities and hand them out to people who need it," Patience explained. "After Reuben, that's gonna be almost everyone."

Patience wasn't kidding. It looked to Natalie like everybody in Liberty City was in line for help. Black folks. White folks. Latino folks. Asian folks. Young families and middle-aged couples and old people. And Patience seemed to know them all by name.

Natalie stood awkwardly with Churro in her arms as Patience moved through the crowd, shaking hands and hugging people and listening to their stories about how they had survived the storm, and what they had lost.

"All right, all right," Patience said. "I want to talk to all y'all, hear how you're doing. But let me get things opened up."

Natalie followed Patience inside and set Churro down on the floor. An older Black woman was setting up a folding table, and she and Patience hugged each other and got caught up on what happened to them during the storm while Natalie and Churro explored Brother's Keeper. The small space was filled with floor-to-ceiling metal shelves. Some of the shelves held things like bottled water and baby diapers and cans of food, but a lot more of the shelves were empty.

"We handed stuff out to people ahead of the storm, but we saved some for after," Patience told Natalie. "Nat, this is Letitia. Letitia, Nat. Nat's the one I was just telling you about who washed up all the way from Hialeah."

"Come here," Letitia said, and promptly wrapped Natalie up in her arms. "I'm a hugger," Letitia told her. "Not gonna apologize for it."

"Okay," Natalie said as Churro circled them and barked.

"FEMA show up? Red Cross? Anybody from the city?" Patience asked.

"No. Not yet," Letitia told her.

Natalie remembered the ocean that surrounded "Liberty Island." Until the water receded completely, the only help they were likely to get would be by boat or by helicopter.

"Looks like it's just us, then," Patience told them. "Let's get to work."

Patience rolled up the big garage door, and Natalie saw even more people outside than there had been before.

Letitia sat at the table and took down people's names and addresses and what they needed. If Brother's Keeper had something to spare, Patience and Natalie went to the shelves and brought it back for them. Churro, meanwhile, had decided he liked Letitia after all, and he climbed up in her lap and inspected everyone who came through the line.

Hauling things back and forth was hot, sweaty work, but Natalie liked it. It felt good to be doing something. To be making a difference in people's lives.

And it took her mind off her mom and Tía Beatriz.

By midday, Brother's Keeper had handed out everything on the shelves, and there were even more people in line. All of them were trapped on Liberty Island with what little they'd been able to buy before the storm, and there was still no sign of help from the outside.

"I'm gonna see if I can get cell phone service anywhere," Patience said. She picked up a clipboard and put it in Natalie's hands. "You and Letitia go down the line. Get people's names and addresses. Phone numbers too for when there's service again. Find out what they need, and tell them we'll get it to them as soon as we can."

"*Me?*" Natalie asked.

"Of course you," Patience said, turning her around and pushing her out the door. "You see anybody else around here who's gonna do it?"

Natalie stepped out into the bright sunshine. The eyes of every person in line instantly shifted to her and the clipboard in her hands, and Natalie gulped. Carrying bottles of water and diapers back and forth from the shelves was one thing. But talking to people? Being responsible for making sure they got what they needed? That was a whole different thing.

I'm just a seventh grader, and everybody else here is an adult, thought Natalie. *Who's going to listen to* me?

IMPATIENCE

At first, nobody did listen to Natalie. The people of Liberty City surrounded her, talking over each other to tell her what had happened to them and where they lived and what they needed. Natalie didn't know where to look, or who to listen to. It was too much. There were too many people. Too many sad stories. There was no way Natalie was going to be able to help them all. At her feet, Churro added to the chaos by barking furiously.

"Everybody stop!" Natalie yelled, and suddenly everyone went quiet, just like Hurricane Reuben had. Even Churro was surprised into silence.

Maybe this is my superpower, Natalie thought, privately pleased with the idea.

"Listen," she said more quietly while all eyes and ears were on her. "Everybody needs help, and everybody's going to get help. But we're only going to get through this if we work *together*, all right? So I need everybody to form a line behind this lady right here, and I promise I will talk to each and every one of you."

The people looked at Natalie, then each other, and then, amazingly, they all did what she told them to do and got into a single-file line. Natalie almost couldn't believe it.

Letitia looked over at Natalie and winked. "All right, you heard the girl," Letitia hollered to the people who surrounded her. "Two lines. Let's go."

One by one, the people in Natalie's line told her what they needed. Food. Bottled water. Medicine. Tampons. Blankets. Fans. Clean underwear. Dry socks. Batteries. Diapers. Baby formula. Hammers, nails, and plywood to repair their homes. Rakes, brooms, sledgehammers, and saws to clean up their streets and yards. It was easy to feel overwhelmed by it all, but Natalie focused on doing what she could.

"The grocery store up on Twelfth Street is back open, but they can't take SNAP cards with the electricity out," a woman named Nevaeh told her, a toddler in her arms. SNAP stood for Supplemental Nutrition Assistance Program. Natalie's mom called it food stamps. It's what the government gave out to people who worked jobs but still didn't make enough money to buy food.

"How am I supposed to eat in the meantime?" Nevaeh asked. "I don't get paid again 'til next week."

"*Nobody's* getting paid," the woman in line behind her said. "Not anytime soon."

Natalie realized she was right. It would take weeks, *months*, for things to get back to normal. If they ever did. How would people survive until then?

The story was the same all the way down the line, and Natalie's heart sank with each new name she added to the list, each new thing somebody needed. She had to flip over the pieces of paper and start using the backs to keep track of it all.

Natalie felt her hope receding like the tide. When she'd been stuck on the boat in the storm, the lady with the two little kids had said everything would be all right mañana. But she'd been wrong. It was tomorrow, and everything was *not* all right. In many ways, it was worse.

"*Do we have any infrastructure concerns?*" Natalie heard Patience yelling from inside Brother's Keeper. She sounded distinctly *im*patient. "I've got hungry people down here, people without any clean water to drink, and you want to send *construction crews?*"

Natalie left her line to peek inside, and her heart leapt. Patience was on the phone. She had cell service! Natalie ran to her and clutched her arm.

"You don't get somebody down here with some food, and fast, you're *gonna* have infrastructure concerns," Patience told whoever was on the call. Churro didn't know why Patience was mad, but he stood beside her and growled menacingly on her behalf.

"Hello?" Patience said. "Hello?" The other person either hung up, or Patience had lost her signal. She closed her eyes and took a deep breath. When she opened her eyes again, she shook her head.

"That was FEMA," she told Natalie. "The Federal Emergency Management Agency. City, state, federal government, they're all telling me the same thing. They can't get us food and water because they're 'too busy handling the emergency.' How do they not see that this *is* the emergency?" She gestured around them. "We've got no electricity, no water, no food. I've got hundreds of hungry people and a whole warehouse sitting here empty. Did the government fill it up *before* the storm, like I asked them? No, they did not. Now they tell me they can't get the food and water through the flooded streets. What did they *think* the city was going to look like after a hurricane?"

Natalie couldn't help but admire Patience all over again. She was out there every day, yelling into the storm, no matter how big and overwhelming it was.

Patience let out a frustrated breath and then softened. "Here," she said, handing Natalie the phone. "I know you need to try your mom."

Natalie took the phone carefully, almost reverently, and punched in her mom's number with shaking hands. Churro hopped around her, as if sensing her nervousness.

The phone rang. And rang. Natalie felt her spirits dropping . . .

And then someone answered.

TAKE A WALK

"Mama! It's me, Natalie!" she cried. But her mom's voice cut in on top of her:

"Hello, this is Elena Torres. I'm not able to answer my phone right now."

Natalie bit back a sob as the rest of the voice mail message played. She felt her knees go weak and she leaned against a metal shelf.

"Hey. It's me," Natalie said after the beep, her voice quivering. "I'm okay. I'm with a woman named Patience Davis, in Liberty City. This is her phone. Call me back at this number if you get this." She paused, not knowing what else to say. "I love you and I hope you're okay," she added, and hung up.

Tears streamed down her face as Patience took the phone back from her.

"It's okay, Nat," Patience said. She put an arm around her and let Natalie lean in and cry. "She probably lost her phone in the storm like you. She'll call her voice mail when she's safe and see you've gotten in touch."

Natalie sniffed back a sob. Patience was being nice, but they both knew what she wasn't saying. That there was every chance her mom would never call back, because she had drowned in the storm along with her phone.

Patience took Natalie's clipboard from her. "You've been at this for a while now. I'll call the Red Cross, get you on their list of people. You take a break. Go for a walk with that dog so he's not growling at me every second in my own place of business."

Natalie laughed through her tears. "He's not my dog," she said. But a break sounded good.

She and Churro left Brother's Keeper and explored the neighborhood. Natalie was glad to be alone for a little while, and Churro was happy to sniff at all the piles of trash and debris and to pee on everything.

The rain had stopped, and the afternoon sky was bright blue and the birds were chirping again. But *everything*—every tree, every electric pole, every car, every roof and window and wall— was damaged or destroyed. And no one from the government had come out to start cleaning it up yet, or help all the desperate people who were staring at their broken homes with nothing to do and no way to fix anything.

Natalie and Churro worked their way around a pile of broken tree branches. They turned a corner at a row of shops that was still standing, and suddenly a big white man in black military fatigues and a black mask stood in front of Natalie, holding an automatic rifle.

"Stop right there," the man said, his voice hard. "Who are you, and what do you want?"

YOU LOOT, WE SHOOT

Natalie froze as a second white man in a black uniform and a black mask came up behind the first. He had a huge rifle too, and on pieces of tape stuck to his bulletproof vest he'd written the words YOU LOOT, WE SHOOT.

"What are you doing here?" the second man demanded.

Churro growled at the men. Natalie scooped him up and hugged him close.

"I'm just walking my dog," Natalie said.

"Well, walk him somewhere else," the first man said.

The men were standing in front of a shoe store, a liquor store, and a convenience store. The storm had broken all the windows and awnings, but as far as Natalie could see, nobody had taken anything from the shops.

"And tell everybody to stay away from these stores, or else," the second man said.

Natalie frowned. Who did she know that was going to go looting stores? She nodded anyway and hurried back the way she'd come, completely rattled. What were men with guns doing in Liberty City the day after a hurricane?

On another street, a young Asian woman was using a long-handled squeegee to push water out the front door of a Chinese restaurant.

"Are you open?" Natalie asked.

The woman shook her head. "Just cleaning up," she said.

Natalie nodded to Churro. "Got any scraps for a hungry dog?"

"No. Sorry," the woman said. "We're not opening our freezer up until the last minute. If we open it up now, the food will go bad that much faster. Probably going to lose all of it anyway." The woman brightened. "Oh, wait. We do have some dog treats, I think!"

She disappeared into the store and returned with a small plastic container of store-bought dog snacks. She handed the whole thing to Natalie. "Here," she said. "So you can keep giving him treats until things get back to normal. Whenever that is."

Natalie thanked the young woman, gave Churro one of the treats, and headed for Patience's food pantry. Churro kept leaping up every few steps to beg for another treat, but Natalie shook her head.

"You can't have them all at once," she scolded Churro.

Letitia was still writing down people's information when Natalie returned, and Patience was hanging up on another frustrating phone conversation.

"Still no help coming," Patience told Natalie. "And no word from your mom. I'm sorry."

Natalie nodded. It had been too much to hope that her mom would call back while she was gone.

"There were soldiers out on the street," Natalie said. "Maybe it's the army or something."

Patience scoffed. "Yeah, I heard. But they're not the army or the National Guard, and they're not the police. Vigilantes is what they are," she said. "As far as anybody can tell, they don't even live here. They came in by boat to shoot people if they start looting stores. But did they bring food with them so people wouldn't need to steal? Water? First-aid stuff? Dry clothes? No. Just their guns."

Natalie couldn't believe it. "And they can shoot anybody they catch looting?" she asked.

"Not legally," said Patience. "But who's gonna stop them?"

Natalie shook her head. She couldn't imagine somebody getting shot for stealing food, or a pair of shoes, or even a TV. That wasn't the way things were supposed to work.

"The Chinese restaurant down the street isn't reopening yet, but they gave me some dog treats for Churro," Natalie said, showing Patience the box. Natalie took pity on Churro and gave him one more treat before putting the plastic container on one of the empty shelves.

"Well, *he's* covered at least," Patience said as Churro ate happily.

Patience's phone rang. She answered it with a tired sigh, but after a moment her eyes lit up and she smiled.

"Nat," Patience cried, "it's your mom!"

MAMA'S STORY

"Mama!" Natalie cried when she heard her mother's voice on the phone. "You're alive!"

"I thought I would never hear your voice again, my angel," her mother said through sobs.

Mama wanted to know everything that had happened to Natalie, and she wept as Natalie told her story.

"I can't believe you're alive," Mama said when Natalie was done. Hearing it all out loud again, Natalie couldn't believe it either.

Mama's story was just as frightening. After Natalie had escaped, the water in their house had kept rising, pushing Mama and Tía Beatriz up toward the ceiling. But the storm surge was so powerful it had done what they couldn't, and ripped the front door off its hinges.

"We took deep breaths, and I dragged Tía down through the open door," Mama said. "I thought my lungs were going to burst, but we made it out and came up gasping for air. Reuben was raging all around us. I looked for you, but you were already gone."

Natalie remembered being swept away by the storm. What a blur it had been. How fast. Natalie's heart broke, thinking about her mom and Tía Beatriz out in the storm and her not being there to help them.

Reuben had dragged Mama and Tía Beatriz to Natalie's old

elementary school up the street, and they had climbed in through one of the broken windows on the second floor and taken refuge in a stairwell.

"But Natalie," Mama said softly, "Tía Beatriz—it was too much for her. She swallowed too much water. I did what I could, but before we could be rescued, she . . . Oh, mija. I'm so sorry. Tía Beatriz is dead."

TÍA BEATRIZ

Natalie put a hand to her mouth. For the past day, she'd been worried her mama and Tía Beatriz might be dead. Hearing her mother's voice again had given her hope. But now, to learn that the woman who had been like family to her was truly gone . . .

Natalie bent double and sobbed. Patience put her arm around her and took the phone, letting Natalie cry. Natalie heard Patience talking to her mother, but Natalie was somewhere else. She was on the floor of Tía's apartment, cutting out blue construction paper butterflies for Mariposa while Tía's telenovelas played across the room. She was in her tía's lap, listening to her stories about face-changing witches defeated with mustard seeds, and beautiful princesses sealed in caves by greedy suitors. She was in Tía's kitchen, helping her stir red beans and white rice and chopped onions on the stove. For Tía Beatriz to have survived a hurricane in Nicaragua as a young woman and come all this way to the United States only to die in another storm—it wasn't fair. No one person should suffer so much loss.

Natalie felt Patience's hand on her back, and she looked up. Her mother was on the phone for her again.

"I can't believe Tía Beatriz is gone," Natalie said, sniffling.

"I know, my angel. I know," her mother said through her own tears. "I can't talk much longer now. I'm safe in a shelter in Hialeah, but there are other people here who need to use this phone, and we only have one generator for power. I've spoken with your friend Patience. She says you can stay with her for now. Are you all right with that?"

"Yes," Natalie told her.

"Good," her mother said. "Stay in Liberty City, then, and I will come to you when I can. Do you understand? I love you, mija. You've been very brave."

They lingered another few moments over their goodbyes, and then they had to go. Natalie gave the phone back to Patience, and Churro crawled up into Natalie's lap, sensing her despair. Little Churro. How would he understand when he never saw Tía Beatriz again? Would he always be wondering where she was?

Natalie took the plastic treat container from the shelf.

"Just one more," she told him. "We'll save the rest for any other dogs that come by so they can have one too."

"I'm glad your mom's okay," Patience said, sitting down next to Natalie. "Sounds like they're getting some help in Hialeah, at least." She lifted the heavy clipboard in her hand. "Me, I got a long, long list of people who need stuff, and FEMA and the city government are still AWOL. I already ran out of all the money I took out of the ATM before Reuben got here, and I don't know who else to call. Not even 911 is answering anymore."

Natalie remembered Tía Beatriz saying something similar about the first hurricane she'd survived in Nicaragua. How there hadn't been any government to help them after the civil war, so they'd banded together. Shared what they had with each other. It hadn't been enough in the long run, but it had helped them survive until they could get out. Go someplace better.

Churro barked at the treat container, wanting another. Natalie wasn't going to give in to him, but she was starting to get an idea.

"You keep asking people in the neighborhood what they need," Natalie said, thinking out loud. "What if we went around instead and asked everybody what they *have*?"

Patience sat up. "You mean like the treats. Like . . . does someone have a lot of meat that's going to spoil?"

"And does somebody else have a grill," Natalie said, nodding. "Or more bottled water than they can drink, or ice that's going to melt. People may not have much, but if everybody puts what they have together . . ."

Patience wrapped Natalie up in a hug. "Nat, you're a genius!" Patience cried. "Let's take this clipboard and go knock on some doors."

WHAT DO YOU HAVE?

In the parking lot outside Brother's Keeper, hamburgers and hot dogs sizzled on the grill, and rice and beans cooked in big pots over a fire pit built with cinder blocks. The smell of good food had brought people from all over the neighborhood, and they stood around eating and talking and laughing as the sun went down on Liberty City.

And all because Natalie and Patience had stopped asking people what they needed and started asking them what they had to share.

Not that everybody they'd asked had been helpful. The first person they'd talked to had flat out refused to share what he had, and shut the door in their faces. Natalie had been devastated, but Patience was undeterred.

The next apartment belonged to a young family with a baby, and peeking inside, Natalie could see they didn't have much. She was sure they would be another no—what could they possibly spare?—but Natalie's heart caught in her throat as the young mother went and got a package of diapers and handed it to Patience.

"We should have enough until the stores open back up," the woman told them. "You make sure some momma that needs these gets them."

Natalie got choked up, but Patience didn't have time for getting sentimental. At the next apartment, a family gave them bottled waters. At the next, a man gave them two packages of hot dog buns. Almost everywhere they went, people had *something* to donate. When a teenage boy came to a door and said he didn't have anything to share, Patience took all the things Natalie had been carrying and shoved them into his arms. "You don't have something to give, you can work," she told him, and soon they had a small army of people hauling food and supplies back to the warehouse on foot.

Now the shelves were full, and people had come to help distribute things. One table handed out bags of chips and bottles of water and apples and bananas. Another table gave out diapers and formula. A really talented teenage girl sat on a stool and played songs on her acoustic guitar, and two men brought their grills and were trying to out-dad each other with their cooking and their bad jokes.

The tasty aromas had brought some of the neighborhood's dogs too. Natalie gave them each a treat, even though Churro growled at every one of them.

Natalie smiled at Tía Beatriz's dog. There was still a hole in her heart that might never heal, but doing what Tía Beatriz would have done—helping other people—took some of the sting away from losing her.

Natalie suddenly recognized somebody standing in line and felt a fire rise up in her. She grabbed Patience by the arm and pointed.

"Look! It's that man from the first apartment we went to. He wouldn't share anything he had, and now he's standing in line to get food other people donated!"

"And he's welcome to it," Patience said, shocking Natalie.

Patience shrugged. "Some people are always going to take without giving," she said. "I'm always going to give without taking."

Natalie was in awe all over again at the way Patience thought about the world. *How can I be like that when I grow up?* Natalie wondered.

"People like him aren't nearly the worst of our troubles now anyway," Patience said with a sigh.

"What do you mean?" Natalie asked.

"Come on," said Patience. "There's enough people helping out here. Let's you and me go up on the roof."

MAGIC CITY

"I like to come up here and think," Patience told Natalie as they climbed up a ladder on the back side of Brother's Keeper. Patience carried a tote bag with cans of soda and a bag of chips for them to share, and Natalie carried Churro. She thought he'd like seeing lots more things he could bark at.

"I used to have a couple of lawn chairs up here," Patience said. "I guess they're all the way to Orlando by now."

She and Natalie sat on the edge of the roof, looking down at all the people laughing and eating. Natalie thought they'd done something good, but Patience seemed unhappy.

"What's wrong?" Natalie asked. "Was this a bad idea or something?"

"No, no, Nat," Patience said, seeing her frown. "I'm sorry. It's great that everybody pitched in to help each other. But what you see down there is the last of the good times. Everybody in Liberty City has already given all they can. When all that food and water and stuff is gone, that's it. We've got nothing else. And then what?"

Natalie hadn't thought about that. She'd felt so good about bringing people together, so good about helping. But Patience was right. It wasn't enough.

Patience scrolled through a news feed on her phone. "So much is gone," she said. "The Keys got flattened. Bunch of buildings came down in Miami Beach. All those marinas along the coast, destroyed. Port of Miami, Miami Airport both gone. Brickell Financial District is flooded. Coral Gables looks like Venice. Freedom Tower's gone. Sawgrass Mills is part of the Everglades again." She shook her head. "Reuben wrecked Fort Lauderdale too. Port Everglades. The fishing pier at Pompano. It's all gone. Basketball arena made it though, so there's that, I guess."

Natalie wondered about Hialeah. It wasn't as high up as Liberty City and would still be underwater. What did her house look like now? Was it even there anymore?

Patience reached across Natalie for a potato chip, and Churro growled at her.

"Okay, Churro," Patience said, holding up her hands. "I'm not going to hurt your girl."

Churro pranced in a circle in Natalie's lap, smug with victory, then settled down and closed his eyes. Natale stared down at him. When had she and Diablito become friends?

Patience shook her head and laughed. "That dog of yours hates everybody but you."

"He's not my—" Natalie started to say, but she had to stop herself. Tía Beatriz was gone. Churro had nowhere to go.

"I guess you *are* my dog now," Natalie told him. She scratched Churro between the ears, and he gurgled approvingly.

In the distance, electric light glowed from the windows of the tall condos that had survived the hurricane.

"I see they got the power back on down in Brickell," Patience said with disgust. "Glad the rich people were first on the list. Needed the power to run their juicers and exercise bikes, I guess."

Natalie thought about Shannon, in her high-rise apartment with its own generator. Shannon, who was only worried about how Reuben was going to ruin her Halloween. Whose father called staying in Miami through the hurricane a "camping adventure."

Natalie couldn't imagine her and Shannon going back to being friends when this was all over. Shannon was a nice person, but it was like the two of them lived on different planets.

Patience shook her head. "They call Miami the Magic City," she said. "But it's only magic for some of the people who live here. It's not real magical for the rest of us."

"When I was little, I made up a magical world called Mariposa," Natalie said. She blushed a little to say it out loud, but it was easier to talk about it up here as night was falling, while she and Patience were looking out over the ruined city. She told Patience about Mariposa's houses and parks. Its libraries and hospitals. The way the people looked out for each other and their world.

"In Mariposa, the king and the queen made sure everybody got what they needed," Natalie said, "and everybody was happy."

Patience nodded. "Sounds like a place I'd very much like to live," she said.

Churro's head perked up, and he started to growl at something down below. Somebody new was coming into the parking lot and causing a stir.

"What's all this now?" Patience asked.

Natalie worried it was the fake army men, come to give them

all a hard time. But these people didn't have guns. They had camera equipment.

Natalie gasped as she recognized a tall, pretty Latina woman in jeans and a blue windbreaker.

"Patience, I know who that is!" Natalie cried. "It's Maria Martinez, from TV!"

A GREAT STORY

"And you run a community food pantry?" Maria Martinez asked Patience, the camera lights bright in the dark parking lot.

"Yes," said Patience. "Even before the hurricane, Brother's Keeper collected donations and distributed food and clothing and other necessities to the folks in our community who needed them most."

Natalie stood just out of the circle of light, watching the interview. The news station had seen what was going on in the Brother's Keeper parking lot while flying drones over the city, and Miami's famous meteorologist had come by motor-boat to Liberty Island to talk to everyone. She'd already interviewed the grill dads, and the girl with the guitar, and a bunch of the people who'd stood in line for food.

Natalie was so excited. Not only did she get to see Maria Martinez, live and in person, but people all over were going to see what was happening here. Liberty City was finally going to get the help it needed.

"Can you tell us more about how all this came together today?" Maria asked Patience.

Patience explained how they'd gone around and asked every-one what they could share, and how people had given what they could, even when they didn't have much to begin with.

"And it was all Nat's idea," Patience said. She turned and gestured for Natalie to join her.

Natalie's stomach dropped. She shook her head and backed away. She couldn't go on camera! She hadn't showered in two days, her hair was a frizzy mess, and she was wearing hand-me-down clothes that were five sizes too big. She was dirty and sweaty and tired. Natalie didn't like having her picture taken under normal circumstances, and she most certainly did not want anybody she knew to see her looking like this.

Patience grinned and pulled her into the light.

"This is Natalie Torres," said Patience. "She's the one who made all this happen."

Natalie was mortified. She tried desperately to pull her hair back into a bun and was sure she'd just made it worse.

"Hi, Natalie," said Maria Martinez. "Tell us a little more about yourself. What grade are you in, and what school do you go to?"

Natalie blinked in the bright lights of the camera. She was standing right next to Maria Martinez!

"Hi," Natalie said.

Patience and the people watching all laughed, but not in a mean way.

"Hi, Natalie," Maria Martinez said again, smiling. "How old are you, and what school do you go to?"

Maria Martinez had asked her something, but for the life of her Natalie couldn't remember what it was.

"I watch you all the time on TV," Natalie told her. "I'm a big fan."

Everybody laughed again, and Maria Martinez laughed with them.

"Well, I'm a big fan of you and what you and Patience have accomplished today," Maria said. She turned to the camera. "It's a heartwarming example of what a community can do when people pull together to help each other. I'm Maria Martinez, Miami News Channel Five."

The bright lights cut off, and suddenly the parking lot was dark again.

"Thanks. Nice job here today, everybody. It's a great story," Maria Martinez told them, and she and her camera crew began to pack up to leave.

Natalie blinked, still seeing stars.

"Wait, that's it?" she said.

Maria Martinez turned. "Is there more to it?" she asked.

"Well, yeah," Natalie said. She remembered what she and Patience had talked about up on the roof. "What do you think things are going to be like here tomorrow, when all this food and water and stuff is gone?" she asked.

"Tell me," Maria said. She turned to her cameraman and signaled for him to start recording again.

Click! The blinding light hit Natalie in the face, and she turned away. No, no, no. She couldn't do this. She couldn't look up into those lights and talk to Maria Martinez *on camera*. Natalie looked up at Patience in desperation. What was she supposed to do? What was she supposed to say?

DIFFERENT BOATS

"You got this, Nat," Patience said. "You can do this."

Natalie shook her head. This wasn't her. She couldn't talk on camera!

Churro sensed her panic and stood at her side and growled.

"Just forget about the camera and talk to me," Maria told her. "Natalie, it looks like everything's great here. The people of Liberty City came together and they're sharing what they have and grilling out and listening to music. How is that not good?"

"It *is* good," Natalie said. She tried to forget the camera was recording her and looked at Maria instead.

"You're right," Natalie went on. "This is amazing, what happened here today. There were so many people here in Liberty City who didn't have enough food after the hurricane, enough water, all the other things they need to survive. There was no way we could help them all, and we didn't know what to do. It was too much."

"So you got people to come together and share what they had," Maria prompted her.

Natalie nodded. "But it's not going to be enough," she told Maria. "People don't have any more to give. Tomorrow they're going to be hungry again. And it doesn't fix the bigger problem."

"What's the bigger problem?" Maria asked.

"You know. You talk about it all the time," Natalie told

Maria. "It's climate change." Natalie felt her pulse quicken as she came back to her old, familiar topic. "We're always going to have hurricanes, but climate change is making them worse. And it affects different people in different ways. Look at those skyscrapers," she said, pointing at the sparkling lights in the darkness. The only lights on in all of Miami. "Most of those rich people, they already got out of town. But they're still the first ones to get their power back. When is Liberty City going to get its power back? Or Hialeah? Or Overtown? Or Little Haiti? People say we're all in the same boat with climate change, but we're not. Some people get to ride out the storm in yachts while the rest of us are clinging to whatever floats by and trying not to drown."

The crowd was with her now, and people clapped and cheered her on. Churro yapped with them.

"We have to *do* something about all this," Natalie said, straightening up. "We rallied together and we helped each other as much as we could. That's great. But that shouldn't be all there is. We need *more*. We needed more to begin with. Patience had empty shelves that could have been filled with food before the storm. And if we'd done something about climate change already, maybe Reuben wouldn't have been so bad to begin with."

"What do you want people to do, Natalie?" Maria asked her.

Natalie sagged again. How was she supposed to know? They were talking about something way bigger than she was. Way bigger than any of them. And she was just in the seventh grade!

She looked all around her for answers. At Maria. At Patience. At Churro. At all the people of Liberty City who'd come together. No one of them had the answer, but the answer was there.

"I don't know," Natalie told Maria. "But I do know that we can't do it alone. It's going to take all of us."

"Great," said Maria, and she signaled to the cameraman to stop filming. "*Now* I think we've got the real story, don't you?" she asked Natalie.

Natalie nodded, and Patience gave her a hug.

I did it, Natalie thought. *I talked on camera. About climate change!*

"You really know your stuff," Maria told her. "Ever think about becoming a climate scientist?"

Natalie laughed. Only all the time! "Yes," she said. "I want to be a meteorologist, like you."

"You should come by the station after all this is over," Maria told her. "Maybe we can do some segments together. You need to get your message in front of more people, Natalie. Get more kids like you fired up about climate change."

Natalie was thunderstruck. "I will," she said. But she wasn't going to stop there. Suddenly she saw it. What she had to do. If it was going to take everybody to fix climate change, she was going to have to find a way to get as many people together as possible. And Natalie had an idea how she could do it.

EPILOGUE

RALLY TIME

Akira Kristiansen stood behind the curtain, trying to calm the butterflies in her stomach. She was about to go speak on a giant, open-air stage at a Kids Against Climate Change rally on the steps of the United States Capitol, and she was having second thoughts.

No, third thoughts. Fourth thoughts.

Akira peeked out at the crowd again. Even though it was a muggy summer day in Washington, DC, people filled the wide, tree-lined lawn that stretched from the Capitol Building to the Washington Monument in the distance. There had to be tens of thousands of people out there. *Hundreds* of thousands of people.

Akira's mom put a hand on her shoulder. "You're gonna do great," she told Akira. "Just remember to breathe."

Middle schoolers from all over the US and Canada and Mexico waited in the wings to speak at the rally, and even more kids were Zooming in from all over the world. Akira and her mom had come here from California—by train, to reduce their carbon footprint—so Akira could experience the rally in person. But now that it was almost time for her to go out in front of everyone, Akira was wishing she'd joined the rally online instead.

Akira glanced at the other speakers waiting backstage with their parents. Most of the kids looked as nervous as Akira felt. The only one who looked calm was a blond-haired boy who was chattering away to his friend like they were standing around in the hall before class.

A pop song blared from the speakers out front, and somewhere backstage Akira heard a little dog barking nonstop. Who had brought a dog to the climate change rally? Akira put her hands to her ears, but she could still hear the noise of half a million people in the crowd like the dull roar of a fire in the distance.

Akira tried to sit with her anxiety, letting it wash over her like a wave, the way her therapist had been teaching her. It had been almost nine months since Akira and her family had escaped from the Morris Fire, but she still got panicky when she had to process an overwhelming situation like this one.

Akira and her therapist had agreed that attending the Kids Against Climate Change rally was a good way to confront what had happened to her. But this was a far cry from riding Dodger up to see the monarchs after the wildfire. What had Akira been thinking? Why in the world had she agreed to do this?

Because my monarchs burned up in the Morris Fire, she

reminded herself. *Because climate change is real, and it's here, and I'm not going to stay quiet about it anymore.*

Akira let out a deep breath and nodded. She could do this. She had to do this. She was just going to have to ignore the butterflies.

Which was funny, because there were blue butterflies *everywhere*. They were the symbol of the rally. Stylized blue butterfly logos decorated the podium, the big screen in the background, the pennants that waved in the slight breeze. Cutout paper versions of butterflies hung from streamers and lampposts. You couldn't ignore the butterflies here if you tried.

The pop song that had been playing for the crowd ended, and another one didn't start.

"Looks like this is it," Akira's mom said.

Before Akira could think about getting more nervous, a girl's voice boomed out through the loudspeakers, across the National Mall. "Friends, allies, and fellow earthlings," the young emcee cried, "please welcome to the stage . . . NATALIE TORRES!"

The roar from the crowd became a raging wildfire. Akira thanked her lucky stars she wasn't the first person to go out onstage and watched from the wings as a pretty Latina girl with curly brown hair and a blue butterfly T-shirt made her way out to the podium. Akira recognized her from rehearsals, but they hadn't officially met yet.

"Hi," the girl told the crowd. "My name is Natalie Torres." She had her speech on a screen in front of her, the way the rest of them would when it was their turn, and she started reading.

"Last October, I survived Hurricane Reuben," Natalie said.

"I was in my house in Hialeah with my mom and our neighbor Tía Beatriz when the storm surge knocked down our back wall and swept me out into the hurricane."

Akira watched on in awe as Natalie told her story and showed pictures of the storm on the screen behind her. It gave Akira chills to think that she and Natalie had both been in danger from different climate change disasters at the same time last year, on opposite ends of the continent.

"Hey, there's my girl," someone backstage said, and Akira looked away from Natalie to see her old friend Patience Davis coming up to her.

Patience gave Akira and her mom each a quick hug. "I'm so sorry we haven't had more time to talk! I've been busy running around making sure everything was working," Patience told them. "How've you been, Akira? Look at how tall you are!"

Akira was so glad to see Patience. Akira had missed their long chats from when Patience was Hildi's babysitter. Patience looked a little older, but just as cool. And her hair was blue now, instead of orange. Blue like the butterflies.

Patience had been the one to reach out and invite Akira to speak at the rally when she heard about the Morris Fire.

As they stood backstage, Akira caught Patience up on her life—how she and her family were rebuilding their home, the anime shows she and her dad were into, the volunteer work Akira was doing with a local environmental club.

"I'm surprised you didn't move after the fire," Patience said.

Akira's mom shrugged. "The insurance would only pay us if

we rebuilt in the same place, so we're right back where we started, in the path of the next wildfire."

The audience *oohed* at one of the pictures on the screen, and Akira's mom turned to look.

"How's your dad with all this?" Patience asked, leaning in close where only Akira could hear her. "You being here, I mean."

Akira sighed. She and Patience might have changed, but Akira's father hadn't.

"He didn't want me to be here," Akira said. "He still thinks people aren't responsible for climate change."

Patience nodded. "I heard it in his voice when I talked to him on the phone. Must be tough, something like this driving a wedge between you."

Akira looked away. It *was* tough. "He'll always be my dad, and I'll always love him," Akira said. "But just because he's going to keep doing things the same old way doesn't mean I have to."

Patience put her arm around Akira again and gave her a squeeze.

Akira focused back on what Natalie was saying onstage.

"You've heard how I survived Miami's 'Big One,'" Natalie told the audience. "But that doesn't tell you the whole story about climate change. To do that, we invited a bunch of kids from all over the world who went through their *own* climate disasters last year to come here and tell you *their* stories. I hope you'll listen to what they have to say and think about how you can make a difference for the future. Because we're all together on this island we call Earth, and we're the only ones who can save it. Thank you!"

Akira watched as Natalie waved to the crowd and left to a huge ovation. The kid who was emceeing the rally announced the next speaker, a girl named Ishani who had survived a rain bomb in India last year.

Natalie joined Akira and Patience backstage while Ishani spoke to the crowd virtually from Mumbai on the big screen.

Patience put one arm around Akira and one around Natalie. "Look at my two girls, all grown up and changing the world," said Patience. "Nat, this is Akira Kristensen. Akira, this is Natalie Torres. You two are my little sisters from other misters!"

One of the stagehands called Patience away, leaving Natalie with Akira and her mom. Akira panicked. Was she going to have to make small talk with a stranger now? Nobody had told her to prepare any small talk! Akira looked to her mother for help, but she gave Akira a look that said, *You talk to her.*

Akira was still trying to think of something to say when Natalie bailed her out.

"So, you and Patience already knew each other? Like, before the rally?" Natalie asked.

"Oh. Yes," said Akira. "Or we did, when she lived in California. And we still do, I guess."

"Oh, cool," said Natalie, looking surprised. "I thought she'd just found you because of the wildfire."

"No, we knew each other before," Akira said. *Which you already said*, Akira thought, kicking herself inwardly.

Akira stood uncomfortably, trying to think of something else to say.

"So, what's with all the blue butterflies?" she asked at last.

"Oh!" Natalie said, perking up. "Well, there's a couple of reasons, actually—"

"Ah, ah, ah," Patience said, swooping back in. "You'll tell her and everybody else all about it in your closing speech," she told Natalie. "For now, you need to go find Churro and keep him quiet. Your mom's walking around with him somewhere. And you," Patience told Akira, "you need to get ready, because you're almost on."

Akira looked up in a panic. The girl speaking from Mumbai was almost done. It was her turn to go onstage next.

NO PLANET B

"Bahut dhanyavaad, Ishani. Thank you," the emcee said to the girl from Mumbai. "Now please welcome to the stage . . . AKIRA KRISTIANSEN!"

Akira knew that was her cue, but she couldn't move. She was petrified.

Patience gave her a little push, and suddenly Akira's legs were carrying her to the podium. She couldn't believe she was doing this.

Akira grabbed on to the podium like it was a life preserver, and stood there uneasily for a long moment after the applause had stopped. Half a million pairs of eyes looked up at her from the crowd, waiting for her to begin. Akira gulped. Her words were right there on the screen below her. All she had to do was say them.

She wanted to do this. She *had* to do this.

"Hello, I'm Akira Kristiansen," she said at last, "and I survived the Morris Fire in California last year."

Once she got started, it was easier to keep going. Akira told the enormous crowd how she'd survived the wildfire with the help of her horse, and Dodger got a big "Awww!" from the crowd when she showed his picture.

"The Morris Fire produced as much energy as a thousand atomic bombs," Akira said. The image of Dodger was replaced by scary pictures of black trees stripped bare of branches and leaves, of hillsides covered in smoking gray ash, of a whole town burned to the ground.

"The wildfire burned out of control for sixteen days," said Akira. "Firefighters were only able to put it out because we got a little rain. In the meantime, the Morris Fire ate up more than three hundred thousand acres of land. That's an area about the size of Los Angeles. That was a record," Akira told the crowd, "until a new megafire in northern California and southern Oregon beat it a week later."

Akira looked down and took a deep breath. This next part was the hardest part of her speech.

"I still have scars from the fire," Akira said. "Physical scars, and mental ones. I wake up in the middle of the night sometimes, gasping and crying out. I dream that I'm surrounded by fire. That I'm burning up and can't escape." She swallowed. "Sue, the girl I was with in the fire, she survived, and we're good friends now. But I knew a lot of people who didn't make it out. Lily Turner, who lived down the hill from me. Marcus Gutierrez, who was in my homeroom. Bethany Stone, who went to school with my little sister, and her baby brother, Eli, and her mom and dad, Helen and Chris Stone." She showed the pictures of all the people she'd named. "For the whole next month, it was like I went to a different funeral every day," Akira said.

Akira paused for a moment, and the enormous crowd was silent with her.

"We also lost a stand of giant sequoias," Akira said at last, showing a picture of the enormous trees. "The trees that died were thousands of years old. If these trees can burn—trees that are built to survive wildfires—how much more vulnerable are we?"

Akira looked out across the huge crowd.

"Nature is big. It's powerful. It seems like we're nothing compared to it, that there's no way we could change it," Akira said. How many times had her own father said something like that to her? She shook her head.

"But that's wrong," said Akira. She was talking to the huge crowd, but really she was talking to her dad, even though he wasn't there. "When a beaver builds a single dam, it can change an entire ecosystem. How can we humans think that all the things we're doing aren't changing the earth?"

Akira took a deep breath and let it out. "It's time to accept that we're responsible for the rise in the earth's temperature," Akira said, feeling the confidence of her own words. "To take our blinders off and get on with fixing things. Because while we're standing around arguing about it, nothing's getting done."

The audience applauded Akira as she left the stage, and this time it sounded less like the roar of a distant fire and more like the steady, reassuring thunder of horses' hooves.

Patience, Natalie, and Akira's mom were all clapping for Akira as she came offstage.

Akira's mom hugged her tight. "I know how hard that was for you," she told Akira. "I'm so proud of you."

"Great job," said Natalie.

"Thanks," said Akira.

"So who's next?" Natalie asked. On the screen, a boy from Switzerland named Wolfgang was showing pictures of the ancient artifacts he'd found when a ten-thousand-year-old glacier melted near his house in the mountains.

"Oh, no," Patience said, holding her clipboard up out of Natalie's reach. "Your work here is finished. At least until you come back up to send everybody home."

"But—"

"But nothing," Patience told her. She looked at Akira. "Get her out of here, will you? Go be a part of the audience, Nat. See what you're making happen."

Akira was surprised to find herself willing to hang out with Natalie. Eager, even. She was done with her speech and was feeling great. After getting up there and talking in front of all those people, Akira felt like she could do anything. Maybe even make *another* new friend. *Two in nine months*, Akira thought. *That has to be a record.*

Akira held her hand out to Natalie. "Come on," she said with a smile.

Natalie seemed to relax, and she smiled and took Akira's hand.

"Just be back before the end, or we'll have to send Churro out in your place!" Patience called as they ran for the stairs.

It was hot and close out in the crowd, but Akira felt an electricity in the air. Everything was in *motion*. Moms and dads bopped toddlers up and down on their shoulders. Elementary kids chased each other through the crowd with blue paper butterflies on strings. Teenagers grooved to their own internal soundtracks.

A bunch of people carried protest signs and wore T-shirts

with climate change slogans, and Akira and Natalie took pictures of the best ones. A girl their age held up a poster that read ONLY FOSSILS LIKE FOSSIL FUELS. The girl's friend wore a shirt that read THERE IS NO PLANET B. A woman carried a sign that read CLIMATE REFUGEES WELCOME, and her baby had on a onesie that read RESPECT YOUR MOTHER. Two grade-school boys held signs that read CLIMATE CHANGE IS WORSE THAN HOMEWORK, and I MISS SNOW DAYS. A teenage girl had one that read I WANT A HOT DATE, NOT A HOT PLANET.

The speaker onstage now was a handsome white boy from Louisiana named Landry. He had the crowd in stitches even though he was telling the story of how his whole town had been slowly swallowed by the sea.

The next person to Zoom in, a boy named Chetachukwu, told a sadder story about how desertification in northeast Nigeria had caused a famine, and Akira stood rapt as he explained how starvation was forcing boys like him to become child soldiers.

A girl from Brazil named Francisca talked about losing her whole village in a jungle fire in the Amazon, and a boy from Australia named Noah told everyone how his suburban Sydney neighborhood had burned up in a megafire. The scenes from the aftermath of the wildfire were so similar to what Akira had lived through that she shuddered and had to look away.

Natalie took her hand again and squeezed it. "It's a lot, I know," she said. "But it's important that everybody hears this."

Akira nodded. Natalie was right. They both knew how bad it was from personal experience. Climate change was affecting young people like them all over the world, and people needed to see it.

The boy Zooming in from Australia finished, and a picture of a polar bear replaced him on the screen.

"Ooh," Natalie said, pulling Akira close to whisper. "You'll want to watch this one. It's those two cute boys from Canada!"

TOURISTS

"All right, everyone, direct from Churchill, Manitoba, the Polar Bear Capital of the World," announced the emcee, "please welcome to the stage GEORGE GRUYÉRE and OWEN MACKENZIE!"

Owen walked out onstage, smiling and waving. He was halfway to the podium when he realized his best friend wasn't with him. George was still standing offstage, looking green.

Owen held up a finger to tell the audience to wait, and he jogged back to George.

"Hey, buddy. That's us," said Owen. "George and Owen. Owen and George. Two great tastes that taste great together."

George shook his head. "I wish Nanuq had eaten me," he said.

"Now, now, you're just saying that because you're scared to death," said Owen, pushing his friend out onto the stage. "Do it for the polar bears."

"Who tried to eat me," said George.

The audience applauded, and Owen waved again as he herded George up to the podium. Owen wanted the moment to last forever. His whole life had been a rehearsal for this.

"Hey there, I'm Mac—" said Owen.

"And I'm really regretting my life choices right now," said George, and the audience laughed.

"Dude!" Owen whispered, the microphone picking up

everything. "You can't go back on the nickname thing now! Not in front of all these people."

The audience laughed again, and Owen smiled. They were killing it right now, but only Owen knew how much George was freaking out. He wanted to keep the audience happy, but had to find a way to help his friend relax too.

"I'm Mac, and he's the Cheese!" Owen said, filling in for what was supposed to be George's line. "See, because his last name is Gruyére, which is a kind of cheese," Owen ad-libbed.

George rolled his eyes and motioned for him to move on, and Owen grinned. There was the George he knew and loved.

"Anyway, we're here because we almost got eaten by a polar bear," Owen said.

"For real," said George.

The picture behind them changed to show a big polar bear's nose right up in the camera, and everyone laughed and awwed.

"Yeah, you think he's cute, but Nanuq here tried to eat us!" said Owen.

"Repeatedly," said George.

"But it's not really his fault, right, George?" asked Owen, and George nodded in agreement. George didn't look like he was about to pass out anymore, and Owen relaxed.

Owen and George went back and forth telling their story, then explained how polar bears spent all winter out on the ice, hunting seals. But as the earth got warmer, the sea ice season got shorter. And the longer there was no ice in the Arctic, the hungrier the polar bears got.

"Which is why they're coming into town more and more, looking for food," said Owen.

"Nanuq here was tranquilized and spent a month in Polar Bear Jail before being released back into the wild," George explained. "Because we saved Nanuq's life, we got special permission to fly out with him when he was released and see him run out onto the ice."

The crowd was mesmerized by their video of the sleepy polar bear being loaded into a net and lifted into the air by helicopter, and Owen couldn't help but turn to watch with them.

"Hey, I think I can see my house from here!" Owen said, pointing to the buildings of Churchill as the helicopter flew over them.

"You can see *everybody's* house from there," George told Owen. "It's a small town," he told the crowd, and they laughed. Owen grinned at his friend. George had made a joke that was off script!

Owen bounced up and down. "Now can I tell them about microbe farts?" he asked, and the crowd laughed again.

"No," said George. "But if you want to hear more about how microbe farts in Manitoba are causing bigger hurricanes in Florida, and other ways that climate change in the north is changing the world," George told the crowd, "check out our YouTube channel, What Happens in the Arctic."

"Nice plug, dude!" Owen said. He was glad to see George was starting to find his stride.

"Uh-oh, Cheese," Owen said, looking at the place on his wrist where he'd be wearing a watch if he owned one. "Looks like it's almost time for us to get our ices out of here."

"Please, Owen, not in front of the kids," said George. "But before we go, we wanted to get serious for a minute and say that, to be honest, climate change never really mattered to us much before."

"In fact, it was kind of helping us," said Owen. "Helping *my* family, at least."

"And it was like, if it's not bothering us, why should we care?" said George.

"Turns out, we were living like tourists," said Owen.

"You know how when you go on vacation, it's like real-life rules don't apply anymore?" asked George.

"You cross in the middle of the street," said Owen. "You eat out all the time and buy stuff you don't need. You don't worry if you drop a piece of garbage on the ground."

"What does it matter if you mess the place up a little? Break a few rules? You're not going to be there forever," said George.

"But everything's connected," said Owen.

This next part of the speech gave Owen legit chills.

"What happens in the Arctic doesn't stay in the Arctic," said George. "And it's the same everywhere else. Mumbai. Louisiana. Honduras. Shanghai. Jakarta. Switzerland. Nigeria. Brazil. Australia. Tokyo. Miami. All the rest of the places you're hearing about today. What we do in one part of the world affects everyone else."

"Because we're not tourists here. Planet Earth is our home. All of it," said Owen.

Owen believed that with all of his heart. As remote as

Churchill was, he felt more connected with the rest of the world now than he ever had before.

"And long after we're gone, our kids will still live here," said George.

"And so will your kids' kids," said Owen. "And your kids' kids' kids. And your kids' kids' kids'—"

"Because we're all one big family," George said, cutting him off. "All the plants and animals too. Including the polar bears." The screen behind them cut to a video of an adorable polar bear cub rolling in the snow, and everyone *oohed* and *aahed* again.

"Save the polar bears, save the planet!" cried Owen. "Thank you!"

The audience roared, and Owen waved as they left the podium, feeling the delicious rush of performing in front of a crowd again. *From the tundra buggy to the stage*, he thought. *Next stop, YouTube star!*

Owen checked his phone when they were all the way offstage. "Dude, we've already got, like, five thousand new subscribers!" he told George.

"My dad's working on a new video about how the Mushkegowuk Council got Parks Canada to establish a National Marine Conservation Area in the southwestern part of the bay," George told him. "We'll have new content loaded by Monday."

Owen and George tapped fists, and Owen beamed. Between running outdoor expeditions and helping them with their video channel, George's dad was now making enough of a living without working at the port. Which meant George and his family were staying in Churchill.

Owen heard the emcee introduce a girl named Daniela, and she went out to the podium to tell her story about riding on top of a train all the way to the United States from Honduras after a drought killed her family's coffee farm. It was an incredible story, but Owen had already heard her speech during rehearsals.

"Hey, we should find that boy from Louisiana, see if we can interview him for the channel," Owen said, trying to sound casual.

"Uh-huh," said George, giving him side-eye. "Well, if you get to interview him, I get to interview the girl from Miami who organized the rally."

"Deal," Owen said with a grin.

Owen's phone buzzed in his pocket, and he took it out to look at it. Yes! It was a text from his dad. The one he'd been hoping would come through.

"Hey, Cheese—" he whispered, trying to get George to look at his phone.

George ignored him.

Owen tugged on his sleeve. "Hey, Cheese, check this out."

"Owen, do you remember when we talked about paying attention?" he whispered back. "This nice girl from Honduras is saying some important stuff right now."

"I know, but we've already heard it and this is really important too," said Owen.

George finally relented and looked at Owen's phone. It

showed a picture of an old yellow-and-black snowmobile.

"I saved up enough money at last!" Owen crowed. "My dad just went and picked it up today."

George blinked. "For real?" he asked. He took the phone from Owen to see for himself. He looked up at Owen, amazed. "I don't believe it. You finally have your own snowmobile."

Owen shook his head. "No, man, I still don't."

"What do you mean?" asked George.

"This one's yours, buddy. I bought it to replace the one you lost in the lake. We lost. *I lost*," Owen said, covering the last bit with a fake cough.

"I— Dude," George stammered. He was speechless.

Owen smiled. It had been absolute *torture* to not give away the secret for nine whole months as he saved up, but the look on George's face was totally worth it.

"We'll share it," George said at last.

Now it was Owen's turn to be stunned. He shook his head. "No, man, I—"

"We'll share it," George said again, and he meant it.

"Deal," said Owen, and they bumped fists again.

The girl from Honduras finished with a call to open the US borders to climate refugees, and Owen and George cheered with the audience as she left the stage.

"I think that's it, isn't it?" asked Owen.

"All right, all you bodacious babies, terrific toddlers, glorious grade schoolers, magnificent middle schoolers, and tremendous teens, let me hear you!" the emcee said, and the audience roared.

"Who *is* that?" Owen asked, looking around. The emcee sounded familiar somehow. He didn't know who she was or where she was, but she was good. Not as good as Owen was, of course. But talent recognizes talent.

"We've got one last speaker for you to hear before we send you off to save the world," the emcee said. "Everyone please welcome back to the stage . . . NATALIE TORRES!"

Owen and George clapped with the rest of the audience, and waited.

And waited.

And waited.

"I think somebody missed her cue," said Owen.

Owen jumped with surprise as a Chihuahua tore out from the other side of the stage. The little dog saw the huge crowd and ran right to the edge of the stage, barking madly at each and every one of them.

The audience immediately erupted in laughter, which only made the little dog bark more.

"Well," said George. "This climate change rally has really gone to the dogs."

THE FINAL CHALLENGE

"I'm here!" Natalie cried. She flew up the steps from the audience, pushed past the two boys from Canada who were standing in the wings, and ran out onstage. She'd been so wrapped up listening to the other speakers with Akira that she'd lost track of time.

And how had Churro gotten loose on the stage? He was running back and forth, barking at everything like they were back in the hurricane.

"Churro, come here!" Natalie cried, chasing him around the stage. The audience loved it. They cheered every time Churro slipped away from Natalie, and they moaned in mock disappointment when she finally got her hands on him.

Blushing mightily, Natalie hurried to hand Churro off to Patience, who stood waiting offstage.

"I told you I'd send him out if you weren't back," Patience said.

"Wait, you mean you—" Natalie started to say, but Patience took Churro from Natalie and turned her around.

"Now get out there and tell them what's what," Patience said, and gave Natalie a push.

Natalie hurried back to the podium. "Hey! Woo. What a day!" Natalie said into the microphone, her heart still racing from chasing down Churro. The audience applauded again, and Natalie took a deep breath and smiled. It was funny—she had expected to be nervous to take the stage again, but running around after Churro had taken her mind off speaking in front of the huge crowd.

"We brought all these amazing young people together to show you that climate change isn't some far-off threat," Natalie said, reading from the screen on the podium. Natalie's mom and Patience had helped her write her closing speech, but the ideas were Natalie's—thought out in the days and weeks and months of difficult recovery after Hurricane Reuben. Recovery that was still going on, nine months later.

"Climate change is real, and it's happening *right now*, all over the world," Natalie said. The screen behind her changed to the image of a rising thermometer. "The average temperature of the world has gone up a little over one degree Celsius since the beginning of the industrial era in the 1800s," Natalie told the crowd. "That's bad enough. But if it hits two degrees, climate disasters like what you heard about today will be happening to all of us, all the time."

The image on the screen behind Natalie changed to a still shot from her television interview in Liberty City.

"The day after the hurricane, I was interviewed by a Miami meteorologist named Maria Martinez," Natalie began.

"Hey, it's the Weather Lady!" Owen Mackenzie cried from offstage. Natalie turned to look at him, and she watched as his friend George Gruyére clapped a hand over Owen's mouth and whispered her an apology. Natalie didn't mind. She'd been surprised, was all. How did two boys from Canada know a meteorologist from Miami?

"I went off about climate change in the interview," Natalie said, continuing her story, "and at the end, Maria Martinez asked me a question. She said, 'What do you want people to *do* about it?'"

Natalie paused.

"I didn't have a good answer for her," she confessed. "Climate change is big. *It's overwhelming.* Sometimes it feels like you're swimming against a hurricane. Like you'll never be able to do all the things you need to do to fix it," Natalie said. "Maybe you and your family already recycle and use public transportation. Maybe you have solar panels on your house, or drive an electric car. Maybe you eat less meat, or have a yard you don't have to mow. You're doing all the things, and that's good. It helps. But the earth is still getting hotter."

Natalie shook her head wearily. "It's enough to make you want to give up and stop fighting," she said. "I know. I've felt that way myself. But we can't. There's too much at stake. So what do we do? Well, a good friend of mine once told me something that changed the way I looked at fixing climate change. *Nobody has to do everything, but everybody has to do something.*"

Natalie glanced offstage at Patience, and Patience put her hands together in the shape of a heart for Natalie.

"So here's my challenge to you," Natalie said to the audience. "Besides the little things we all need to keep doing to prevent the earth from getting warmer, what is *one big thing* you can do to stop climate change? What's the one thing you're really good at that you can do to help?" Natalie asked.

"If you're an artist, maybe you can paint signs or murals that get people thinking about climate change," she went on. "If you're a musician, you can write songs about climate change. If you're good with words, you can write letters to the editor of your local newspaper. If you're rich, or good at raising money, you can donate to climate change charities."

Natalie caught sight of a familiar face in the crowd, and she smiled and waved. Her friend Shannon had come to Washington with Natalie and her mom, but Natalie hadn't seen her since the rally began.

During the storm, Natalie hadn't been able to imagine the two of them ever finding common ground enough to go on being friends. But after seeing Natalie's interview with Maria Martinez on television, Shannon and her family had done what they could by showing up in a motorboat with food and water and money for Liberty Island.

Natalie and Shannon might have been from very different parts of the city, but they were from the same planet after all. A planet they could save together.

"Are you good at science?" Natalie said, returning to her script. "Figure out a way to explain climate change so everybody understands it. Are you good with a shovel and love playing in the dirt? Plant more trees in your community. Do you love clipboards and spreadsheets? Organize a rally!"

The audience laughed.

"And even if there's nothing you're really good at yet," Natalie said, "you can do what I and the rest of the young people did here today. You can use your *voice* to speak up about climate change."

Natalie clapped with the rest of the crowd as the other speakers came out and took a final bow, and the kids who'd Zoomed in waved from the screen.

"There's a place for all of us in this fight," Natalie told the crowd on the National Mall. "But one thing I learned on Liberty Island was that even when every single person does everything they can, it can still not be enough. We can't do it all by ourselves. There are some things that could fix climate change that we're *not* good at, but our government *is* good at. And it's time for them to step up and do their part too.

"That's why we're here today, on the steps of the US Capitol," Natalie said, pointing at the big white building behind her. "Even if we're kids, even if we can't vote, our representatives are still supposed to work for *us*. We have to tell them how we want them to use our resources. Our power. Because it *is* ours. The government isn't somebody else. We are the government, and it is us!"

The crowd erupted in applause again, and Natalie hoped that everybody in the Capitol and in every other building in Washington could hear them.

"That goes for every level of government, big or small," said Natalie. "Tell your principal you want climate change in the curriculum. Tell your city council you want more parks and less concrete. Tell your state government to require solar panels on new houses, and to install charging stations for electric cars at rest areas. Tell the federal government to stop giving subsidies to fossil fuel companies and to give that money and those tax breaks to renewable energy instead. To really move the needle on climate change, it's going to take all of us—including our government."

Natalie paused for a moment as the people in the audience cheered again. The screen behind her returned to the blue butterfly image that was on all the signs and banners and flags for the rally, and Natalie took a deep breath. The end of her speech was the hardest part, because it was the most personal.

"When I was little," Natalie said at last, "I made up a fantasyland called Mariposa. Its symbol was a blue butterfly." She turned and pointed to the screen.

"Mariposa was a place with dragons and castles and magic. But it was also a place where the air was clean and the water wasn't dirty, and if you needed help, you got it. There were no poor people in Mariposa, and everybody was happy all the time."

Natalie looked out over the quiet crowd. "I would show you the pictures and maps and flags I drew for Mariposa, but they were all destroyed during Hurricane Reuben, along with everything else I owned," said Natalie. "I *can* show you a picture of the real butterfly that inspired Mariposa though."

The screen changed to the image of a beautiful blue butterfly, only an inch wide from wing to wing. "This is the Miami blue butterfly," Natalie said. "When I was a kid, these butterflies lived all over South Florida. Now, thanks to climate change, there are only a few of them left on a single, tiny island in the Key West National Wildlife Preserve."

Natalie sighed. "The Mariposa I created was a little kid's dream. We can never create a perfect world, no matter how hard we try. But even if Mariposa can't be our reality, there's no reason it can't be our inspiration. We don't need the world to be perfect. We just need it to be *better*."

Natalie looked up from her speech. "The Miami blue butterfly is almost extinct," she said. "*Almost*, but not yet. It's not too late. We can save the butterflies. And the polar bears," she said, looking over at Owen and George. "And the giant sequoias," she said, looking at Akira. "We can still save all the other plants and animals around the world that are in danger. Including *us*. But only if we do something about climate change *right now*. All of us. Together. Because the earth can't wait another minute."

TWO DEGREES

Natalie left the podium riding high on a wave of cheers and applause from half a million people. She was *pumped*. Nine months ago, standing in the parking lot of Brother's Keeper with Patience and Maria Martinez, a Kids Against Climate Change rally had just been an inkling of an idea. Now here it was, a full-blown reality.

And it was only the beginning.

Patience and Natalie's mom and Churro and all the other kids who'd spoken that day were just offstage waiting to congratulate her. Then all the speakers went back out for a final curtain call.

We did this, Natalie thought as she bowed with the others. *We're just in middle school, and we made this happen.*

When all the bowing and waving goodbye was over and pop songs blared through the speakers again, Natalie found Patience and Akira backstage. The two boys from Canada were with them, and Natalie shared a little smile with Akira.

"Awesome speech," George told Natalie.

"Thank you," Natalie said, blushing a little. George was even cuter in person.

"Yeah. You made me want to write a letter to the president, and I'm Canadian!" said Owen.

"So write one to the prime minister," George told him.

"Oh, yeah," said Owen.

"You were all great," Patience said, hugging Akira again.

"Where's your dog?" Akira asked Natalie.

"With my mom," said Natalie. "He kind of reacts to crowds the same way he does hurricanes. And everything else." Natalie turned to Owen. "So, hey, how do you know Maria Martinez?"

Owen nudged George. "*That's* her name," he said.

"Yes, Owen. She said it before," said George.

Natalie laughed. Owen and George were like a nonstop comedy routine.

"The Weather Lady—Maria Martinez—she comes up to Churchill every year with her film crew," Owen explained to Natalie. "My family takes her around on tours."

"Hunh. I found these guys on YouTube," said Patience. "I had no idea they shared a connection with Maria."

"Akira and I had a connection already too," Natalie told the boys. "Turns out we both knew Patience, before we met each other."

"Wow," said George. "How random is that?"

"Dude, what would *really* be spooky is if you and I knew somebody *Akira* knew," Owen said to George. "Then we would all have a connection!"

"Owen, we live at the ice end of nowhere," George reminded him. "We're not connected to *anybody*."

"I do know *someone* from Canada, and she's got the same accent as you two," said Akira. "Here she comes now. Hey, Sue!" Akira called and waved.

Natalie turned and saw the girl Patience had recruited to be their emcee. So that's where Patience found her. Sue was a friend of Akira's.

"Sue and I survived the fire together," said Akira. "She wanted to be a part of the rally, but she didn't want to get up onstage."

Natalie said hello again to Sue, then realized that George and Owen were staring at Sue in stunned surprise.

"Suzy?" said George. "Suzy Tookoome?"

"What's up, lugnuts?" Sue said to the boys.

"Wait," said Akira. "You're not saying you actually *know* each other."

"Yeah, I went to school with these two for years in Churchill," Sue said to Akira. "Thanks for not coming over to say hello or anything when you heard me on the loudspeakers," Sue told the boys. "Not that I couldn't smell you a mile away."

Owen's eyes went wide, and he grabbed George's arm. "She said she could smell us a mile away," Owen whispered, even though everyone could hear him. "Just like a polar bear!"

"What are you talking about?" asked Natalie.

"She's the Polar Bear Girl!" said Owen.

"We call her that because she was attacked by a polar bear," said George.

"And also because she's a polar bear in disguise!" Owen cried.

Sue rolled her eyes and shook her head.

"Weren't you a competitive swimmer?" asked George. "Polar bears do love to swim."

Sue raised her hands like claws and said, "Rawr."

"Were you really attacked by a polar bear?" Patience asked Sue.

"I don't like to talk about it," said Sue.

"The scars on your forehead!" Natalie said. She'd seen them when Patience had introduced her to Sue at rehearsals, but Natalie had been too polite to ask about them. She clapped a hand over her mouth now, embarrassed that she'd said anything.

"I've got scars too," Natalie added, trying to make things better. She pulled up the bottom of her shirt to show the scar Reuben had left on her stomach after hitting her with a kitchen stove in the storm surge.

"I've got a bunch too, from the fire," Akira said. She rolled up her shirt sleeve and showed everyone a lumpy red welt under her arm.

"And we have a matching set," George told Sue, parting his hair to reveal the scars Nanuq's claws had left on his scalp.

"Ooh! I have a scar too, from where Nanuq bit my leg," Owen said. He started to unbuckle his pants, but George stopped him.

"Owen, no," said George.

"Oh. Right," Owen said, turning red. "Sorry."

As the others laughed, Natalie shook her head in wonder. All of them had gone through different climate disasters at the same time last year, and they had each been scarred by them. But there was something else that linked them too.

"So wait," said Natalie, doing the math. "If you and Akira both knew Sue," she told the boys, "and Akira and I both knew Patience..."

"And you and the boys know that meteorologist..." Akira said to Natalie.

"Then we really *were* all connected," George said. "I mean, before we met here at the rally."

They all stood and looked at each other for a minute, and Natalie got goose bumps. What were the odds that each of them knew somebody else in common?

Patience shook her head, as stunned as the rest of them. "This is some six-degrees-of-separation stuff happening right here," she told them.

Natalie didn't understand.

"Six degrees of separation is this idea that everybody in the world is at most six people removed from everybody else," Patience explained. "Like, if my boyfriend knows me, and I know Natalie, and she knows Akira, and Akira knows Owen, and Owen knows George, then my boyfriend is six degrees of separation from everybody else that George knows, even though they've never met. You get it?"

Natalie had a hard time following all that, but she thought she understood. At a certain point, everybody was connected to everybody else in the world by people they'd met. Like when a social media app recommended a new friend for you because that person was friends with a bunch of other people you already knew.

"But we're *not* separated by six degrees," Akira said. "We're each connected by just *one* person. That's two degrees of separation."

Two degrees, Natalie thought, and she felt a shiver go up her spine. Two degrees separated each one of them from the other, and two degrees of temperature change separated the world from disaster. They were linked together the same way an invisible web connected pollution to wildfires, wildfires to melting ice caps, melting ice caps to rising sea levels, rising sea levels to storm surges.

"Whoa. How many other people who spoke at the rally do you think we were connected to before we got here?" George whispered.

"How many other people in the *world*?" asked Akira.

"Pakoom," Owen said, making fireworks with his fingers like his brain was exploding.

Natalie looked around at all her new friends. At all the other young people who'd come together to speak. At all the thousands of people leaving the National Mall to go home and rally their own communities against climate change.

Even if everyone in the world didn't know *how* they were connected, thought Natalie, maybe it was just enough for them to know that they *were* connected.

Maybe, she thought, that's what it would finally take to save the world.

AUTHOR'S NOTE

Climate change is the term scientists use to describe long-term shifts in the earth's temperatures and weather patterns. Shifts in the earth's climate may be natural, but since the beginning of the industrial era (around the year 1800), human activities have been the major cause of climate change.

People primarily affect the climate by burning fossil fuels like coal, oil, and gas. Those fossil fuels power our cars, trucks, ships, trains, and planes; run our electric power stations and factories; and heat and cool our homes. Burning these fuels releases greenhouse gases like carbon dioxide and methane, which linger in the atmosphere and trap the sun's heat, causing the earth's temperature to rise. Warmer temperatures create a number of problems, including melting Arctic glaciers, rising sea levels, severe droughts, extreme heat waves, stronger storms, and animal and plant extinction.

Scientists have long known about the human impact on climate change, but it was only when I was a kid in the early 1970s that "global warming" became a household term. In the fifty years since, as the governments of the world dithered about our role in climate change and what, if anything, we should do about it, the temperature of the earth has only continued to rise and climate disasters have become more frequent and more devastating.

In recent years, I've been heartened to see young activists like Greta Thunberg take to the streets to lead protests against climate change and challenge the world's leaders to take action. But besides marching with them and voting for leaders who promise to do something about climate change, what more, I wondered, could I do to help boost their signal?

This book, *Two Degrees*, is my answer.

I considered many different locations and scenarios for each of the three stories in *Two Degrees*. Akira's story, for example, could have been set in Australia, Chile, Portugal, Greece, Turkey, Russia, or China, all places that have suffered recent and devastating wildfires. George and Owen's polar bear story may be specific to the Arctic, but I could also have written about how climate change is threatening the habitats of any number of animals, including cheetahs in South Africa, giant pandas in China, Asian elephants in the Greater Mekong region, Adélie penguins in Antarctica, and green sea turtles around the world. And South Florida is not alone in dealing with flooding and hurricanes. Cyclones, typhoons, "rain bombs," and other flooding disasters endangered lives and destroyed property in many places last year, including Canada, the Caribbean, Ecuador, Brazil, the United Kingdom, Germany, Belgium, the Netherlands, India, Bengal, Nepal, Japan, Indonesia, Fiji, and the Philippines.

I ultimately settled on three climate crises in North America for my novel, but even then, there were many other effects of climate change I didn't have room to write about, like tornadoes, droughts, desertification, deadly heat waves, food scarcity, and forced human migration.

It was, I confess, incredibly overwhelming. There was so much science. So many people suffering from the effects of climate change in so many different ways. It took me a long time to even know where to begin, and far longer than usual to find the focus of my story. As the novel evolved, Natalie's character became a voice for how overwhelmed I, the author, was feeling, and how intimidating just the *thought* of climate change can be. Like Natalie, it was important in the end for me to understand that I couldn't do everything. I just had to do something.

Climate change is real, but the specific events I've written about in this book are fictional. There was no Morris Fire in California. Two boys were not pursued for miles by a polar bear in Churchill. And Miami, thankfully, has not been hit by the "Big One." But the things Akira, Owen, George, and Natalie experience and do in their stories have all happened to real people during recent climate disasters.

AKIRA

Akira's story is based primarily on the 2020 Creek Fire, which was centered in the Sierra National Forest, and the 2018 Camp Fire, which is the deadliest and most destructive wildfire in California's history. To better understand what Akira and Sue's ride through the Morris Fire would be like, I watched many harrowing videos shot by people fleeing wildfires in their cars. Metal cars do burn in wildfires, and the flames can be so hot and come up so fast that the passengers are burned alive, as Akira and Sue discover. Wildfires can burn hot enough to melt asphalt too, and just walking on pavement in a wildfire can melt the soles of your shoes off.

Lightning is the main cause of natural wildfires, but the US National Park Service estimates that 85 percent of wildland fires in the United States are started by humans, either intentionally or unintentionally. The cause of the 2020 Creek Fire is still unknown, but investigators believe the devastating 2018 Camp Fire, which killed eighty-five people and destroyed the towns of Paradise and Concow, California, was sparked by a faulty electric power line. And yes, the 2021 Fawn Fire was accidentally started by a woman trying to boil drinking water she thought contained bear urine.

Dodger's dip in the pool is based on a true story as well. Following the Camp Fire in 2018, a man was surprised to find a horse sitting half-submerged on the cover of his neighbor's backyard pool. How and when the horse had gotten there no one knows, but waiting out the fire in the pool saved the horse's life. Many other animals were not so fortunate, as untold numbers of pets and wild animals were tragically caught up in the blaze.

Burning monarchs are unfortunately a real thing too. California's wildfires have become so big and so intense over the past six years that the National Park Service estimates that 85 percent of all giant sequoia grove acreage across the Sierra Nevada has burned. The 2020 Castle Fire alone burned one-third of all sequoia territory across the Sierra Nevada, killing an estimated 7,500 to 10,600 large sequoia trees. Many of the trees killed in the Castle Fire were more than two thousand and three thousand years old.

OWEN AND GEORGE

Churchill, Manitoba, is a real place, and tens of thousands of tourists from all over the world come to Owen and George's hometown to see the polar bears that gather there every fall. Tundra buggies like the one Owen's family owns and operates are real, as are all of George and Owen's polar bear facts. And yes, polar bears really do know how to camouflage themselves by lying down in the snow and covering their black noses with their white paws. Polar bears are crafty hunters, and Churchill residents really do leave their cars and houses unlocked in case anyone has to run for cover from a polar bear that has wandered into town.

Human encounters with polar bears can be deadly. In 2018, a young man was attacked and killed by a polar bear on Sentry Island, about 165 miles north of Churchill. And just like Sue, a young woman was attacked by a polar bear in Churchill on Halloween night in 2013. She survived, but only after the polar bear tore off part of her scalp and a piece of her ear. The people of Churchill regularly carry shotguns and rifles with them any time they're outside of town, just in case they run into a polar bear.

And run-ins with polar bears are happening increasingly as bears are forced to spend more time on land and less time out on the ice. According to a study by the University of Manitoba, Hudson Bay is now ice-free for forty-seven more days each year than it was in 1980. That means polar bears are fasting much longer than they used to, which is particularly dangerous to momma bears. The average weight of pregnant polar bears in the Churchill area declined 15 percent over that same period, and momma bears that used to have twins now often have one baby polar bear, or none. The number of polar bears in Western Hudson Bay has decreased by 30 percent since 1987, and some scientists worry that the polar bear population there is on its way to extinction.

As the Arctic sea ice shrinks, there is less of it to reflect sunlight back out into space, warming the oceans and making the earth hotter. That warming is also being accelerated by the release of methane gas, which is a by-product of bacteria consuming newly unfrozen biomatter from the permafrost. According to the US National Oceanic and Atmospheric Administration (NOAA), sea ice cover throughout the Arctic has shrunk by 13 percent per decade since 1980. That's a loss of 31,100 square miles—an area the size of South Carolina—each year.

NATALIE

Many hurricanes have hit Miami indirectly, and I used those storms and others that hit major metropolitan areas—including Hurricane Katrina, which hit New Orleans in 2005, and Hurricane Sandy, which impacted New York City in 2012—to imagine what a direct hit on Miami would look like. Natalie's back wall collapsing from a wave and her desperate survival in the storm surge, for example, was inspired by something similar that happened to a woman escaping her home in New York City during Hurricane Sandy.

According to NOAA, storm surges can push water tens of miles inland, causing flood levels of thirty feet or more far from the coast. Just three feet of water can lift and move a four-thousand-pound car, and yes, storm surges often carry thousand-pound manatees into strange places, like golf course lakes, backyard pools, and even deep into forests. A six-foot storm surge is enough to completely flood the first floors of homes and businesses, and nine feet of storm surge is almost impossible to survive without getting to higher ground. By National Hurricane Center estimates, storm surges account for nearly half of all Atlantic tropical hurricane deaths, mainly due to drowning.

Miami is a unique case because it experiences flooding even when there is no storm. Sea levels have risen three inches globally since 1993, and more than five inches locally in South Florida. That, combined with unusually high tides, creates what is known as "sunny day" flooding, where seawater is pushed back up through Miami's drainage system, flooding streets and buildings. Once an infrequent occurrence, NOAA believes Miami will be flooding on sunny days ten to fifty-five days a year by 2050. Add to that a storm surge of any height, and Miami is in serious trouble.

Liberty City, where Natalie ends up, is one of the Miami communities that sits on the Atlantic Coastal Ridge, an area of high ground about eleven feet above sea level—nearly twice the average height of the rest of Miami-Dade County. Developers looking to avoid Miami's rising tides have begun buying up land and building expensive residential and commercial projects in these areas, driving out many of Miami's Black and Afro-Caribbean communities. In the end, though, it may be impossible for *anyone* to live in Miami. If ocean levels rise another five or six feet, as some scientists believe will happen by 2100—a date many of the young readers of this book will live to see!—large parts of Miami-Dade County will be underwater, and a third of its current population—almost a million people—will have nowhere to live.

Everyone, everywhere, is affected in some way by climate change. Recognizing that, nearly every country in the world came together in 2015 to sign the Paris Agreement, a landmark international accord that committed each nation to working together to cap global temperature rise at two degrees Celsius above preindustrial levels by the end of the century—and eventually reduce that number to 1.5 degrees or lower. There is still a great deal of debate over *how* to halt global temperature rise, let alone whether it will be enough. But if the bad news is that humans are causing the climate crisis we now face, the good news is, we have the power to fix it.

It's your world. Your future. It's up to you to decide what you want that future world to look like, and what you can do to make it happen.

Alan Gratz
Asheville, NC
2022

ACKNOWLEDGMENTS

Thanks first and foremost go to my amazing editor, Aimee Friedman, whose patience and guidance helped see me through one of the most difficult projects I've ever tackled. (Note to self: Maybe don't choose to write about such a heavy, dispiriting subject during a pandemic.) Thanks too to my publisher and cheerleader, David Levithan, and to my copy editor, Shari Joffe, and proofreaders, Jody Corbett, Jackie Hornberger, Jessica White, and Bonnie Cutler. You guys make me look good.

And a big thank-you to everyone who works behind the scenes at Scholastic to make my books a success: Ellie Berger, president of Trade Publishing; Seale Ballenger, Erin Berger, Alex Kelleher-Nagorski, Jordana Kulak, Rachel Feld, Jordin Streeter, Illianna Gonzalez-Soto and everyone in Publicity and Marketing; Lizette Serrano, Emily Heddleson, Michael Strouse, Matthew Poulter, and Danielle Yadao and everyone in School and Library Marketing and Conventions; Aimee's former associate editor and now editor in her own right, Olivia Valcarce; Aimee's new assistant, Arianna Arroyo; Janell Harris, Elizabeth Krych, Erin O'Connor, Leslie Garych, JoAnne Mojica, and everyone in Production; Christopher Stengel for the terrific cover and interior layout; Jazan Higgins, Stephanie Peitz, Jana Haussmann, Mariclaire Jastremsky, Kristin Standley, and everyone with the Clubs and Fairs; Jennifer Powell and her team in Rights and

Co-editions; Alan Smagler, Elizabeth Whiting, Jackie Rubin, Savannah D'Amico, Dan Moser, Nikki Mutch, Chris Satterlund, Roz Hilden, Terribeth Smith, Sarah Sullivan, Jarad Waxman, Betsy Politi, and everyone in Sales; Lori Benton, John Pels, and Paul Gagne for their amazing work, as ever, on the *Two Degrees* audiobook; and all the sales reps and Fairs and Clubs reps across the country who work so hard to tell the world about my books.

Special thanks to Jorge Duany for reading Natalie's sections and giving me notes, and to Suzanne Methot for reading the whole book—particularly Owen and George's story—and giving me invaluable feedback. Big thanks to bookseller and horsewoman Angie Tally of The Country Bookshop, who got on the phone to talk about horses with me at the beginning of this book, answered my strange and random texts about horses for the next year and a half while I wrote it, and then read Akira's story at the end to rein things in. Much appreciation to Mary Olson, founder and co-CEO of Climate School Asheville and now network manager for The Collider, a collaborative nonprofit in Asheville, North Carolina, focused on solutions for climate change; Miles Kish, co-director of membership and project manager at The Collider; and Dave Michelson, applied research software designer at the University of North Carolina Asheville's National Environmental Modeling and Analysis Center. I learned so much from everyone who spoke to me and read the manuscript. Any mistakes that remain are definitely my own.

Massive thanks to my literary agent, Holly Root at Root Literary, for always being in my corner, and to my publicists and right-hand women Lauren Harr, Caroline Christopoulos, and Aya Phillips at Gold Leaf Literary—the work you do allows me to do the work I do. Thanks to my friend Paul Harrill, who listened to me complain, and to Bob, who's been with me right from the start. And thanks as always to all the teachers, librarians, and booksellers out there who continue to share my books with young readers. You're awesome.

And last but never least, much love and thanks to my wife, Wendi, and my daughter, Jo, my greatest champions and friends.

Like Natalie, I don't have all the answers. I just know we can't succeed alone.

ABOUT THE AUTHOR

Alan Gratz is the #1 *New York Times* bestselling author of several acclaimed and award-winning books for young readers, including *Refugee, Ground Zero, Allies, Grenade, Projekt 1065, Code of Honor*, and *Prisoner B-3087*. Alan lives in North Carolina with his wife and daughter. Look for him online at alangratz.com.